OVERTURE

THE SONGS OF AARDA
BOOK TWO
BY
K. R. SCHULTZ

THE SONGS OF AARDA SERIES

Prelude
Overture
The Heretic's Song (Prelude and Overture combined)

(Forthcoming)
Nocturne
Rondo
Crescendo
For updates and special offers on other works by K.R. Schultz, sign up on his Author Homepage at:
http://krschultzauthor.com

Author Facebook Page
https://www.facebook.com/pages/K-R-Schultz/237124209712175

Twitter @krs1952

ISBN 13: 9781090717894
Printed in the United States of America

To those who dream and dare to believe, and to Patricia and all the others who encouraged me to continue writing, dreaming, and believing.

To Stevie, Jovie, Aidan, Roan, Nate, Benjamin, and Ripley. May you find truth and adventure in equal measure throughout your lives.

Special thanks to Dean Ellis for the cover image, Christie Stratos my editor, and Patricia for putting up with me and Beta reading my work.

MAPS

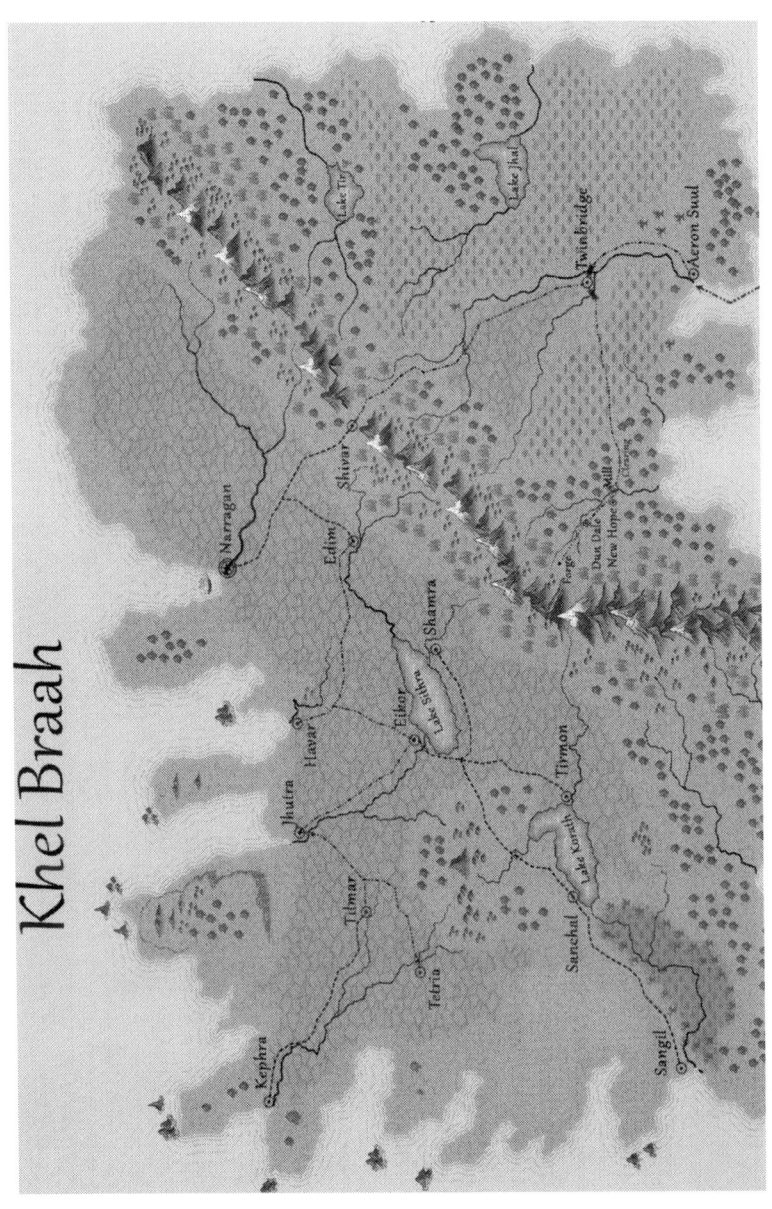

Khel Braah

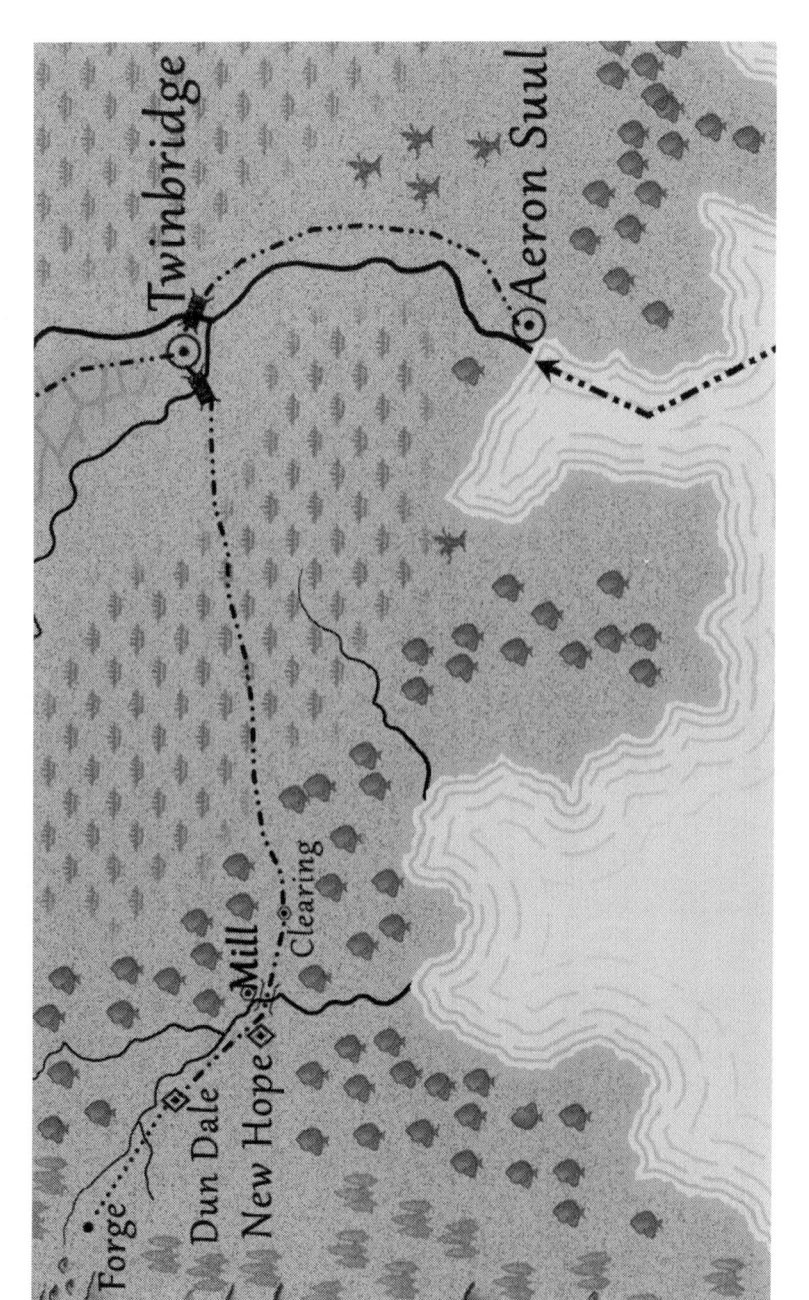

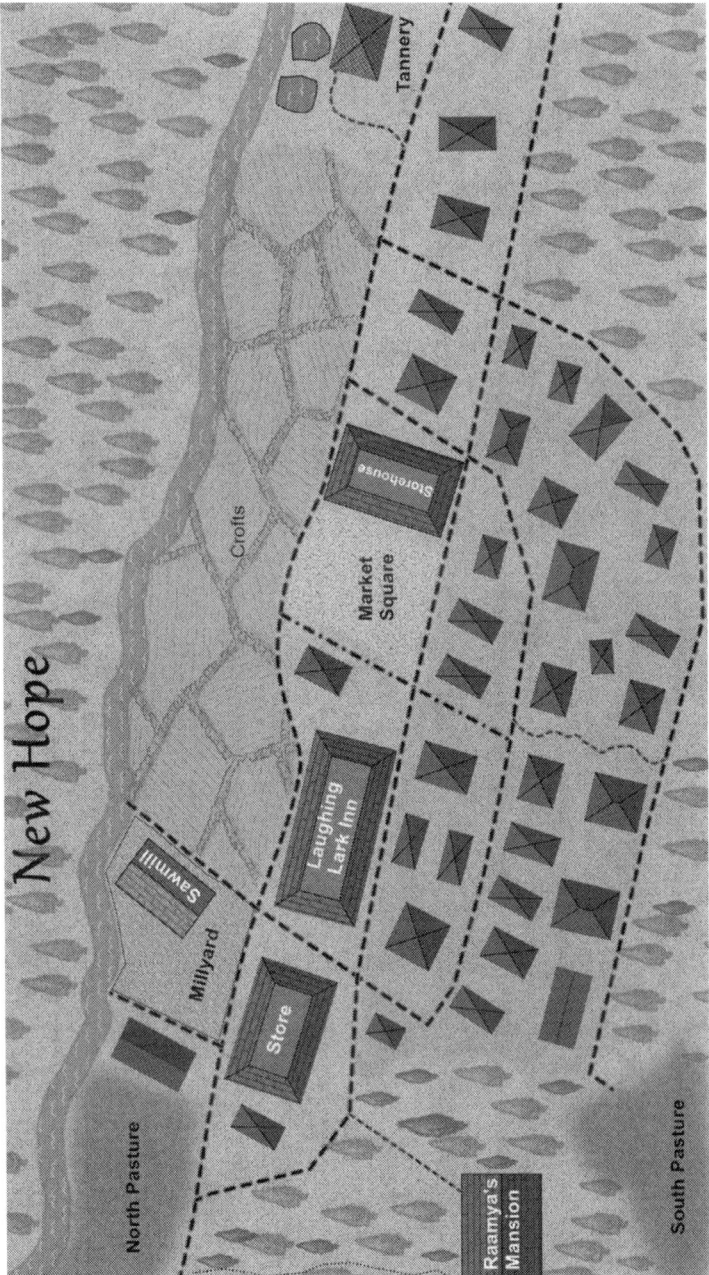

New Hope

North Pasture

Millyard

Sawmill

Store

Laughing Lark Inn

Crofts

Market Square

Storehouse

Tannery

Raamya's Mansion

South Pasture

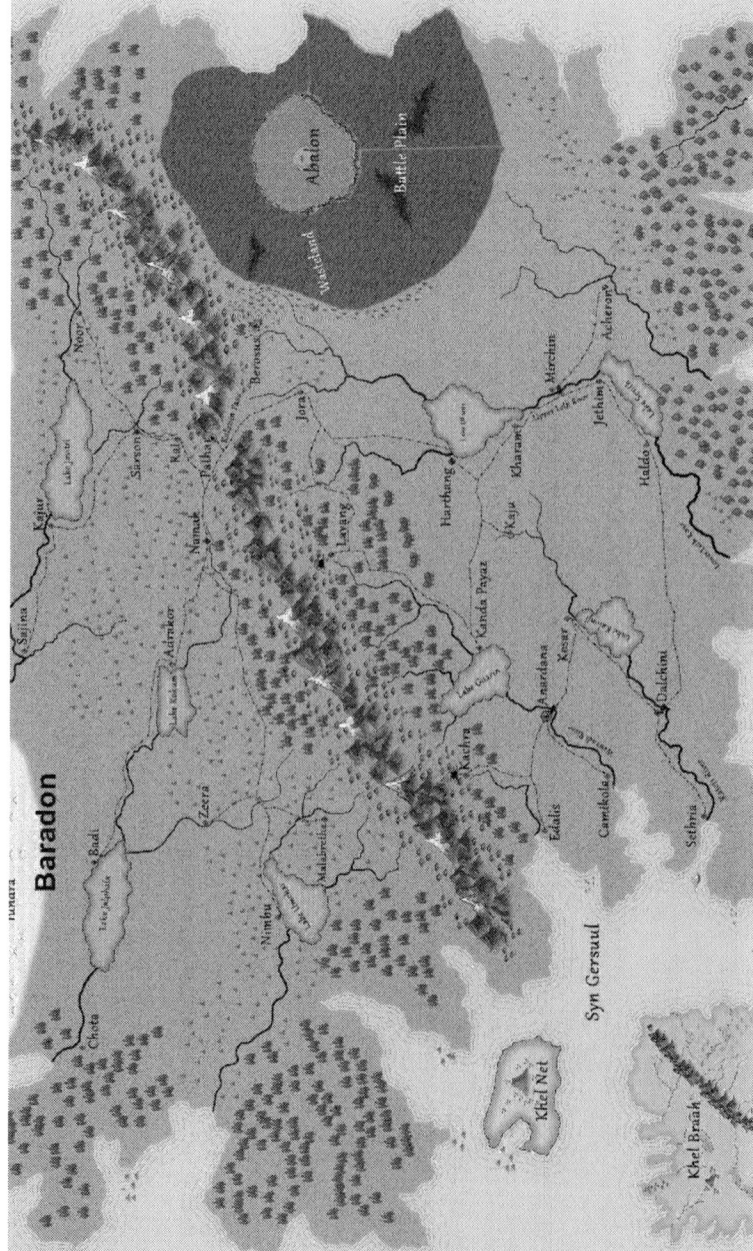

HOME

Everyone needs a home, a place where they are valued and protected. Some are born into it. Home surrounds those lucky few from the moment of birth like the air they breathe. They inhale support and approval, unaware of the blessing they have received and heedless of its worth unless that gift is suddenly lost.

Others wander lonely roads, desiccated by the winds of chance, stripped to the bone by adversity, and yet they never find a place to belong. Their souls shrivel as they breathe the poisonous dust of disappointment. Bitterness stings their eyes like sand and blinds them. They blunder past places of refuge. They forever seek their home but never reach it.

Still others wander those roads reaching a home only after a prolonged search. They arrive bruised and broken, their vision sharpened by adversity, forever grateful for the precious gifts of family and home.

Reflections on Traveling by Amur Auriga-Plafox

CHAPTER ONE

DISCOVERY

Isil and Rehaak awakened to the sound of rain dripping from the thatched roof of Laakea's home. While Rehaak gathered kindling, lit a fire in the hearth and made breakfast, Isil straightened her bed and then swept the flagstone floor. Isil poked her head into Laakea's room, meaning to wake him. "Wake up sleepyhead." Puzzlement replaced the smile when she spotted the rumpled blankets strewn across the empty bed. They were the only evidence he had slept there.

"Laakea must'a gone to light the forge mighty early this mornin'. I'll holler at him if breakfast be ready," Isil said.

"Yes, please do. By the time Laakea washes up, breakfast will be on the table."

Isil swung open the door and shouted into the downpour, "Laakea, breakfast be ready. Come wash up so's we can eat." Rain splashed on the wet earth outside, and dishes clattered inside the house behind her. She shouted louder, "Laakea, stop what you're doin'. Breakfast be ready. It ain't like you to miss a meal." After her second attempt to hail Laakea got no response from the workshop, she said to Rehaak, "I'll just go fetch him and tell him. He likely couldn't hear me over the sound of the storm."

Isil grabbed her coat, draped it over her shoulders, and dashed toward the smithy in a vain attempt to stay dry, but the frigid droplets soaked her hair, ran down the back of her neck, and left her shivering after the first few steps. Clouds shrouded the clearing in gloom, and her feet squelched and slipped on the muddy earth as she sped across the space between the house and the smithy. Once inside the building, she wiped the raindrops from her eyes. There was no fire in the hearth, and deep shadow filled the building's interior. The structure appeared deserted. "Laakea, where in all the hells did you go, lad?"

Isil was about to leave the smithy, but when her eyes adjusted to the gloom, she spotted Laakea's naked body between the anvil and the hearth. She shrieked, sprang across the distance, and knelt beside the boy. She bent to touch Laakea's brow, yelped in pain, and jerked her scalded hand away. Water dripping from her hair steamed when it touched his skin and hung in the chill air like smoke above his body. She slipped off her coat, turned it backward, knelt beside Laakea, and slid her hands into the arms so she could comfort him. Despite the layers of cloth between them, sweat beaded on her forehead. "Rehaak, come quick!" Isil shrieked as she knelt on the earthen floor, supporting Laakea.

Within moments, Rehaak skidded to a halt in the smithy's doorway. "What's wrong? Where's—?" His eyes dropped, finding Isil kneeling near Laakea's body. "The boy is steaming like a kettle. What happened to him?"

"No idea. I found him like this. He's burnin' up. Let's get him into the house where we can doctor him. You must have herbs to cure a fever."

"I do, but this is no ordinary fever." Rehaak knelt beside them and held his hand above Laakea's brow. "The youngster's skin is searing hot. I dare not touch him without gloves." He motioned for Isil to rise." An Abrhaani could never survive a temperature that high. Fetch a blanket so we can carry him." Rehaak stood watching over Laakea as he waited for Isil's return. The boy's body, as he lay on the packed earth floor of the forge-house, still steamed like hot porridge on a wintry morning.

The moment Isil returned with the blanket, Rehaak rolled Laakea onto it, protecting his hands, then wrapped him in it. He grabbed Laakea under the arms while Isil fished gloves out of her coat pockets, donned them, and grasped his ankles. Together, they hauled Laakea out into the rain. "He's heavier than I remember from the last time I dragged him through the rain," Rehaak said.

Isil kept a firm grip on Laakea's ankles. Her gloves made the heat tolerable. They carried him toward the house while the rain misted and evaporated off his face as fast as it landed. Isil and Rehaak struggled to keep their footing while avoiding becoming entangled in the floppy blanket, which dragged on the muddy pathway. "Do you s'pose we ought to stow him outside to cool him down?"

"You are right, Isil. I think Laakea's skin has cooled from the rain while we carried him. Fetch another blanket, and I will stay out here with him. If the fever subsides, we will bring him in and lay him on his bed."

Rehaak leaned back against the wall cradling Laakea against his chest while he waited for Isil to return. *If Laakea dies, it is my fault. Once he is gone, I will leave before Isil falls victim to my foolishness and the curse that seems to follow me. I don't know what caused this or what to do about it, but I won't let it be said that Laakea perished because I didn't provide adequate care.*

Once they reached the house, Rehaak plopped on the bench beside the door and propped Laakea beside him. "This is all my fault, Isil. I should never have allowed this child to stay with me. I should have taken him to Twinbridge or sent him somewhere far away from me. I am toxic."

"That be utter nonsense." Isil slung a blanket over Rehaak's shoulders as he cradled Laakea in his arms. "Let me bring you somewhat to eat afore you catches a fever yourself."

"The pain in my gut is more guilt than hunger."

About midday, Laakea's temperature had dropped, so Rehaak and Isil brought him inside and laid him on his bed. As they covered him with the rain-soaked blanket to further cool him, Rehaak's brow furrowed. "It's my fault, Isil. If Laakea had not met me, I would not have drawn him into my quest, and he would not lay there near death," He stooped over Laakea and tugged the sodden blanket around the boy's chin. "It is dangerous for anyone to stay near me. I am a threat to you too. You and Laakea would be safer if you never met me. I am cursed."

"Stop talkin' nonsense. You rescued the boy from an icy death in the rain, and from what Laakea says, you gave him a place to hide out from his pa. More'n that you gave him a place to belong. We's both *lucky* to have met you. I can't speak for Laakea, but I's been searchin' for you ever since I heard 'bout you back in Narragan."

Rehaak straightened up and gaped in wide-eyed astonishment. "You knew of me in Narragan?"

"When you prayed over that first meal we ate together, I figured out you was the fella what got exiled for heresy. I went a-lookin' for you, but you skedaddled afore I got to The Gilded Swan. When I met you in the grassland, I had my suspicions, but until you prayed to the Creator, I weren't sure."

Rehaak raised his open palms to his sides. "You never mentioned it. Why not?"

"Never thought it were important till now." She pointed her bony forefinger at him. "You needs to understand…there be a purpose to our meetin."

"I felt guilty about keeping my secret. If you knew about my message of the Nethera invasion, why didn't you say something?"

"I figured it weren't my business to pry it out o' you. You would tell me at the right time. The Creator brung us together, and He is the one what guides us. We doesn't see His plan, but he works through us and even in spite o' us. Even when we makes stupid mistakes, He is wise, and He is powerful enough to change things.

"We belongs together. The Ecclesiarches turfed you out o' Narragan because o' your message. Laakea had to run away from home because he thunk his pa wanted to kill him. You left your family behind to follow the Faithful One, Laakea lost his ma and his pa, and I lost my folks too. We were all exiles, but together we're a family, a family created by the one what created everythin'. We have to stay together and have faith. You told me you prayed for another chance just afore Laakea stumbled into your life. Don't that mean nothin' to you? Don't it tell you we needs each other?"

"I want to believe that, but whenever I do, tragedy strikes, and people around me get hurt." Rehaak pointed at Laakea lying on the bed. "That's man-child is merely the latest example." Rehaak scowled and bit his lower lip. "There's no more we can do for Laakea now. We should eat, keep up our strength."

Isil's jaw clenched, and her eyes filled with steely determination. "We can't stop just 'cause things gets hard. Our mission be too important. Trust me, Laakea will recover, and we'll all be fine,"

CHAPTER TWO

EIDERON'S DREAM

Eideron awoke, uneasy, bothered by his dreams. Nightly visions had troubled his sleep for weeks now, but once he awoke, he never remembered the details. Still, the omens bothered him. Eideron wished he understood what they meant or at least recalled the warnings they contained. He rose as usual and prepared for his day at the Synod Council.

Eideron's halo of curly white hair framed the weathered ocher skin of his wrinkled face. He stretched to ease the pain in his arthritic joints and ran his fingers through his hair. Trapped between darkness and dawn with a sour taste in his mouth, he washed the sleep from his eyes, rinsed his mouth with water, and spat it in the bathroom sink. The sink, like his dwelling, was carved from the stone walls of the caldera where the Sokai lived.

The burden of leadership lay heavy on his weary old shoulders this morning. How could he lead the Sokai when he, a senior leader, could not discern the path? Eideron supposed that he represented, in miniature, the rest of his beloved people. Thoughts spun in his head like dust caught in the desert winds outside their protected sanctuary.

The Sokai feared the violent madness of the Abrhaani, and the Eniila would taint them. They fled to

Abalon centuries ago, to live protected and isolated from the rest of humankind. During their long years of isolation, they succumbed to their own peculiar form of madness. The Synod met daily and engaged in endless debates, and the discussions always centered on which activities and actions comprised purity and sanctity. Eideron hated the internal conflict but couldn't escape the endless rounds of nitpicking and navel-gazing. That interminable strife led nowhere, except to prevent new insights. The Sokai had become fearful of change; they believed any divergence from the status quo threatened their way of life.

We should abandon this valley, but I doubt I ever will. It has become a prison. Abalon is my birthplace, and it will be my tomb. My wife's grave is here, and her bones lie in the crypt atop thirty generations of our forebears. I am too old to cross the barren desert and seek the Abrhaani and Eniila. If I was younger—

He broke from his thoughts and instead spoke aloud as if addressing the council. "We have become like insects trapped in amber. Perfectly preserved and permanently incapacitated by the instrument of our preservation." Eideron smiled. *I like the analogy, and I will use it in the Synod Council if the opportunity arises.*

Eideron's anxiety was not unique. Several other Synod members had shared similar misgivings from their dreams or intuitions. Curious events brewed inside their protected haven, and his dreams left him wondering if similar things were happening outside Abalon too. The nature of those phenomena was unclear. The council still faced months of debate and strife before they reached a conclusion and fashioned a response to the events.

Speaker Amoreya will not approve any action unless she sees the world ending in front of her. Amoreya is a righteous woman who tries to preserve righteousness and integrity. All the councilors pursue clarity of thought and purity of heart and seek to avoid the violent tendencies of the

Eniila and Abrhaani. They work hard to maintain order and discipline, but they also remain rooted in place, too bound by fear and tradition to move forward. Eideron revised his thoughts. *History is not the problem; it is the answer. Amoreya and the Synod are shortsighted.*

A long-forgotten passion stirred within Eideron, and he spoke aloud, practicing his oration. "We are shortsighted. Our history begins long before we arrived in Abalon, but none of us look beyond the time when our ancestors arrived in this valley. They built sheltered lives for us within Abalon's protective walls. Protection became a dependency, and now we are addicted to safety and security.

"We must gaze farther back in history for inspiration. Our forebears risked everything to cross the wasteland and build homes for us here, but now we, their offspring, dither over the slightest hazard. We must focus beyond the centuries of warfare our ancestors fled, beyond the Sundering, back to the time when the three species of mankind worked together in harmony. We Sokai must understand the Creator's purpose for us. Instead of the blind, selfish, and complacent lives we now lead, we must grasp our destiny with both hands and become the people the Creator intended.

"The Creator fashioned us to be the Seers and Speakers for humankind's three species, and yet for eight hundred years, we have talked only to ourselves. We Sokai have become dotty old fools who mutter into our beards in our rooms while nobody listens.

"Nobody hears us because we no longer have anything meaningful to say. We never leave our sanctuary and never invite anyone into our refuge. We must send someone to investigate the situation outside Abalon. We must follow the example of our ancestors, face danger, take risks, and return to our place among the other species."

Eideron hoped the speech would convince the Synod to move ahead. *Even if I persuade them of the truth, they still must act. Who will the Synod send, how many will go, and where will they send them? The decades of debate engendered by such a mission make my head ache.*

A crash in the kitchen interrupted his ruminations. *Sounds like Simea's broken another plate. My crockery won't survive that boy's clumsiness.* Eideron ignored the racket and called out, "Simea, is breakfast ready?"

"Yes, Master Eideron. I tried to be quiet, but I dropped a plate. I am sorry if I disturbed you."

"Do not fret, youngster. I was awake and shall come out once I am dressed."

The lad grows half a span every tenday and thumbs have replaced all his fingers. Simea trips and stumbles around my quarters, and the youngster's presence puts any breakable objects at risk. I'm in no mood for company this morning. Eideron listened for more sounds of catastrophe in the kitchen. When there weren't any, he hoped his young apprentice had left.

Eideron sighed and looked heavenward, and muttered, "I know, I'm being ungracious and grumpy." *Simea is a talented lad with an eager mind and a good heart, and he often perceives what I and others miss. The youngster shows incredible potential. Even at the cost of shattered china, my latest disciple is worth the effort.* Eideron dressed and entered the kitchen, where breakfast and a silent apprentice both waited at the low wooden table. *Simea hasn't left after all.*

"Can I do something else for you, Master?"

"No, lad, you have done enough damage for one morning." Eideron smiled at Simea to soften the sting of his caustic humor. Eideron expected the lad to bow and leave. Instead, the youngster continued to stand at the table like a trapped animal, uncertain of his fate but powerless to prevent it. "Don't worry about the plate, Simea. I can replace it."

After Eideron had absolved Simea of the broken dish, Eideron expected the boy to let him enjoy his breakfast alone. He settled onto his cushion.

Simea, instead of leaving, hovered over his master and looked more uncomfortable by the second. Eideron reclined on the pillow at the low table, ignored the boy's distress, ate his breakfast, and waited to see if the lad had the nerve to speak. *My friend Himish says I derive a guilty pleasure from my apprentice's discomfort and rejects my claim that it builds character in the lad. Instead, he accuses me of a devilish streak of perversity.*

Simea was the fifth apprentice the Synod assigned to him, the fifth to undergo Eideron's efforts at character building. *The others were undoubtedly characters once I finished with them. Anyone headed for service in the Holy Orders needs a stiff backbone.* Eideron suppressed a smile at the memories of other young men who served him in previous years and sighed. *Sadly, I have outlived two of my former charges.*

"Master," Simea began, tentative as usual.

Eideron pretended not to hear. He continued to scoop up his breakfast and feigned a distracted thoughtfulness. Simea opened and closed his mouth while he fidgeted and blushed, reminding Eideron of a fish. *I'll bet he will turn and run.* Instead of leaving, the boy swallowed hard, squared his shoulders, and began again.

"Excuse me, Master."

Well, at least this time he was polite. He looked up at the boy with a stare calculated to instill panic. "If you must interrupt my breakfast, it had better be important." He brandished his spoon at Simea like a sword and scowled at the youth. "Well, out with it! I don't have all day!" He feigned impatience and enjoyed the way his contrived annoyance made it even more difficult for the lad to continue. "Well, spit out whatever has gotten stuck in your craw."

"Master, I have a question for you, I understand you are busy, but this girl—"

"If you have questions about girls, ask one of the other masters—a younger one, or at least one whose wife has not been dead for many summers. Better still ask your parents—it's their job to teach their children about romantic and biological functions."

CHAPTER THREE

KYONNA

Kyonna stood on the edge of the precipice, ready to plunge into the empty air beneath the ledge. She perched like a sparrow on the lip of the chasm, her tiny body dwarfed by the wingspan of the glider she piloted. Her body, clothed in the tight-fitting windproof flight suit, and her black ringlets, mostly secured under her padded cloth helmet, made her look even more birdlike. The ocher skin of her face, high cheekbones, and chiseled facial features accentuated the look.

Kyonna grinned her crooked-toothed smile as she prepared to step into the void. The glimmer in her violet eyes betrayed her eagerness to get airborne. She pushed off into empty air and felt the familiar rush of excitement. The thermal embraced the wings of her glider like a lover. Today's busy freight schedule meant she could spend the entire day airborne and soar above Abalon looking down on everyone instead of everyone looking down on her and her family. "Ah, the rush of the wind, the freedom from prejudice, the bugs in my teeth." Her smile broadened. The air rushed past and whipped her black ringlets against her padded cloth helmet.

As a Windrider, she carried freight across Abalon, and she had risen to prominence because of her talent. Her instincts and skill at detecting and riding the shifting air currents and dodging the steel cables of the overhead trams gave her elite status among her fellow Windriders. Ky's loads, the heaviest of any Windrider, always arrived ahead of time and undamaged. When airborne, she ruled the sky, but in the valley, on the ground, she and her family faced constant prejudice and hostility.

Her beauty and vivacious personality offset her social stigma as the daughter of a corrupted woman, especially with young men who vied for her attention. She harbored no illusions that their interest went beyond sexual conquest.

Knowing their intentions, she teased and tormented her suitors and never gratified their desires. The only boys she trusted were Eideron's apprentice, Simea, and her close friend and mentor, Rais. Simea was like a brother to her and her older sister, Aibhera. Ky suspected Sim held romantic feelings for Aibhera, but he was too shy to speak of his love, and Aibhera was clueless that his interest in her was more than brotherly.

Rais was several years older than Kyonna, and he had been her instructor when she became an apprentice Windrider. Their relationship had grown into a deep friendship. They often bantered and teased each other like lovers, but nothing serious ever grew from their mutual attraction other than deep respect and mutual trust. Neither of them seemed willing to change the status of their relationship and risk their friendship. Other Windriders believed Ky and Rais were lovers, and neither of them denied or confirmed their coworkers' suspicions.

The sun completed its arc above the crater's rim while she glided back and forth above Abalon's patchwork of fields and gardens. Most of the caldera had held lush forests when the Sokai first arrived. In the last thousand years, out of necessity, the Sokai converted the forest into farmland and orchards. The only remaining native trees existed on the island in the center of Lake Selatan. Nowadays, wooden objects were rare treasures among the Sokai. The Sokai had selected the island as a park and preserved the original vegetation there.

Since the Sokai needed agricultural land to support the valley's population, they had replaced the trees with farmland and roadways. Several decades ago, their engineers replaced their original roads with trams. The wind-powered trams carried agricultural produce, work crews, and passengers. Leoned, Kyonna's stepfather, and his team of engineers built and maintained the thick cables anchored to the crater's rim. It took a full day to cross the caldera in the tram's light baskets, but it was faster and easier than walking.

Wind turbines powered the irrigation pumps, elevators, and all the other technology except for the systems that required thermal energy. Pipes and ducts collected heat from the pool of lava that still boiled below the surface of the caldera. Kyonna knew little about the systems that provided the Sokai with levels of comfort unavailable to their refugee ancestors. She didn't bother herself with such things. She soared above all that, and it was enough for her…almost.

It took over three days to cross the crater on foot. Thermals around the crater's edges lifted the gliders skyward. It was dangerous work dodging the tram cables, but gliders crossed the valley with speed impossible on foot or by tram. Fame and freedom appealed to Kyonna. Sudden gusts of wind sometimes blew the gliders into the wires and sent glider pilots plummeting to their deaths. Windrider's lives were often short, which made anniversaries important celebrations.

Sunlight sparkled like polished jewels off the surface of Lake Seletan, the caldera's central lake. The sun glittered on the black basalt columns and warmed the moisture-laden air, which gave her more lift than usual. By dusk, she had crossed and re-crossed the caldera three times. Exhausted, she parked her glider and folded the frame and wing membranes. Once she had safely stowed it in its niche carved into the crater wall, she picked up her pack and marched to the dispatcher's booth. "I'm off," she said as she breezed past his workplace on the way to the lift, which would carry her to the crater's floor.

Windriders had little use for the class divisions common among the Sokai. They soared the thermals far above the currents and eddies of intrigue that blew the rest of their people back and forth. Family origin did not matter, and wealth was irrelevant. Skill alone determined status among the Windriders, and through her talent as a pilot, Kyonna had gained prominence among them.

Tonight promised to be exceptional. Kyonna's fellow Windriders were gathering at The Greenhouse to celebrate her second anniversary and her promotion to elite pilot status. She was the youngest ever to achieve such recognition. There would be drinking and dancing until the early morning. *After a long day, I deserve some me time. I've let Ma and Aibhera know I won't be home until late, so it's all good.*

Since she was the last to leave the landing pad, she had the elevator to herself. Once inside the wire cage, she engaged the lift mechanism. It creaked and groaned its way down to the caldera floor. *It's celebration time, and I've earned my party, so nothing is going to stop me from enjoying myself to the max.*

Alone in the wire cage, Kyonna took the opportunity to change from her flight gear into her party clothes. She stripped off her flight suit and stowed it in her pack, slid the dress over her head, and smoothed the fabric down her body and thighs. Kyonna's scarlet party dress ended mid-thigh and hugged her curves as snugly as her flight suit. *Aibhera would never expose this much leg or wear clothing this tight. My sister always wears those baggy formless gray things she calls dresses. My friend Aiyo could turn flour sacks into high fashion, so I'm glad I convinced her to whip up this little number for the party tonight. It cost me a week's worth of extra flights, but the cotton feels like silk against my skin, and it hugs every curve.*

The lift ground to a halt on the caldera floor. Kyonna stepped off and strolled along the familiar streets that bordered the planted fields. She knew every pebble, dust mote, and doorway of these streets since her family home lay among the squalor of the field hands' lodgings. Several people greeted her when she passed by their doors. The older women shook their heads and commented about Ky's scandalous garment choice. Old Lady Boon, the spinster who lived a few blocks from Kyonna, yelled, "Go home and put some clothes on, young lady, before trouble catches up to you."

Young men gawked at her, and older men did too—until their wives noticed.

Kyonna swayed her hips as she flounced past the married men and muttered, "And that's how the fight started." She grinned and tossed her ringlets provocatively at old man Conger, who smiled and waved, appreciating the display she put on. *He's such a brazen old fart.* She blew a kiss in his direction and waved back at him. *It's a good thing his wife is inside preparing supper, or she'd box his ears and he'd be sleeping on the floor for weeks.*

CHAPTER FOUR

REVELATION

Eideron tilted his head forward and pressed his lips together, hiding his smile, lest it ruin the austere image he projected. *So, a girl has Simea tied in knots. His hormones have finally made an appearance.* Memories of his feelings during the courtship of his wife, Fierra, flooded his mind, but the boy interrupted Eideron's reverie.

Simea wrung his hands and stammered, "No, sir... It's...it's not what you think." Simea's speech picked up speed. The words gushed out of him. "It's my friend Aibhera, who lives below us on our street. Aibhera and I have been playmates since birth, and we talk a great deal about things like your work in the Holy Order and the future of our people. Our nightmares trouble us." He paused and waited for encouragement from the older man. When Eideron remained silent, Simea took a deep breath and continued, "In recent nights Aibhera and I have dreamed identical dreams each night for the last several tendays."

Having been troubled by his own dreams of late, the word *dreams* caught Eideron's ear. He listened, suddenly attentive. "Continue." It came out as a command, although Eideron no longer intended to appear harsh.

Simea took a deep breath and began, "At first, we dreamed of an ominous cloud of death and disaster obscuring the sun. The cloud darkened the western sky, but now the cloud moves toward our valley. Its expansion threatens Abalon like a tsunami of darkness headed in our direction." Simea paused.

"Nightmares are common, but I've never heard of people experiencing them in tandem. Do your dreams happen on the same night?"

"I understand that sir, and yes, we dream them on the same night. Last night, for the first time, we dreamed of three strangers amid the darkness. These people are a mystery to us since they stand directly in the path of destruction and yet remain whole and alive. One is young like me but tall as a tree and fair as ripened grain, disconnected from his heritage, and driven from his home.

"The second man is older than the first, with olive-green skin and ebony hair. He is shorter and weaker, but he is mighty in lore and knowledge. Filled with doubt, he dithers and blunders along, skirting destruction with every careless choice he makes. He seeks something lost long ago, hoping it will answer all his questions and put an end to doubt.

"The last, a woman, seems older, jade-skinned, and black-haired like the second man. She has seen much and endured much but has forgotten the hard lessons her past has taught.

Because the Nethera want to work in secret, they have tried to silence them without success, but these people are about to expose the Nethera's actions and schemes. When they bring the Dark Ones' plans into the light, they will move openly, and we will be unable to withstand them. These three beings are a beacon of truth, but without aid, the Nethera will snuff out their lives.

Simea paused, emboldened by Eideron's silence. "Are these things symbolic, or do we dream of actual events?" He waited for a response from his mentor.

Eideron pondered the information. The nervous boy stood by, shifting from foot to foot until the older man spoke.

"How long have you had these dreams?"

"We dreamed of the darkness for several months but didn't realize the nightmares were significant. When we dreamed of the three who stand against the Nethera last night, Aibhera and I panicked and thought it best to tell you immediately."

"I must meet your friend…Aibhera, was it?"

"Yes, Master, I will fetch her straightaway." He dashed toward the door.

"Hold!" Eideron shouted. "There is no need for haste. Since your visions have waited several months, they can wait a bit longer. I am uncertain how to help those people or even find them since Aarda is vast. We live deep in the Eastern Wastes, and your three strangers are probably far away. If the Creator wants us to help them, He will have warned us well in advance. I must attend a Synod meeting this morning, so when I meet my friend Himish, I will seek his advice."

"Sorry, Master. When shall I fetch her then?"

"Bring her for the midweek evening meal. We can dine together then. Now be off and let me finish my breakfast in peace."

"Yes, Master." Simea bowed and scurried from the room. On his way out, he bumped a vase filled with crystalline flowers set near the doorway. Eideron grimaced, fully expecting the vessel to share the fate of the dish the boy had broken earlier, but Simea caught it as it tipped from its perch. He bowed to Eideron and, with shaking hands, set it back in place.

After the boy left, Eideron lost his appetite. *The boy has given me food for thought, along with my morning meal.* Despite his inner turmoil, he forced himself to eat, and once finished, he opened the door of his quarters. He squinted in the sunlight and stepped out onto the balcony connecting all the dwellings on this level. He realized he was late, troubled by Simea's story, he hurried along the walkway toward the lift.

Eideron usually enjoyed watching the Windriders soar across the caldera before he descended to the valley floor. His home on the ancient crater's lip provided a vantage point to appreciate their acrobatic skills. He had never flown a glider but often imagined the freedom Windriders felt while they soared high above the valley floor. But today, preoccupied with Simea's revelation, Eideron ignored both the magnificent view of the caldera below and the gliders overhead. The almost deserted lift platform near his quarters emphasized his tardiness. He had neither the desire nor the time for imaginary flights this morning.

CHAPTER FIVE

RECOVERY

For three days and nights, Laakea burned with fever and lay motionless while Isil watched over him. She bathed him with moist cloths to reduce his temperature and sang every prayer-song she knew over him. Neither Isil nor Rehaak had seen a fever so severe. The boy's labored breaths and rhythmic heartbeat were the only evidence he still lived.

"It's the morning of the fourth day." Isil leaned forward with her hands hanging limply over her knees and her head down. "The long nights fearing that any breath might be his last has brung me near to breakin'. My faith has grown thin." Her voice broke. "Are you sure we can't do no more for the lad?

"We did all we could, but without knowing what happened to him, I am reluctant to give him an herbal febrifuge. I doubt he could swallow it." Rehaak chewed the inside of his cheek. "I do not know what caused this, and if I guess wrong, he is so weak it could kill him. We are both helpless, and I know nothing else we can do to break the fever. As you told me before, Laakea is in the Creator's hands. Whether he lives or dies is up to Him."

"Why didn't we hear the lad at work? We shoulda heard him a-bangin' on the anvil while he made them swords and that there breastplate." She pointed to the smithy where the items lay gleaming on the workbench.

Rehaak shrugged. "I can think of no explanation. If he ever wakes, we will ask him, but for now, we can only monitor his condition and make him comfortable." Rehaak left the room while Isil continued her vigil over Laakea's fevered form.

Exhaustion and lack of sunlight weakened her and muddled her thoughts, but she refused to leave Laakea's bedside. Isil understood Rehaak's reluctance to act, but she wanted to do more. In desperation, she spoke to Laakea. "We needs you back, laddie. You got your weapons, but they be useless if there be no one to wield 'em." She hoped her words penetrated the coma.

Despite the hot, moist tears blurring her vision, Isil's eyes burned like she had sand trapped under her eyelids. She wanted to stomp and shout in frustration but refrained. "If my son had lived, he'd be your age. You are a brave, strong lad, and no mother could ask more from a son," Isil said and closed her eyes while she waited.

Another interminable day lay ahead, and Isil felt like an eggshell in an empty nest with the hatchlings fledged and flown—fragile, empty, and alone. Sorrow surfaced in her thoughts like sulfurous bubbles from the depths of a swamp. To ease her despair, she poured out her heart to the Creator.

"I's lost and helpless. I just met Laakea, but I loves him like my boy Eyhan. If You be takin' him now, that be Your right. Laakea belongs to You, but what'll I do if I loses him? How can You 'spect me to continue if I loses this boy too? My life will be like water poured onto dry ground and absorbed without a damp spot to prove that I were ever here. I done lived without direction, purpose, and meanin' to my life for too long now. I gave up everythin' to join these men on this journey, and if You takes him, if it be over, I'll just drift aimlessly till the cold, bony fingers o' death reaches out to claw me into the next life.

"It used to be simple and clear what I should be doin' next. Now, that seems fruitless. Meals made, dishes washed, mithun tended, freight hauled from one place to the next don't mean squat. Is that all my life amounts to? Is my life just a list o' tasks completed with tally marks beside each one? I wants more'n that. I were somebody to someone once, and I had folk what cared about me. This here young'un has got to live 'cause to him I'm somebody. Please don't be takin' another child away from me now that I got a son to love again." Her head sagged until it rested on the bed beside Laakea. Consciousness slipped away, and she slept, troubled by her fears.

Isil awoke to a hand stroking her hair. She jerked upright and blinked in the morning light, which streamed through the window. Laakea looked pale and drawn, but his blue eyes glinted in the sunlight—he was awake at last! She grasped his hand in both of her calloused palms. It felt cool to her touch.

"Praise the Creator!" she shouted, then threw herself across Laakea and enfolded him in a hug that threatened to squeeze out his renewed life.

"Isil," he panted. "Let me go before you smother me."

"Sorry, laddie." She released him, embarrassed by her thoughtlessness, but flooded with relief that he was alive. "Rehaak, come quick, Laakea's awake!" Isil shouted.

❖

Rehaak bounded into the room and halted beside her.

"You are alive." Rehaak's eyes shone, and he bounced on his toes.

"Spot, your keen grasp of the obvious amazes me."

Laakea's weak grin was a healing balm to Rehaak's heart, but it didn't ease the guilt etching his soul. "And your sense of humor is still as bad as your cooking," Rehaak rubbed his hands together.

"Stop it, the pair o' you," Isil scolded, though there was a hint of a smile at the corners of her mouth. "Is that the best you can do for someone who has laid at the gates o' death these past four nights? Rehaak, get this young man vittles afore he wastes away."

"Yes, mistress," he mocked. "Welcome back, Laakea. While you were sick, she was an unbearable tyrant. I need your help to deliver me from the scourge of her incessant demands."

Isil stood and raised her hand as if to cuff Rehaak.

"See what I mean?" he said. He scampered to the doorway in mock terror. "Please don't flog me anymore. I promise I will behave. I will show you the scars and bruises later, Laakea."

Laakea chuckled at Rehaak's antics. He got out of bed with Isil's help, but he wobbled like a newborn lamb when he tried to walk. After he had dressed, gone to the privy, and washed, he dragged his exhausted body to the kitchen table. While he waited for Rehaak to bring breakfast to the table, he drank mug after mug of water to quench his fierce thirst.

Rehaak set a steaming platter heaped with food onto the table and slid a generous portion onto Laakea's plate.

The boy tore a massive chunk from the loaf of bread Isil pushed toward him and speared a sausage with his fork. "I…had…an…interesting…dream," he said between mouthfuls as he wolfed down eggs, and sausages and sopped up the egg yolk with the rest of the bread.

Isil and Rehaak looked knowingly at one another but remained silent while Laakea related his experiences in the Garden of Flame. Neither Rehaak nor Isil interrupted his story. Laakea told Rehaak what he had discovered about selfishness being the source of all mankind's problems. Rehaak nodded in agreement.

When Laakea finished the tale, Rehaak rose from the table. "Stay with Isil, I must get something from the smithy," he said.

"What's going on, Isil?"

"You'll see soon enough, I imagine."

Within moments, Rehaak returned with a large bundle wrapped in oiled skins. It clanked when he set it on the table in front of Laakea. He did not comment but watched Laakea closely as he eyed the bundle.

"What's this? Is it a 'glad you didn't die' present for me? You shouldn't have."

"It is a present alright," Rehaak said with a cryptic smile. "Isil and I hoped you could tell us how you got it, but you have already solved that mystery for us."

CHAPTER SIX

AERON SUUL

Blue-gray morning came, moist and misty around him. It wasn't freezing, but the light breeze and the fog-tinged air gave the day a sharp bite that accentuated the morning's shadows. A hot breakfast would have lifted Aelfric's spirits. There was plenty of wood, spray-dampened, salt-impregnated, and impossible to light; besides, he had nothing left to cook. After Aelfric lost the boat and most of his provisions to the surf, he had reached shore but only found his weapons and duffel bag the next morning. Two tendays of hard marching brought Aelfric near the port at Aeron Suul. Near enough to spot the outlines of masts in the harbor against the silvery morning sky.

The ocean stretched toward the horizon and reflected the light like a sheet of beaten metal. Aelfric made out the darker blue and purple colors of the inlet's opposite shore. Khel Braah's mountains, their indigo edges silhouetted against the sky, cast hazy outlines at the limit of his sight to the west and towered above the green wall of the forest behind him. The beach gravel slid and grated underfoot, slowing, and tiring him, but it had proved easier than thrashing through the brush farther from the shoreline laden with his weapons and heavy pack. There were no thorny branches here to tear at his face and hands and no obstacles hidden in the undergrowth to snare his tired feet.

Aelfric pulled some jerked meat from his pouch and chewed it as he slogged toward the harbor. Few people strolled the rocks and gravel beaches of Khel Braah. Those he encountered circled wide to avoid him. The Abrhaani sensed Aelfric's anger and resolve, hardened to a brittle crystalline edge, and they knew by instinct he was deadly. They were right since; he was returning home to cause bloodshed and violence, and to reap vengeance.

He needed a ship to cross Syn Gersuul, and that was why he had come. Vessels waited here, and Aelfric knew he would find one, and with it, a way home to Baradon. Determination propelled him forward, overruling his tired legs. He strode onward, lost in his thoughts until he reached the town, and marched down the street toward the pier, intent on reaching his destination before his strength failed. The townspeople eyed him from their shop windows and peered at him from the doorways of their houses made of squared stones.

Aelfric walked alone and outnumbered several hundredfold, but they still feared him. Sixteen years of living among them had altered his viewpoint. Aelfric realized the Greens, for all their shortcomings, were more tolerant people than his species.

The Abrhaani were kinder and more understanding than even the members of the Brotherhood, the Eniila holy men who guarded their cities of refuge. The Greens' tolerance and understanding were their greatest strengths and their biggest weaknesses, but even the Greens' broad-mindedness had limits. If anyone threatened their precious trees or animals, they became as violent as anyone else.

Aelfric smiled grimly. He imagined how he looked now, no longer the quiet village smith, but a strange warrior, armed, lethal, and hard as the metal of the sword hanging across his back. Aelfric personified their nightmares. Death incarnate visited Aeron Suul today, dressed in Aelfric's scarred face and body.

On the battlefield, before he came to live among them, he had faced thousands of their little soldiers in countless skirmishes and cut them down like a sickle mowing grass. He had killed better men than these on his way to an actual battle and might do so again, he hoped later rather than sooner. The score he intended to settle was not with the Greens but with his own kind, those who betrayed him.

Aelfric rounded the corner and stalked onto the dock. He ignored the Abrhaani townsfolk and strode confidently down the center of the pier, past crates of cargo. The smell of creosote, salt, rotting seaweed, and freshly caught fish hung in the air. Aelfric ignored the dockworkers and deckhands, who glared at him. Except for these men, most townspeople had never seen an Eniila. Aelfric strode past the ships unloading goods since they likely wouldn't leave port again before the winter storms. He had no more time to waste. A new brigantine called the *Sea Witch,* loading trade goods, and preparing to leave port attracted his attention. Sixteen years had passed in a heartbeat. He had lost his wife and son. All he had to show for the time spent on Khel Braah was an empty ache in his heart. Cold anger and bitter vengeance were all that remained to move him forward.

Aelfric halted. Work stopped. Deckhands stared.

Aelfric waited a moment before fixing his gaze on the Abrhaani deckhand nearest him.

"Where is the master of this vessel?" he boomed.

Although the man looked ready to dash away, he stood his ground while a crowd grew around Aelfric. If he let them get up enough nerve, they might try to overwhelm him with their numbers. No doubt, men among this group had fought in the war and had old scores to settle with any Eniila warrior. Tired and footsore, he was unwilling to pay the cost of an encounter if they attacked him. *Best to press on before tempers flare and the situation gets out of control.*

"I said," he thrust out his chest, put his hands on his hips, and watched the crowd. They didn't back away. *Confidence in their numbers is making them brave.* "Where is the master of this vessel? I wish to book passage to Baradon."

"I will take you to him, sir," the deckhand answered with a steady voice, his courage bolstered by the growing number of Abrhaani hovering around the battle-scarred giant. "Follow me, please." The deckhand walked past Aelfric toward the town, back the way he came.

The crowd on the pier parted to let them through, and the murmur of the Greens' voices, as they talked in hushed tones, faded behind him. *I'm not out of danger yet, but if they intend to ambush me in an alley, their numbers will be useless against my strength and skill.*

Just when Aelfric was sure he had earned his safety through sheer audacity, he noticed a bowman scrambling onto a roof. The archer cocked and aimed his crossbow at Aelfric's chest. Aelfric pretended not to see, but he tensed for the release of the bolt. He'd seen Abrhaani fighters use crossbows once before, during the battle of Edalis. An Abrhaani with a crossbow meant only one thing: this Abrhaani was an old campaigner who fought the Eniila in Baradon. *I pray he releases his bolt soon. If I haven't gotten too old and soft from my years of exile, I might be able to swat it aside or dodge it.*

Each step brought him closer to his potential killer and reduced his chances for survival, but he pressed on behind the man leading the way. Aelfric considered using his guide as a shield, but the man was too far ahead. This bowman knew his craft. It was one of his own axioms: "Be sure of your first shot, or you may never get a second."

Aelfric walked on, trying to exude confidence he did not feel. "Tell that fool on the roof to put away his weapon before I climb up and feed it to him," he growled to his guide. "I have no wish to begin a fracas, but I swear it will end badly for you and your town if you force it upon me."

CHAPTER SEVEN

RUMBLE

The Greenhouse, a dance club in a dilapidated warehouse, sat near the caldera's north wall among other storehouses. The storehouse always sat in shadow. Its moss-covered exterior made it appear like a massive squarish mound of green fuzz nestled against the crater's steep side and gave the structure its name. Light and noise from inside spilled out into the street as Kyonna pulled the door open. The place hummed with energy, and young Sokai packed the dance-floor. Ky spotted her friends amid the crowd and shouldered her way through the dancers gyrating bodies to join her workmates. "Thanks for waiting for me," she shouted above the noise and the music.

"You shouldn't have taken that last job, Wild Child," Kyonna's friend Rais said, using Kyonna's Windrider nickname. "It could have waited until tomorrow. You risked your ass doing it. One of these days, you'll tangle with a suspension cable in the poor light, and that will be the end of your career and your crazy life. We began wondering if we would celebrate your funeral and your anniversary at the same event."

"Never fear. I lead a charmed life," Kyonna waggled a forefinger in his face. "Where's the drink you promised me?"

"Follow me," He took her hand and dragged her along as he danced and elbowed his way across the crowded floor toward the bar. Halfway there, he turned to Kyonna and said, "Stop staring at my ass, you perv. I can feel your eyes burning holes in my pants."

"If you don't want the attention, you shouldn't display the merchandise in those tight jeans, Rais," Kyonna countered.

Once they reached the rectangular bar enclosing the bandstand near the center of the warehouse, Rais ordered drinks for them. Ky leaned her back against the bar counter and surveyed the room while they waited for their beverages.

Kyonna's Windrider friends gyrated and bounced to the rhythm of the music out on the dance-floor. Nearby, her friend Aiyo danced with Loran, a lanky fellow Windrider. She nudged Rais and pointed at them. "Look at the way they're dancing. How long have those two been together?"

"Pretty much since spring."

"The little minx never said a word to me, and I'm her best friend. I'm deeply offended, and I'll make her pay." Kyonna cackled and rubbed her hands together in mock villainy.

Rais shook his head and pursed his lips in simulated disgust. He paid the bartender and reached for the drinks. "The house band sounds better than usual tonight." He perused the murals and graffiti art from young lower-class Sokai artists, which covered the polished basalt walls and glowed in garish neon colors. The eclectic mixture of street-art paintings and social commentary covered the walls to the lofty ceilings, where thousands of tiny blue lights sparkled like a sky full of stars.

Rais was about to hand Kyonna her beverage, but suddenly looked away and stared past her left shoulder. "What's going on over there?" Rais pointed, and Kyonna turned to see what had attracted his attention. A wedge of burly figures in black masks and dark clothes sliced through the swirl of dancers and headed straight toward the bar.

"Oh crap. Not again, and please not tonight," Kyonna said through gritted teeth. Rais put their drinks back on the bar.

The music faltered and stopped mid-song because the band had seen the commotion. The musical group scrambled to pack their instruments and fled the stage, and once they reached a safe distance, they peered at the confrontation.

Rais put his fingers in his mouth, creating a shrill whistle to other Windriders in the crowd that carried above the confused babble of the manhandled dancers. The Windriders responded to his signal and moved to cut off Virtue's goons before they reached the bar.

"You troublemakers don't want to stand in our way." The black-masked leader of Virtue, perpetual protesters, glared at Kyonna, Rais, and the other Windriders who stood between them and the bar that surrounded the bandstand.

"Why not?" Rais said. "Are we supposed to fear you because you wear black masks? You're not as scary as you think. Do the math. Windriders outnumber you, and we won't let you crash our party tonight. We've come together to honor one of our members, and you're disrupting our celebration."

"Virtue aims to close this den of iniquity and social unrest. Don't stand in our way, or you will be judged."

"Sounds like you've already judged us," a tall, bony Windrider chimed in.

"He sure sounds judgey to me," Kyonna added.

Rais scoffed, "Social unrest? We promise to be perfectly restful if you leave. There were no problems in The Greenhouse until you arrived and caused them. How many people did you injure when you pushed your way through the crowd? How many do you intend to harm to reach the bar? You brand us troublemakers, and yet there was no trouble here until you arrived. So who are the real troublemakers?"

"Enough talk." A masked goon stepped forward and grabbed Ky by her ringlets to move her aside and gain access to the bar. "Get out of the way, slut. We're shutting this down right now."

"I'm sorry, I think I misunderstood you," Kyonna said. The Windriders surged forward to help her. "It sounded like you called me a slut."

"You understood me just fine, skank. I said, move aside." The masked hoodlum yanked her hair to force her obedience. Kyonna staggered but stood her ground with gritted teeth and fire in her eyes. She grabbed the thumb of his free hand and bent it back. Her attacker leaned to the side to relieve the pressure on the joint.

"Let go of my hair, asshole, or I'll break your thumb." He released his grip on her curls. "Now, apologize for calling me a slut." The fellow groaned and gritted his teeth against the pain as Kyonna applied additional force. Rais and the other Windriders surrounded Kyonna and her assailant and pushed the other black-clad bullies away from the confrontation.

"Do you need any help, Wild Child?" Rais grunted and stood nose to nose with Virtue's leader. The spokesman for the group tried to push Rais aside and rescue his friend, but Rais pushed back; the men were too evenly matched for either to make any progress.

"Nope, I've dealt with handsy jerks like this all my life. I live under a curse. Guys think I'm an easy mark because I'm tiny and beautiful. Everybody wants to touch me." Kyonna flipped her curls with her free hand, smiled her most alluring smile, and applied more force to the offender's thumb. He whimpered and dropped to his knees but still refused to apologize. "Last chance before I dislocate it. I'll help you get started. It goes like this. I'm...sorry..." Kyonna gave the thumb a little extra twitch of encouragement and flashed her victim an expectant look.

"All right...I'm sorry...I called you a slut."

"And...you'll never do it again...right?" Another little twitch of encouragement elicited a scream.

"I'll never do it again, all right, I'll never do it again."

"That's good because I find that language demeaning. I imagine it's as humiliating as a girl making you cry like a baby with only one hand." She released her grip on the offender's thumb. "Okay, you can go now. I forgive you." She raised her voice. "It was an obvious case of mistaken identity. You mistook me for—your mother."

Several Windriders near enough to hear the exchange laughed.

Aiyar and her dance partner had elbowed their way through the crowd. Aiyar giggled at the exchange, elbowed Loran, who stood beside her, and they chorused, "Ouch. That's gonna leave a mark."

By the time Kyonna's assailant regained his feet, everyone in The Greenhouse, encouraged by her actions, had surrounded Virtue's posse. The goons realized they could never carry out their mission in the face of such united resistance. "We'll be back." The leader backed away from Rais and glared at the crowd. "And there'll be more of us next time. A lot more. We won't stop until we close this hell hole."

"Everyone is welcome here, but next time leave your mask at home so we can discuss your issues face to face like civilized people, no pun intended. Remember, tolerance *is* a virtue." Rais' eyes narrowed, and he pointed toward the entrance. "The door is over there. "Don't let it hit your asses on the way out."

"Only gutless whiners hide behind masks." Kyonna's violet eyes blazed with fury at the fellow who cradled his injured hand. "If you want to change things, take your concerns to our leaders. Don't barge in here and threaten people,"

"Okay, Ky, dial it down. We won this round," Rais said. "Virtue is headed out the door. It's your party—oh, here's the drink I promised." Rais picked up their drinks and handed Ky her beverage. The band returned to the stage, tuned up, and prepared for their next number. "You must be thirsty after that scuffle. Chug that drink, and let's dance."

"Thanks, humiliating bullies is hard work, and it always makes me thirsty." Ky downed her brew and tossed the cup to the bartender, who caught it and winked at her. "Try to keep up, old-timer." Kyonna grabbed Rais's hand and dragged him to the center of the dance-floor, where the Windriders had gathered.

Ky and Rais led the gyrating, bobbing crowd. Anger fueled Kyonna's energetic moves where she and Rais danced, surrounded by their friends, who chanted, "Wild Child, Wild Child" in time to the music.

CHAPTER EIGHT

HIMISH AND LEELA

"Good morning, my dove," Himish said as he watched Leela's unique amber-colored eyes flutter open. Most Sokai had eyes in shades of violet or blue. He had watched his wife sleep while sunbeams lit her face and crept across the floor of their Upper West Rim apartment.

The residences on the west side of the crater's rim, reserved for senior members of the Synod Council, provided the most prestigious accommodations in Abalon. Housing assignments confirmed every Sokai's social status and authority. Councilors and senior officials lived high on the rim while common laborers lived on the south side near the caldera floor. It meant that laborers needn't ride the overcrowded lifts to their workplaces. Workers merely walked out their doors to tend the fields and orchards, but the steep caldera wall perpetually shaded their homes. The upper classes looked down on *shadow folk* their term for the working classes.

Himish and Leela had married forty summers ago. Although her physical beauty had faded, Leela's compassion and tenderness increased over the years. Her strength of spirit shone through her aged flesh with more brilliance than when she was younger.

"Good morning to you too, you old fool." Leela's eyes widened. She rubbed the sleep from them, yawned, and stretched. "Were you watching me sleep again?"

"Yes, I was. Does that bother you?"

Leela shrugged and pursed her lips. "It's your time, and you can waste it looking at an old crone if you wish."

"Time spent admiring your beauty is never wasted, my love. I still see the beautiful woman who captured my heart all those years ago."

"Sweetheart, you must have incredible eyesight to see past the wrinkles and gray hair. You should have fallen in love with someone who could cook."

"I credit your cookery for my youthful vigor and boyish build. Unlike most of my friends, I lack the corpulence of my contemporaries, who could pass for pregnant women." Himish arose, turned sideways, sucked in his stomach, and pointed to it with both hands. "See what I mean? I shall live forever because of your culinary prowess, my dear. Besides, I wouldn't want you any other way. Our life together, just the two of us, has been full of adventure and passion."

Leela giggled. "Adventure, yes, and passion, ha, precious little of the latter lately." Leela feigned anger, but her eyes betrayed amusement at her husband's antics. "Your flattery will get you nowhere, husband. Since I'm no longer the young innocent you courted, I'm immune to your honeyed words."

"It's an altered form of passion, my love. We have found alternative ways to express our love, is all." Himish loved their verbal scuffles as much as he loved the woman he sparred with. Leela's wit and wisdom had attracted him as much as her beauty. Leela's black hair had gone snow white over the last few years. Wrinkles lined her face and age spots dotted her hands, but her mind remained sharp as flint.

"Enough of this flattery. You know I don't believe half of the nonsense you spout." Leela sat up and slipped her robe over her nightdress to ward off the chill in the room. "I'll make breakfast for us; besides, don't you have appointments?"

"I have appointments every morning, but my most important appointment is time spent with you." Himish snuck behind Leela, wrapped his arms around her age-thickened waist, nuzzled her silvery hair aside, and kissed the back of her neck.

Leela pushed his hands away, twisted around to face him, and threw her arms around his neck. Her eyes sparkled with mirth. "There was a time when that trick would earn you a return trip to the bedroom, and you would miss *all* your appointments," she teased.

"I know, but we are oh so much more responsible in our old age, aren't we?" Himish changed the subject. "Eideron and I have a meeting before the Synod assembly. Shall I give him your greetings?"

"Of course." Leela paused, her eyes focused on some distant object, deep in thought. "I have an idea. We should invite Eideron to our quarters for supper sometime soon. I could invite Ayana Sesani—her husband died two winters ago. Ayana and Eideron would be a perfect match." Himish held his hands over his eyes and shook his head until his wife asked, "What's the matter, Himish? Eideron's been alone too long, and they are a perfect match."

"The reason he rejects your invitations, my love, is not your cuisine. It's your ceaseless efforts to marry him off to one of your widowed friends. So, Ayana is the widow of the month, is she?"

"But—"

"No buts," Himish interrupted. "Eideron won't visit unless I can promise him you won't ambush him with another of your friends. I know you want him to be happy like we are, but he has no space in his heart for another love at this late stage of his life. After Sidi died fifteen years ago, he swore he would never remarry, and his apprentices are his life since her death. Your intentions are pure, but stop meddling, for the sake of our friendship with him…and my sanity."

"But the Housing Commission is about to evict her from her apartment. The commissioners say she takes up more space than her allotment. Ayana is a single woman with no dependents, and the committee will move her to the widows' barracks, and conditions are horrible down there." Leela stared at her husband and waited for his response.

"Yes, horrible conditions are everywhere. The Housing Commission and the engineers chisel more quarters from the crater walls every day. But it won't be soon enough to save your friend from the widows' barracks." Himish's attempt to calm his wife failed.

Leela scoffed and stomped into the kitchen of their quarters, muttering about men and their shortcomings. Himish thanked the Creator that his hearing was not what it used to be: he didn't need to hear her disparage him and men in general. Himish hadn't won the battle or even achieved a truce. It was a cessation of hostilities and only that. Once Leela seized an idea, he could never dislodge it without high-powered explosives—Himish wasn't sure he could withstand an all-out verbal war with his tenacious wife. *A man must choose the hill he wants to die on, someone once said, and I'm not ready for the afterlife yet.*

CHAPTER NINE

EHLBRINGA WEAPONS

Rehaak pushed the large bundle wrapped in oiled skins toward the youngster. Laakea unwrapped the package and instantly recognized the objects inside it. "How is this possible? Did I make these?" Eyes wide, he ran his hands over the shiny objects inside the skins.

"We had hoped you could answer that question for us," Rehaak said. "Now that we have heard your dream, I understand. It was no dream. These items were beside you when we found you on the floor of the smithy, burning with fever and pale as a corpse. You must have made them while you slept, though I doubt you experienced any actual sleep. You made the blades and breastplate, and the process of their creation almost destroyed you."

The ehlbringa was different now, brighter, almost translucent, and Laakea knew the runes inscribed into the guards meant Truth and Justice. He also knew the rune worked into the center of the breastplate denoted Righteousness. The swords glowed as if light trapped within the metal tried to escape. Both swords had perfect weight and balance. Laakea tested their sharpness with his thumb and only realized he had cut himself when he saw blood oozing from the wound. The breastplate, thin and light as thistledown, when worn padded and concealed under a shirt, would protect his torso from any weapons the assassins could use against him.

"I reckon that explains the fever too," Isil added. "You was in the forge o' the Creator, and it took you a while to cool off again."

"Well, Rehaak, I suppose we can continue your quest since I have the tools to protect you." He attempted to stand, but Isil pushed him back onto the bench.

"You still needs to rest, laddie. Makin' them things took too much out o' you, and you nearly died doin' it."

"I suppose you're right, Isil." Laakea looked at Rehaak for support, but his friend glanced away. "But Rehaak tells me we Eniila heal much faster than you Abrhaani, and I know it's true. It won't be long before I'm back to normal. I can wrap the sword grips with rawhide and attach straps for the breastplate. That won't take long, and it's easy."

"That's right, Isil. He *will* heal quickly, but he will eat a mountain of food first," Rehaak fell silent, looking pensive and troubled.

"What's wrong, Spot?" Laakea asked.

"Oh, just thinking," Rehaak answered, "At least we know the meaning behind your father's song. Do you think he ever worked ehlbringa?"

"No, he didn't because he had no ehlbringa to use. To him, it was a work-song, set to the rhythm of hammer blows on the anvil. Pa said no one since Selvyn had worked with ehlbringa. I had a thought. I could be one of Selvyn's descendants! Ma taught me her genealogy through twenty generations, and someone named Selvyn was on the list fifteen generations ago." Laakea paused in his recollection, his face solemn. "But that leaves me with an uncomfortable conclusion about the assassin's blades."

"What conclusion?" Rehaak tilted his head to the side and pursed his lips.

"The flame creature claimed Selvyn was the last Eniila who worked with ehlbringa. If Selvyn was the last blacksmith who worked with it, then Selvyn himself made the assassin's blades. That is the only explanation."

"Why is that important?"

"Selvyn is an Eniila hero. How could a hero do such wickedness? Those weapons were perversions of the pure metal, designed to murder people for the Dark Ones. We all felt the evil in them when we handled those things because they served the Nethera's purposes."

Isil sat up straight, eyes wide. "That be why they done gave us the creeps." She slapped the table with her palm. "I knew I weren't imagining it!"

Laakea scratched the downy stubble on his chin. "I wonder what happened to Selvyn that caused him to turn away from the light and create those perversions of smithcraft. I said I might misuse power if I received it, and the flame creature said, 'You have spoken the truth. To Selvyn's disgrace, he strayed from the Maker's plan and became corrupt.'"

"It must be difficult to believe a hero of your species followed the Dark Ones," Rehaak said.

Laakea shuddered. "How could Selvyn twist ehlbringa to serve the Dark Ones and bend such beauty to the service of evil? Good has triumphed, despite evil's nastiest efforts, and now I have weapons to protect you." He rewrapped the breastplate and the swords in the oiled skins. "Although this metal is immune to rust, these are holy items and must be treated with reverence." Laakea paused, then said, "I already have rawhide, and I can wrap the grips before tomorrow afternoon."

"You best go slow, young'un," Isil cautioned.

"It won't take much strength or energy to wrap the grips." Laakea rose from the table, lifted the lid of a trunk near the kitchen, and rummaged through it. "See, here are the strips. I can start right now." Laakea brought the rawhide strips to the table and got a bowl from the kitchen. "Isil, can you get water to soak this leather? I will wet it and wrap it around the hilts, and when it shrinks, it will tighten on the grips."

When Isil left to fetch the water, Rehaak lingered near the boy, disposed of the breakfast leftovers, scant as they were after Laakea finished eating, and began washing the dishes. He worked in silence, periodically looking at Laakea over his shoulder.

He watched as Laakea unwrapped the swords, unable to resist staring at them. The boy caressed the blades carefully to avoid cutting himself again, admiring the craftsmanship they embodied.

"Rehaak, can you go to the village soon? I will need broad leather straps for the breastplate. Father and I made hundreds of buckles I can use. I just need leather straps."

"I shall leave first thing tomorrow morning to see the tanner. You shall have the finest and strongest leather he can supply."

The day slipped away, and work kept them busy. By nightfall, Laakea had wrapped the swords' grips with rawhide.

The next morning, Isil, Laakea, and Rehaak arose at sunrise. At breakfast, Laakea looked as fit as he ever had. He tried to ask Rehaak about the next step in his quest for the Aetheriad, but Rehaak avoided answering his questions. Laakea gave up and went out to the forge to find buckles for his breastplate, while Rehaak gathered his things for the trip to the village.

"You best not lollygag," Isil chided.

"I shall hurry as if my life depends on it…because it does." Rehaak left the house and closed the door behind him. "Farewell, friends," he whispered.

Laakea and Isil are precious to me, and the only way to protect my foolish friends is to leave them behind. This quest has already cost everyone too much. I can save them only if I abandon them. Their lives are too precious to waste.

Rehaak strode away from the house and smithy, his heart brittle as a shard of stone in his chest. The powerful bonds that bound him to Isil and Laakea waged silent warfare with his resolve to abandon them. Although his feet still led him away, his heart always lured him back to his friends.

Rehaak struggled to keep his emotions at bay as the distance between him and Laakea's house increased. *It is better to leave now. Fate constructs the twists and turns of my life, and circumstances beyond my control force me to take paths I would otherwise avoid.*

Rehaak vacillated, his mind in utter turmoil, while he made and unmade his decision to abandon his friends. Rehaak couldn't decide which was more critical—Isil and Laakea's friendship or their safety. He couldn't think of another way to protect them, aside from abandonment. *Perhaps I will get the leather from the village; maybe not. I have all day to decide whether to return.* He followed the trail to the Dun Dale road. For most of its length, it ran beside a stream. Mist curled along its banks. Rehaak was so busy with his thoughts; he did not notice the shadowy shapes watching him from the forest's edge.

CHAPTER TEN

SIMEA'S FRIENDS

As Simea waited to meet his friends in the predawn darkness, dew clung to the shrubs around the meditation garden. Water gurgled over decorative rocks and splashed into the pool at the fountain's base. Sim warded off the dampness and the chill of the stone bench with the hem of his coat, closed his eyes, and replayed his conversation with Eideron. *I wish I could express myself better, but Eideron makes me nervous. I'm such a coward.*

Footsteps crunched on the gravel pathway leading to the fountain. Nailah's and Pippali's voices heralded their presence. Their arrival interrupted Simea's bout of self-deprecation. "Hey, Sim, did you hear about the raid on The Greenhouse last night?" Pippali grabbed Simea's arm, and his words came out in a rush.

"No, I didn't, what happened?"

"Members of Virtue raided the place and tried to shut down The Greenhouse for the third time this season."

"Harmless fun is one thing those idiots from Virtue can't stand. Were you there when it happened and why didn't you tell me earlier?" Nailah crossed her arms and tapped her foot on the ground.

Pippali waved away her objection. "I had just arrived when they burst in and headed for the bar, which is always their prime target. I guess they think nobody will hang out there if they can't drink and dance. Virtue protests everything offensive to them, but they are so easily offended. I assigned an acronym to them. I call them C.A.V.E. people."

"What does that mean?" Simea asked.

Pip smirked, "Citizens Against Virtually Everything." Pip spread his arms and grimaced like a comedian who sought applause. "I have a million jokes, and I'll be here all week. Please hold your applause until the end."

"Hilarious." Simea's face displayed no amusement despite his words. "Was anyone hurt?"

"I saw them burst through the door, so I avoided them, but I imagine some of the dancers are sporting a few bruises. Virtue knocked down anyone who got in their way. Once the band saw Virtue, they stopped playing, people realized the threat and let them pass. The Windriders were hosting a party last night, so there were a lot of glider pilots present, and they squared off with Virtue's hooligans. Simea, your friend Aibhera's sister—what's her name?"

"Kyonna," Simea said. "Ky's a firebrand, but did Virtue and the Windriders fight?"

"I didn't see much after a crowd gathered around them and blocked my view. Except for a lot of shouting, nothing much happened. Once those black-clad goons left, the band returned, and the party resumed. Welcome to The Greenhouse. Nothing stops a party there."

Simea said, "I'm worried because Virtue seems more militant now, and their numbers increase every tenday. Last year, they only paraded out front with signs, but now they are belligerent, and I heard rumors of goons battering anyone who opposes them. If things escalate, more people will get hurt."

"Let's change the subject," Nailah said. "Where's the rest of our study group?"

"They abandoned us since we can't get access to the material we requested from the library. They locked every book we want in the secure section. Unless we get authorization from our masters or the Synod Council, they are off-limits to us," Pippali frowned and pursed his lips. "My master won't permit me into the secure section until I am recognized and endorsed by the council, and that's a year or more away. What about you, Sim, will Eideron grant you access?"

Simea's face burned. He stared at the gravel and answered with a half-truth. "No, Eideron hasn't given me permission to access that section of the library."

"You didn't answer the question. That means you haven't asked Eideron for access." Nailah raised her voice. "Simea, I can't believe you haven't asked yet." She folded her arms across her chest, her lips pressed tightly together, and stared at the top of Simea's bowed head. Her gestures of disapproval escaped Simea since he refused to look at her, but he couldn't miss the anger and frustration in her words and tone.

"Come on, Sim," Pip said. "All the other apprentices tried, and all the masters rejected our appeals. Eideron is our last hope."

"You don't work for him," Sim said. "You don't know him. Eideron's fearsome when he's angry, and his sharp tongue can strip the metaphorical flesh from your bones."

"Stop exaggerating. Eideron's a man, not a fire-breathing monster. You won't burst into flames when you ask. What's the worst that could happen? He could say no, that's all. Eideron can't punish you if you ask questions. You need to grow a spine and take a stand, or you'll never become a councilor."

"Don't you think I understand that?" Simea shouted. "I hate the way I am, but I don't know how to change, and I don't need *you* telling me I suck. I can't be the person *you* want me to be; I can't even be the person *I* want to be, and I hate myself because of it." Tears trickled down his flame-red cheeks. He turned away from Nailah and Pippali, consumed by the pain and shame of his failure.

Nailah moved toward Simea and put her hand on his shoulder. He wrenched away. "I don't want your pity."

"It's not pity, silly. It's moral support. The Creator made us all different. We each have a purpose and a destiny. You just need to find yours."

"Chances are you are right, Simea, Eideron would reject your request. If he refuses to grant access to us, there may be another way into the secure stacks," Pip said.

"What way?" Nailah asked.

"Sim's friend, the one who works in the library, might pull some strings and help us."

"Aibhera? Can she get access to the secure stacks, Simea?"

"I don't know."

"Can you ask her? You grew up next door to her. At least she won't browbeat you if you ask," Nailah reached toward Simea but then withdrew her hand. "I've only met her a few times, but she seems sweet."

"I can ask her, but Aibhera may not have access to the secure stacks either, and I wouldn't want to cause trouble for her. Aibhera and I must approach Eideron about another matter. We have an appointment with him for the midweek dinner. That's only three days from now."

"Why are you meeting with him?"

"Aibhera and I had several disturbing dreams, and we hope he can interpret them for us."

"It's almost sunrise. We should all get to work at the Grand Hall before the meetings start, or Simea won't be the only one who faces his master's wrath."

CHAPTER ELEVEN

MORNING MEETING

Himish kissed Leela on the cheek, patted her rump, and headed for the lift platform. When he arrived, councilors, other bureaucrats, and their apprentices already packed the platform. He scoured the crowd for his friend Eideron, but the puffy white cloud of Eideron's hair was not among the ebony heads nodding in conversation. Himish and Eideron were the oldest members of the Synod Council, and Himish had heard rumors that a faction of younger councilors felt it was past time they withdrew from active service.

Several senior councilors nodded greetings to Himish while conversing with their apprentices. A few stopped and inquired about his health and that of his wife. The youngest members of the group ignored Himish and focused their attention on Councilor Herron, a rising star in Abalon's politics. Himish had never liked the smarmy, arrogant upstart. Even as an apprentice, Herron was overly fond of celebrity and sought the limelight at every opportunity. The apprenticeship process, designed to weed out people like Herron, had somehow failed, and he had slithered his way to the top despite the vetting process.

Outside the platform, a heavy mist glowed golden in the sunlight and obscured the caldera floor. Himish took it as an omen about the future of the Sokai. If egotistical pedants like Herron led the Sokai, Abalon's future looked as nebulous to Himish as the mist outside the lift platform.

The elevator arrived, and the lift operator cranked the doors open. After the fellow crammed everyone into the metal cage for their descent to the caldera floor, Herron's admirers surrounded Himish. He ignored the sycophants and focused instead on the view from the lift cage. Once they plunged below the fog bank, the fields and orchards became visible, and the mist disappeared. Beneath the cloud cover, Lake Selatan, the lake in the caldera's center named after the visionary leader who brought the Sokai to their present home, came into view. Its water, gray as a pool of molten lead this morning added to Himish's increasing melancholy. *How strange. I was in a pleasant mood earlier. The weather rarely affects me this way, so it must be the company. I shouldn't let these fawning upstarts get under my skin.*

The elevator creaked and shuddered to a halt, and its passengers streamed out of its metal mesh cage onto the crater floor's paved plaza. People hustled off to their workplaces while Himish stood alone for a moment and stared down the tree-lined boulevard toward the council chamber. The cherry trees cast no shadows under the overcast sky, but their blossoms littered the avenue, painting the black stone pavement bright red. Himish shook his head to dislodge the image of a river of blood leading toward the semicircular bulk of the Synod Council's Grand Hall.

Centuries ago, the Sokai built the Grand Hall from the stone of the crater's western face. Behind the council chamber, a labyrinth of passageways penetrated deep into the cliff that formed the building's curved rear wall. Those passageways and rooms provided offices for the officials and bureaucrats who managed the business of keeping over a million Sokai fed, clothed, and housed. Below those offices, other passages led to sewage recycling facilities that produced fertilizer for the fields. Lower still, geothermal chambers harvested heat from the lava beneath the caldera and created steam to run turbines and generators.

Himish's aged knees carried him up the series of broad steps, past the carved basalt columns, and into the portico. The tall wood-panel doors stood open and allowed the cloud-filtered sunlight to brighten the interior of the antechamber. Councilors and supplicants jammed the entrance hall with their bodies, and the hiss of conversation hung in the air like steam escaping from a pipe. The domed skylight in the council chamber brightened as the morning mist burned away. Himish made his way to his usual spot and chatted with one of his neighbors until he felt a hand on his shoulder. He turned.

"Aha, Eideron. What kept you?" Himish asked. "You are always among the first to arrive. You look troubled. What disturbs you this morning and upsets your schedule?"

"Simea, my apprentice..." Eideron began his explanation, but the Speaker pounded on the dais with her staff of office, called the meeting to order, and cut off his answer.

"We'll talk later, Himish," he whispered.

The assembly dragged on while councilors wrangled and debated. Himish remained semi-aware of the proceedings. A mixture of curiosity and apprehension deepened within him.

When the session ended, Eideron called him into a private room to explain the source of his distraction.

Eideron sat with his hands folded in his lap and spoke slowly. "Simea has a friend, and they dream identical nightmares of the Nethera. The Dark Ones are active again. At least that is the way I interpret their dreams."

Himish's jaw hung open for a moment. He raised his voice, "What? Both? The same dreams at the same time?"

"Yes." Eideron raised his hands, signaling Himish to speak in hushed tones. "Beware of eavesdroppers. I don't want to start a controversy until we understand their dreams' significance. They dream of great darkness headed our way, and only three people stand against the tide of destruction. Even more important, the three who stand together are two Abrhaani and one Eniila."

"Eniila and Abrhaani...allies?" Himish looked solemn. "Improbable."

"Foretold, not improbable, and you know what that means," Eideron said.

"Simea is one of our most gifted apprentices, Eideron, but the girl, whose apprentice is she?"

"I don't know her. No one has mentioned an apprentice by that name. Simea doesn't talk about his life or relationships outside the Order—"

"And when he talks, he mostly stammers," Himish interrupted. "You should not intimidate your protégés."

"Nonsense. Intimidation is good for apprentices. They need stiff backbones, and that's the best way to build character, but let's not debate that again. I want a second opinion about their dreams. Could you join me for midweek supper?"

"Of course I can. I can always use a delicious meal." He patted his stomach. "That boy cooks far better meals than Leela does."

Eideron replied, "No doubt about it. Leela is a saintly woman, devout and dedicated—"

"And unable to boil water," Himish interrupted. "But Leela fills my life with joy."

Eideron smiled. "One reason I work hard is to avoid her persistent invitations for meals...and her tireless determination to pair me with one of her widowed friends."

"You know her well, old friend. On the bright side—" Himish patted his stomach. "I attribute her lack of culinary skills to prolonging my youthful vigor. She enables me to avoid indulging in gluttony. I only eat when necessary, and never more than I need, unlike your rotund self." Himish poked Eideron's belly with his forefinger.

"You're just jealous."

"Forsooth, you have exposed my inner darkness. Spirits of gluttony and jealousy possess me. Will you report me to the Speaker so they can expel me from this solemn assembly?"

Both men chuckled. Eideron and Himish had been cronies for decades, and they did not have many secrets left between them. In private, they often bantered this way. The Speaker would have reprimanded them if she knew, but she didn't, and they would never tell her. Himish and Eideron's bond of friendship, developed over decades of fellowship, ran deep.

"Arrive before sundown if possible," Eideron said and started toward the door.

"Both I and my appetite look forward to it; I will walk as fast as my skinny old legs can carry me."

CHAPTER TWELVE

BOOKING PASSAGE

The guide looked back. Aelfric spoke again, "Tell him to put up that crossbow, or you'll be the first to taste my anger."

Aelfric's guide turned toward the figure on the roof and shouted to the bowman, "Put down your weapon, you stupid ass, unless you aims to get the both o' us killed. If he wanted to do us harm, he woulda done it long afore now, and he wouldna come alone."

The archer hesitated, nodded, and lowered his crossbow. Aelfric bowed to the bowman with a flourish. The fellow descended the far side of the sloped roof, and once he disappeared below the peak, Aelfric relaxed. With that crisis averted, he focused on the street ahead.

Aeron Suul differed from the village near his farm. The Abrhaani here made their houses and shops from squared blocks of stone, not timbers like the ones in New Hope and Dun Dale. Thatch, not wooden shingles, covered the sloped roofs. Aelfric saw plenty of trees farther inland, but there were many squarish broken stones along the shoreline, and the nearby grassland provided plenty of material for the thatched roofs. Materials at hand and the Greens' reluctance to cut timber dictated construction methods in every Abrhaani town.

Each house along the street had the usual garden planted with various herbs and vegetables. Aelfric's guide turned onto a side street, walked a few more paces, and stopped in front of a small shop with a colorfully painted sign. Aelfric could not read the characters on the sign, but the pictogram showed that it was a trading house.

"The master be in here." His guide pointed to the door.

"I suspect you had best go first and give me an introduction."

"I reckon you be right. The master might think we been invaded if'n you was to go first." His guide smiled and stepped through the darkened doorway into the shop. Aelfric had to duck to get through the door built to accommodate Abrhaani physiques. The average Abrhaani stood chest height to Aelfric. Few stood as tall as his broad shoulders.

Shelves and crates, organized in neat rows, lined the walls in the shop's dim interior. Trade goods of all kinds lay displayed on the containers and boxes. At the far end of the room, curtains separated the store from the office. Muffled voices came from behind the drape.

"The master be in the back, sir; I'll fetch him for you."

Aelfric stood among the crates near the entrance so he could see both doors and escape if negotiations went awry. The conversation in the back room subsided when his guide disappeared behind the screen.

The voices began again at a diminished volume that built to a shout of disbelief. When the curtains parted again, an overweight Abrhaani man emerged, followed by Aelfric's guide and another Abrhaani of similar build to the guide. The men approached through the semi-gloom and stopped just outside arm's length.

The overweight man leading the group looked at Aelfric, grinned, hooked his thumbs into the waistband of his trousers, and leaned back against a barrel." It's been a long spell since I laid eyes on you. The last time we met, you offered me a king's ransom to bring you to the Southland. I warn't sure you survived the boat ride to the shore. Now you be standin' in front o' me again after— a double handful o' years? And where's that woman o' yours?

"My compliments to you, Captain Harmish. Glad to see you again after not ten, but sixteen years. I would have believed you drowned long ago in that leaky tub you sailed," Aelfric said, avoiding the question about Shelhera.

"Well as it so happens, that schooner sank off the island of Khel Nett two years back. But I warn't on it. Sailors swear that island is cursed, and I believe it's true. Never ventured near that rocky wasteland myself." Harmish's raucous laughter sounded more like a seal's bark. "I sold it to an unfortunate fella and bought me a fine new brig with what you gave me for your fare and what I got for the other as payment. The extra mast, sail, and hull length make for better speed, and I can even sail her backward if'n I has a mind to." Harmish held out his arm in welcome.

Harmish and Aelfric clasped each other's forearms in a friendly greeting. "I need your services again, Captain, to bear me in the opposite direction. I cannot pay you much for this trip, only a small purse of gold, some fine silver jewelry, and a few silver bars."

"Should I ask why you be wantin' to go back, or am I better not knowin'?"

"Let's say I want to pay my respects to my family."

"Nuff said. You can keep your gold, but how much silver do you have?"

"I have nine bars in my pack."

"You found a place to settle somewheres, I reckon. How far inland did you settle?"

"I built a house near the village called Dun Dale. It's a two-day walk from the town of New Hope. Do you know it?"

"Gods, man! Does I know it? I trades for lumber and rope from there for our shipyard. It takes a month to get there! How long was you in getting here?"

"Two tendays ago I left my house with what you see on me."

"So you was on the road twenty days luggin' that great heavy sword, nine bars o' silver, and provisions? I'm surprised you be still standin'. You set a good pace too, with them long legs o' yourn."

"I suppose I did well enough for an old man, but part of my journey was by boat."

"By boat! Who'd a brung you by boat?"

"No one. I came alone in the dingy you gave me."

"Well then, where's this doughty little craft. It'd be good to see her again."

"I lost it in a storm ten days ago. It broke apart on the rocks, so I walked the rest of the way."

"And you done it all in twenty days loaded like a pack beast!"

"You might say I took a shortcut, and it was nearer to twenty-two days. I would've been here half a tenday sooner if I hadn't lost the boat in the surf."

"Stumblin' over them rocks and a-slippin' on that gravel, that'd be no shortcut I'd be takin', either old or young. You might say the gods arranged our meetin', since I just made port the day before yesterday. But enough o' this jawin', we got a bargain to strike for a fare to Baradon."

"If possible, I wish to leave now, and the price is whatever you name."

"Well, we be leavin' with the tide this evenin', and because o' the luck you brung me after the last trip, you can keep your silver too. I coulda been on that ol' boat o' mine had you not paid so handsomely, so I reckon I owes you that much at least, for causin' the gods to favor me somewhat."

"The gods… Ha! I want no involvement with the gods. I'm glad the gods favored *you*, but they have shown *me* no kindness."

"Well, be that as it may, they seems involved with *you*, whether you likes it or not. So get to the *Sea Witch* and stow your gear. Hermad here," he pointed to Aelfric's guide, "will show you to your berth. We leaves in three hours. You might want to stop and get a good feed—or mebbe not. As I recollects, you warn't able to keep it down last time. Maybe it'd just be a waste o' good vittles." Harmish grinned at Aelfric amused that such a powerful man had succumbed so horribly to seasickness on his last trip.

Aelfric nodded. He and Shelhera had spent most of the previous voyage bent over the ship's rail while they spewed until their sides ached and their throats burned. Aelfric preferred good solid ground beneath his feet. The constant roll and heave of the Syn Gersuul wreaked havoc on him and Shelhera. Their infirmity provided the sailors with hours of amusement. *An empty stomach might be better.*

"Oh, by the by, the *Witch* has another passenger besides yourself, a fine gentleman from Narragan, headed east, just like your lordship. It'll be my last crossing afore the winter storms begin. It be a short run to Sethria. I won't risk a longer voyage like Camikola or Edalis at this time of year."

"Sethria will do just fine, and I keep my own company, so I expect no problem for either of us."

"Kinda hard to keep your own company on shipboard. It's close quarters, my friend."

The prospect of sharing the voyage with a dandy from the big city displeased Aelfric, although he wondered what business an Abrhaani gentleman had in Baradon. "Take me to the ship, Hermad, and show me where to bunk and stow my gear," Aelfric clasped the captain's hand to seal their bargain, wheeled, and headed for the door. Hermad trundled after him like a faithful hound.

CHAPTER THIRTEEN

OPTIONS

After Rehaak left Aelfric's home, he hurried along the road toward New Hope. The mist had risen higher than the stream's banks and swirled around his feet as he approached Dun Dale. Bogged in a morass of conflicting thoughts, he passed through the village. When he reached the tannery at the village's outskirts, he wrestled with his choices once more.

If I return to the house where Laakea and Isil wait, I endanger their lives. The assassins will kill anyone who aids me in my quest, but without their help, I face the dangers ahead unaided. I suppose I could ignore the Creator's command and abandon my mission again. That worked out so well the last time.

The more distance he put between himself and his friends, the farther it was to return and jeopardize their lives. Rehaak hated to abandon Laakea and Isil, but he passed the tannery without stopping, almost convinced they were better off without him.

Lost in his conflicting thoughts, Rehaak ignored his misgivings and continued away from Dun Dale. The winding wagon trail toward New Hope grew straight, and when the mist lifted, he gained a better view of the road ahead. A lone man strode down the straightaway toward him. Instead of the work-worn, patched clothes typical of locals, the traveler's garments fit well, and their style indicated wealth and power. The fop was a member of the Abrhaani elite, no doubt a high-level bureaucrat from Narragan.

Strangers who wear expensive clothes and ooze political power seldom visit the village. What is he doing here? Rehaak stopped walking. His eyebrows furrowed and then released as he watched the man draw closer. *I must discover why this man travels to Dun Dale. Influential people never visit our backwater village, and most wealthy folks remain ignorant of Dun Dale's existence. His presence shows that someone high in the government has taken an interest in our little corner of the world.*

Rehaak resumed walking, but a roiling in his stomach and tightness in his chest made him suddenly wary. Rehaak's dark eyes evaluated the traveler as the distance between them narrowed. This man's presence could be good news or bad news. As Rehaak approached, the man ahead stopped and leaned on his ornate carved staff.

"Hello!" The man said, his smile barely visible under the thick mustache and braided beard. He extended his hand to Rehaak. His many rings sparkled and flashed in the noonday sun. Rehaak reached forward, and when the fellow clasped Rehaak's hand in a forceful handshake, the jewelry left imprints on Rehaak's fingers.

Rehaak winced and broke free of the man's grip. "Well met, friend," Rehaak responded. "Where are you headed, if I may ask?"

"Dun Dale is my destination. Have I taken a wrong turn?"

"You made no mistake. This road leads to the village. I did wonder if you had lost your way since I only recently heard of the place myself, and I am more familiar with these parts."

"Dun Dale is indeed my goal, as it has been all the weary way from Narragan. I would relish your company if you walked with me, although my journey takes you in the wrong direction. I fear the trees are closing in on me in this isolated area." He extended his arms wide, gesturing at the forest around them. "These vast empty spaces without people set me on edge. This, I fear, is no fit place for one accustomed to city life."

If I return to Dun Dale with him, I might discover what this stranger's presence here means. He could be a source of vital information. After a moment's hesitation, Rehaak said, "I have no objection to your offer, sir."

"Dreynar var Asan is my name." Dreynar used the second name, customary with the nobility. "Call me Drey. I am on an inspection tour." Drey's eyes glittered with energy and enthusiasm, and he oozed charisma, but there was a sharp edge to his polished manner and charm.

Should I give my actual name, since this outsider is a nobleman from the city that exiled me for heresy?

Drey did not say what he inspected, nor did he mention who had sent him on this long journey without an escort. Rehaak chewed his lower lip. *Does he have anything to do with the assassins sent to kill me? Nobles do not wander the countryside without an entourage.*

Despite Drey's friendly manner, alarms continued to sound in Rehaak's mind and left a sour taste in his mouth. He chose caution over honesty. "Saarik is my name, noble sir."

"Unless I am mistaken, your speech tells me you are a man of breeding." Drey paused and peered into Rehaak's eyes as if to gauge his honesty.

"Not of breeding, noble sir, but I am an educated man, the result of ambitious parents," Rehaak lied a second time.

"Ah, I suppose all parents have that inclination to a greater or lesser extent. It is natural for parents to want better for their children than what they've received at the hands of the gods. Let us continue our conversation if you would be so kind as to accompany me."

"With a good will, sir. Lead on." Rehaak turned, extended a hand toward Dun Dale, and gave a shallow deferential bow.

"No doubt you wonder about my retinue, or rather my lack of retainers."

"I admit the thought crossed my mind. It is...unusual...for one of the gentry, such as yourself, to journey this far without companions."

"Ah yes, they deserted me along the way when brigands set upon us. The blackguards left me to fend for myself, but I am handy with this staff I carry." He brandished and twirled the showy rod he carried. "I managed to make the villains wish for an easier target. Although I lost my baggage in the encounter, I escaped with my life and limbs intact. I should have taken *my* men instead of hiring mercenaries for the journey. I will not repeat that error, Saarik." He nodded, his expression the very personification of regret.

Drey's story rang false, and Rehaak's apprehension increased.

"What is it that brings you so far from the capital, if I may be so bold as to inquire?"

"You may indeed ask, but I am not at liberty to explain my mission...financial matters. I cannot say more than that. What brought *you* to this hinterland, Rik? May I call you Rik? Or do you prefer Saarik?"

"Rik is fine, most people know me by that nickname. I grew tired of the city, and I chose this direction on a whim and settled here for a long while. It has suited me well until recently."

"Ah, do I detect the winds of change tugging at your cloak? I suspect you would make an excellent traveling companion and delightful company. Do you seek new adventures to satisfy your soul, my friend?"

"You might well say that, Drey. I have traveled widely for most of my life, and perhaps only my custom calls me onward, but I believe it may be time for me to move along once more. Life has grown tedious in these environs."

Dreynar said, "I can well believe that life in this hinterland could become monotonous. So few folk of culture hereabouts and so little entertainment for people with refined tastes. To journey together would be wonderful! I could use a stalwart companion such as yourself. You should join me. Our encounter may have spiritual significance, and we may gain mutual benefit if we join forces."

Rehaak hesitated and swallowed hard. "I must first ask a question. Where are you bound after you inspect Dun Dale?"

CHAPTER FOURTEEN

KYONNA BEGS

Since her summons to Eideron's home, Aibhera's mood oscillated between flattered and flustered. As the time approached for the dinner hour, she began pacing. *Mother and Leoned will arrive soon, bringing the younger sibs back from the communal crèche with the other field hands' children.*

Kyonna, her sister, flounced into their shared bedroom and sprawled onto a sleeping mat. "I just bumped into Sim on the way home. Why didn't you tell me you were going upslope to hobnob with the rich and powerful tonight?" She sat up. Aibhera stopped pacing, and Kyonna leaped to her feet. "I have a brilliant idea—I should come along." Before Aibhera could speak, Kyonna began rummaging through a pile of clothes scattered across the floor.

"Stop that!" you can't come with us." Aibhera grabbed her sister's arm.

"But why can't I come with you, Aibby?" Kyonna stamped her foot, garments clenched in her fists.

"Because Eideron didn't invite you, silly." Aibhera ignored her younger sister's pouting. Kyonna was two summers younger than Aibhera, but despite the similarities in appearance, the sisters were as different as frost and fire.

Both had the slight builds, black hair, ocher skin, high cheekbones, slightly pointed ears, and chiseled facial features typical of their Sokai ancestors. Aibhera, the eldest of four children, had the edge on her sister in height by a finger width. She and Kyonna were the offspring of Riessa's first husband, Kerrik, who had been a Synod councilor, until his mysterious death.

Riessa, their mother, took Leoned, their stepfather, as a lover not long after Kerrik's death, and they produced two children. The twins, Lissa, and Lara were much younger than either Kyonna or Aibhera.

A few ultra-conservative members of Sokai society frowned on remarriage. If the husband of a childless couple died, those zealots expected his wife to join him in death and be composted alongside him. Those same few expected widows with children to remain unmarried, but neither option suited their spirited mother's style. The majority disliked those strict notions but were too timid to voice their opinions since disagreement with those attitudes often brought reprisals.

Leoned, their stepfather, was an engineer who built and maintained the wind and steam turbines that provided power for the generators and pumps serving the valley. Abalon needed his unique talents with sophisticated machinery, so despite his relationship with Riessa, he kept his position. Leoned moved downslope to live with them because the council had forbidden Riessa and the girls to join him in his upper-level quarters. His sacrifice proved his devotion to Riessa and her daughters.

Their union affected the entire family. Many of Abalon's upper classes shunned Aibhera's mother and her children. Ultra-conservative Synod members considered Riessa a loose woman and tried, judged, and passed sentences on Kyonna and Aibhera too. Innocence was no protection from their prejudice.

The Synod drew members from the ranks of the most learned men and women of the Sokai and governed every aspect of life in Abalon. Synod Councilors were the elite of Sokai society and had the power of life and death over their people. Any decision by the Synod carried grave implications for individuals, either for good or for ill. No one wanted conflict with a Synod member. Many councilors acted petty and vindictive, so the ordinary folk feared them. People held others like Master Eideron, the most senior man on the council, in high esteem because of his firm, impartial judgments.

Aibhera's reaction to their treatment was poles apart from Kyonna's response. Kyonna acted out, while Aibhera became a model of propriety and purity. Kyonna, impetuous and flirtatious, provoked, and alienated Abalon's elders, while Aibhera, careful and demure, attempted to boost the family's honor. Aibhera's organizational skills won her a low-level job in the library and saved her from sharing her mother's banishment to the fields.

Riessa never complained. She adapted and made the most of her life and her lack of status. Riessa often told her daughters that living without the weight of expectations that burdened upper-class women had its benefits. She could do as she pleased, while those women must keep up appearances.

Despite their differences, both girls had their mother's strong will and determination to succeed and rise above adversity. Aibhera felt the burden most keenly since she bore that load for the entire family. Young men circled Kyonna like bees around flowers while Aibhera had few close friends, and none of them were male. The lone exception to this rule was Simea, Master Eideron's apprentice.

"Simea is my friend too," Kyonna protested, reluctant to accept Aibhera's refusal.

"Master Eideron invited Sim and me, not you. I doubt if Eideron even knows you exist." Aibhera cocked her head and held out her hands to her sister. "I'm sure he didn't know *I* existed either until Simea mentioned me to him this morning." She pursed her lips and looked past Kyonna. "Besides, I'm not even sure *I* want to go. According to Simea, Eideron is more than a little scary."

"Nonsense, Aibby, he looks like a nice man. If I meet him, I can show him how wonderful I am."

Kyonna produced her most delightful grin, made even more charming by the flash of her violet eyes. Her smile, despite her slightly crooked teeth, enhanced rather than detracted from her charisma. Her grin was like a secret sunrise. With a coy tilt of her head, she curtsied, her black ringlets framing her attractive face and blazing eyes. Kyonna waited for her sister's reply.

Aibhera pondered an appropriate response. *Could I trust her not to cause a stir if she joined us? I suppose Ky's ability to adapt makes her such a great Windrider. It takes guts and quick reflexes to ride the thermals back and forth across the valley. Ky would be grubbing in the dirt, beside our mother, if not for her exceptional ability with the gliders. No. Ky is pure trouble; if she weren't so attractive and charming, someone would have throttled her long ago. There are days when I want to choke Ky myself...today, for example.*

"Eideron is not one of your love-crazed beaus, Ky. Eideron's an old man and a Synod Councilor, for heaven's sake. I doubt that your flirting will turn his head. Besides, someone must stay and help Ma with the young ones when they get back from the crèche."

"But if he could just see me." Ky turned her head to hide the tears welling in her eyes.

She's withholding the real reason she wants to join us, but Ky is too impulsive to attend this meeting. Liable to say or do something that causes more problems for us. It is dangerous for our family members to attract the ruling elite's attention. While Kyonna escapes notice, she lives without interference.

Once the Synod scrutinizes anyone's life, hell breaks loose. After our father died, our mother lost her position because of the council's animosity. I often wonder what made them hate us so much. Kyonna mustn't jeopardize her status as a Windrider. Losing that job would destroy her.

Tired of Kyonna's protests, Aibhera said, "Enough! Eideron did not invite you. It would be impolite to arrive without an invitation, and that's final! I don't understand why you are interested in this meeting. Why do you want to come anyway?"

Aibhera scowled at her sister, who pouted back at her. Despite her words, Aibhera thought she understood Ky's wish to join them. *It's not every day someone from our family gets an invitation to the house of a notable person like Master Eideron. In fact, it's not every day that someone from the Liara family gets invited anywhere nowadays.*

"I don't know, Aibby." Kyonna seemed to soften her stance on the issue. "I want to come with you because it will involve politics, and you may need protection."

"You never wanted political involvement. Why the sudden interest in politics?"

Kyonna said, "Because politics has never involved a member of my family."

"That's not true." Aibhera glared at Kyonna. "Politics affect our family every day of our lives.

"Before father died, we held a much higher place in Sokai society. Mother was the head archivist, but after he passed, our status changed." Aibhera stopped long enough to draw a breath. "Have you forgotten how the Synod stripped Mother of her position and forced us to live down here with the field hands? Our mother, the smartest woman in this valley—no longer fit to research materials and catalog records." Tears welled up in Aibhera's eyes. "Now she breaks her back, grubbing in the dirt, planting, and harvesting. It's drudge work, but it's the only job they allow. How can you say politics never affected us till now?"

"Have I forgotten? What a stupid question. I miss tending our little sisters. According to the mothers who leave their children at the crèche, we aren't pure enough to care for the kids. According to them, we might pollute their little darlings by our mere presence. They sent our sisters there because Lissa and Lara's attendance mitigates the damage from our immoral influence. Have I forgotten? Please!" Kyonna poked her sister in the chest. "How could I forget when the stench of the manure from the fields outside makes me gag?" She raised her voice. "How could I forget when Mother returns home every night, her hands cracked and bleeding and stinking of it?" Kyonna scoffed, pushed Aibhera aside, and stomped out, leaving Aibhera to her pacing.

CHAPTER FIFTEEN

UPWARD

At seventeen, Aibhera had ample freedom from her parents' control, but her thoughts tumbled over one another while she prepared to leave. *Simea should arrive any moment to escort me to Eideron's quarters, high up the west wall of the valley. I hope he comes before my parents get home, so I won't have to explain my absence to Mother. I can leave the explanation to Kyonna, once she stops sulking.*

This invitation to the upper levels should have me soaring like a Windrider. Ky once flew me across the valley on one of the freight gliders. It left me breathless, free of the problems that face us in the jumble of fields and homes on the crater floor. But all I can think of is, what are we going to tell Eideron, and what will he think of me?

Simea called out to her from their front door and interrupted her contemplation.

"Aibby! Hurry. We must leave. It's a long climb to Master Eideron's home, and I still must prepare the meal."

Aibby rearranged her dark ringlets one last time in the small mirror by the door of their quarters. She straightened up, threw back her shoulders, and glanced at her reflection before she answered him. "I'm coming!" Aibhera hurried to the door where Simea waited. "Sim, I hope we're not making a mistake. Maybe you shouldn't have mentioned our dreams to him."

Simea quivered with nervous energy, bouncing on his toes as if he were about to take flight, "I had to tell him. I can't deal with these nightmares any longer. I'm so tired that I can hardly think."

Aibhera nodded. "I suppose so," she said. "If nothing else, I hope we can get a good night's sleep once we turn this problem over to your master."

"I hope so too. We don't want to keep Eideron waiting for his dinner." They walked side by side as they started the long climb to the upper levels.

Aibhera grinned and nudged Simea. "I can help you with the meal prep, and I'll break less of his crockery."

"I'll never tell you anything again!" Simea protested. When stressed, his voice squeaked and quavered since puberty played tricks with his vocal cords. "I'm nervous around him."

Aibhera said, "I fear I won't know how to act around him either. You are with him every day. Why haven't you gotten used to Eideron?"

Simea looked at the ground, his shoulders sagged, and his voice caught. "I sometimes think Eideron makes me uncomfortable on purpose. It's like he's trying to make me quit."

"Now why would anyone want to rid themselves of the smartest, handsomest young man in the entire valley?" She batted her eyelashes at him and tilted her head in a parody of her younger sister's mannerisms.

"You do that well," Simea gave her a playful shove. "But you'll never match Ky."

"I wouldn't want to. I love Ky to death, but sometimes she is just so—"

"So Kyonna," Simea finished her sentence. "There are no adequate words, and I love her too. I wish she didn't flounce about the way she does. She behaves so vulgarly."

He looked down and kicked a pebble with the toe of his shoe.

"That's the look she aims for." Aibhera put her hand on her friend's shoulder.

Simea stopped walking and looked up at her touch. "But why does Ky act up? Is she determined to prove herself every bit the hoyden that people think she is? I hear so many awful stories about her. I've begun to wonder if they are true. That's not her true nature, is it?"

"No, it's not. Don't be silly; I've heard the lies and the gossip too. I'm her sister, and I know they aren't true. Ky has a big, tender heart. She's so strong, and she sees deeper into people's hearts than anyone in Abalon. It's her way of fighting back. Ky doesn't want them to see how deeply people's disapproval of our family hurts her."

The conversation fell away as the exertion of the climb up the stairs and ramps to the upper levels claimed their breath. They could have taken the elevators, but the Synod frowned on lower-class people using them. Instead of the exquisite view of Abalon from the lifts, the bustle of life on the streets surrounded them. As they climbed higher, the traffic on the ramps and stairs decreased, and the aroma of cooking meals mingled with the perfume of flowers that grew outside the homes.

Simea occasionally stopped for Aibhera to catch her breath and enjoy the view of the gigantic caldera they called home. A spring-fed lake in the crater's center, Lake Seletan, provided their drinking water. It glimmered like a blue-gray jewel in the fading light. The small island in the lake's center, preserved as a nature park, appeared like a dark spot on the lake's luminous oval. The trees and plants that grew on the island had once covered the entire floor of the caldera. Those plants were the last remnants of the crater's original vegetation. Over the centuries of occupation, the Sokai transformed the rest of the caldera into gardens and fields to supply food for their growing population.

Gigantic hydraulic elevators lifted the crops from the valley floor to the storage caverns and storehouses carved into and out of the cliff faces. When the Sokai had first arrived in Abalon, they converted barren caves that had pockmarked the cliff faces into homes and storehouses, leaving the fertile valley floor free for food production. Over the centuries, the Sokai excavated more living quarters in the basalt walls of the caldera to accommodate their increasing numbers. In recent years, the council converted some of the lower dwellings into terraced areas, which created more land for crops.

Aibhera's family lived among the terraces at the base of the slope, displaying the Liara family's lowest-of-the-low social status. Simea's family lived only one level above, yet the Synod chose him to train as Master Eideron's apprentice. Many people thought Simea's selection was a concession to the lower classes, a sop for the ordinary folk, to convince them that their sons or daughters could gain higher status someday. Aibhera knew it was because her friend was brilliant and spiritually sensitive. Simea's abilities alone won him his position. He had scored top marks in the tests for prospective apprentices.

Aibhera and Simea had been friends since birth. Simea's mother and father remained friends with Riessa and stood by her when she took Leoned as a lover and gave birth to twin girls before they married. Despite social pressure to disown Riessa, Simea's parents remained loyal friends until his father died, and it cost them their social status. No barriers stood between her and Simea, and Aibhera was confident they would be friends for life.

Simea and Aibhera had borne the burden of their dreams for months now. Tonight, they carried them to Eideron's house to unload their weight on Simea's master. In their minds, once they told Master Eideron, he and the Synod would take the proper action, and once they shared their story, their lives would return to normal. At least that was their hope.

CHAPTER SIXTEEN

CHOICES

As Rehaak pondered his options and waited for Dreynar's reply to his question, they drew near the outskirts of Dun Dale. *Has the Creator sent Dreynar to end Laakea and Isil's foolhardy commitment to me? If I join Drey, I may complete my search for the Aetheriad without risk to Isil and Laakea. Dreynar presents a fresh alternative, but if he is Narragan bound, it means trouble for me.*

Dreynar interrupted Rehaak's thoughts. He smiled and said, "In answer to your question, I am headed to Aeron Suul to meet my master, who voyages to Baradon on business. Once I have overseen his interests in this region, I shall journey southward along the coast to the port. I shall miss my scheduled appointment with my master because of my encounter with brigands on the road here. Though it is late in the season, I will seek passage to Baradon on another vessel and meet him there later. I sense your reluctance. This is no doubt a difficult decision for you. Perhaps you have friends you are reluctant to abandon."

"No, I have no attachments here," Rehaak lied for the third time since he met Drey. He calculated the risks and benefits of joining Dreynar. *Laakea has sworn a Sword Oath, and he will protect me even at the cost of his own life. He risked his life when he fought five brigands to rescue me and nearly died when he forged his ehlbringa weapons. My continued presence in Isil's and Laakea's lives makes them a target for the assassins dogging my path.*

Laakea is young, and his death is more than my conscience can bear. No one knows the time frame of the Nethera attack. Both Isil and Laakea might live long, productive lives before the Nethera threat becomes a reality. If they follow me, their lives might end swiftly and brutally, but if I disappear, I free them from the quest. They can have safe, anonymous lives without me. But can I trust this man? I suppose time will reveal the answer to that question.

Rehaak offered his hand to Dreynar. "That sounds excellent. I accept your offer of companionship." Rehaak pretended confidence, but doubts still lingered about Drey and his mysterious master. *I can always disappear later if I discover I can't trust Drey.* Rehaak discounted his pangs of conscience for deserting his friends and masked his uneasiness with jokes and banter until he and Drey reached the village.

Once they reached Dun Dale, the pair separated, and Rehaak went to visit the village's tannery. He planned to buy the leather Laakea asked for and send it back to the boy by messenger. The tanner and his wife had left to visit their premises in New Hope, leaving their daughter Ebrill to watch over the business.

Local gossip mentioned that the girl had fallen into a tanning vat as a child. But when he met Ebrill, the stories about her strange appearance proved true. Despite her childhood mishap, Ebrill was still a strikingly beautiful young woman. The caustic liquid had burned away the webbing of her hands and changed her skin color to an odd shade of greenish-orange. Her eyes, lighter in color than most Abrhaani, were almost amber instead of the black or dark brown of typical Abrhaani eyes. Her eyes so fascinated Rehaak that he almost forgot why he was visiting the business.

When he recovered his wits, he asked, "Do you have any leather straps precut. They would need to be at least two thumbs wide and an arms-length long."

"How many would you need?"

"A half dozen should suffice."

"I don't have any that width, but if you wait, I can have them ready by this afternoon."

"I suppose that will do. Shall I pay you now or when I return? How much will they cost?" Rehaak forced himself to look away from her amber eyes. "I'm sorry for staring, but your eyes—are unusual—and quite lovely."

Ebrill blushed and turned away. "You are Rehaak, the healer, are you not?"

"Yes. That is what people hereabouts call me."

"Pay me when you return, if my work is acceptable."

Rehaak stood a while and watched Ebrill at work, then wandered the streets alone until he reached the log structure of the Dancing Dog Inn, where he ordered a pint of beer and a meal. Aert, the innkeeper at the bar, and his wife, at work in the kitchen, were the only people present except for two patrons seated near the door. Rehaak always picked a table in the dark corner far from the entrance, which allowed him to stay inconspicuous but observant when in town.

A fragrant blend of beer, spices, and wood smoke hung in the air. Aert returned moments later and placed a mug of brew, and a bowl of spiced roasted vegetables in a thick sauce, on the table's rough planks. While Rehaak enjoyed his meal and his beer, the inn's door swung open. Sunlight streamed into the dining hall and illuminated the dust motes floating in the air beneath the timbered ceiling beams. Rehaak mulled over his encounter with the young woman at the tannery while he sipped his ale.

Four men filed into the room and settled onto the benches around a table opposite Rehaak. Each of them wore cloaks and hoods, despite the midday heat. A sinister aura surrounded the fellows across the room. Rehaak fidgeted and became uneasy as the men ordered food and drink. He shrank into the shadows, away from the window and door. *In hindsight, I wish I had picked a spot nearer the door, so I might slip unnoticed from the inn, but that ship sailed and left me stranded on the shore.*

Aert scuttled to the table, radiating tension, shifting from one foot to the other as he took their order. He hustled away, fetched their drinks, and hurried back again, mugs in hand. Once Aert deposited their cups, he crossed the room and stopped at Rehaak's table. "Can I get you more food or drink?"

Rehaak ignored Aert's question, lowered his voice, and nodded toward the newcomers. "Do those fellows come here often?"

"Aye, they does," Aert responded. "They first arrived a tenday ago, and they gives me the shivers just lookin' at 'em. They is up to no good. Anyone can tell that right off. Why does you ask?"

"I may have met similar men several months ago."

"And you survived to speak of it? Consider yourself lucky then. I hear they be assassins, but who they wants to kill in these parts is beyond my reckonin'. They'll leave soon enough, thank the gods. They never stays long."

Rehaak groaned, alarmed by Aert's words. *I could run for the door, but if they leave soon, I can wait them out.* Rehaak sank lower in his seat, pulled his hat over his eyes, and tried to blend into the shadows. He checked that his staff still leaned against the wall beside him, and his hand slid toward the comforting weight of the knife in his belt.

Once he had steadied his nerves, he cupped his tankard in both hands like a determined drunk, lowered his head, and furtively watched the men. Long moments crept by. Rehaak waited for them to finish their meal and leave. He nursed his beer, his eyes fixed on the strangers from under the brim of his hat. He sat, shoulders hunched, and slumped against the log wall behind him. His knees bounced with nervous energy. *Dreynar's arrival might provide my excuse to leave and escape these men who look so much like the assassins I encountered earlier.*

CHAPTER SEVENTEEN

DINNER PARTY

As Aibhera and Simea prepared the evening meal, the door swung open with a creak. Eideron arrived ahead of his usual time, and Simea almost sliced his finger instead of the vegetables. He turned and stammered, "Good...evening Master Eideron. Th..this is my fr...friend Aibhera."

Eideron met Simea's words with a curt nod and turned to Aibhera. "I am very pleased to meet you, young lady." His brown eyes twinkled with a mixture of mirth and curiosity as he took her hand and raised it to his lips.

"As am I," she replied and curtsied to the old man. "Simea and I have wanted to speak with you for quite—"

A loud crash interrupted her. Simea muttered, "Sorry, Master," and began scooping up the pieces of the serving bowl and the vegetables strewn across the floor.

Simea's clumsiness shocked Aibhera, unsure of how to react, she stood in stunned silence. A smile ghosted across the old man's face before a somber mask replaced it. He surveyed the mess, then stooped to help Simea, and his reaction revealed the humility and gentleness hidden beneath his crusty facade. She instantly respected him, and his temperament matched her sincere and straightforward disposition.

Simea had mentioned that Eideron's wife had died many years ago. At the time of her passing, Eideron was still young enough to remarry but chose to remain single. A powerful image of the old man grieving his wife's loss came unbidden to Aibhera's mind. *He has likely lost many friends throughout his long life, and those losses have cut him, so he shields himself. It hurts too much to lose comrades. He cares passionately for his friends and our people and builds walls around his heart to keep it from breaking. In that way, Eideron is much like my sister Kyonna. I can trust him, and I like him.*

I think Sim is right to believe Eideron is testing him. Eideron never lets people into his heart until they prove their trustworthiness beyond doubt. He probably plays the bad-tempered old codger to strengthen Sim's resolve and courage. I wonder how many apprentices buckled under that strain and how many toughened because of it? It's too bad Sim can't understand it, but Sim is a gentle, timid soul.

Eideron's smile betrayed chinks in the old man's emotional armor, but he was still an imposing presence, a force that commanded respect and obedience. *I understand why people call him the "Old Lion of the Synod." I pity the unfortunates who fall prey to his fangs and claws.*

Aibhera's thoughts ran on as Eideron explained, "I returned early because my friend Himish will join us this evening. Make sure everything is in order and ensure there is enough food for our extra guest."

"Yes, Master Eideron." Simea's hands shook, and an awkward feeling hung over the room while Eideron lingered to watch the preparations. When Simea reached into the storage bin for more potatoes, he fumbled the paring knife, and cut his hand.

Eideron flinched at the sight of blood. "Do you need my help to bandage that? It looks painful."

"No, Master. I can manage it myself."

Simea found a dressing for his wound in a nearby drawer, "I've had plenty of practice with bandages," he muttered.

"Sim, please let me help you." Aibhera took the rolled bandage from Simea's hand. "Let's clean the cut first, then I'll help you wrap your hand. It's hard to do a decent job one-handed."

Eideron lingered watching the youngsters, and when they finished dressing Simea's wound, he said, "If you are certain you don't need my assistance, I will leave you to it. I must change out of my council robes before Himish arrives. I trust you will be able to finish without further bloodshed."

Simea sighed as Eideron departed and whispered, "I'm glad he's gone. I could feel his eyes boring into me while I worked. He hates me."

"No, he doesn't hate you. He pushes you hard to bring out the best in you. Crankiness is a wall he's put up to protect his big soft heart."

"I see nothing soft in him at all—"

A knock on the door interrupted Simea's complaint. He stopped to let Himish in. "Master Eideron awaits you in the dining room."

"Thank you, young man," Himish said and left Simea and Aibhera to finish cooking the meal.

As the two friends worked, they heard Eideron and Himish talking in the next room, but neither youngster could overhear the conversation. When Simea finished fussing over the meal while cradling his bandaged hand, he and Aibhera carried it into the dining room.

"S-s-s-supper is ready, m-m-master," Simea stammered, doubly intimidated in the presence of Eideron's guest.

"Well, let's eat it then." Eideron harrumphed and gestured for them to sit on the cushions around the low table.

As they took their places, Eideron introduced them.

"Himish, I am pleased to introduce Simea, my apprentice, and Aibhera, Simea's young lady friend."

Simea changed color like a chameleon, but instead of blending into the surroundings, the head-to-toe blush made him more conspicuous.

Aibhera bowed her head in a gesture of respect to Himish and responded in an even voice, "Pleased to meet you, Councilor Himish."

"Not as pleased as I am to meet a beautiful young woman such as you," he teased. "I look forward to what you youngsters can tell us old fossils." He winked and elbowed Eideron.

She smiled to herself. *What a shameless old flirt. I like Himish almost as much as Eideron.* The meal proceeded with pleasant conversation about the weather and other innocuous topics until Simea, out of nervousness, knocked over his water glass. Bolting from the room to get a towel, Simea almost turned the low table over as he shot up from his seat.

Once he was out of the room, Himish said, "I have always said you should not intimidate your apprentices. The boy acts like a hungry mouse in a granary full of sleeping snakes. The mouse is afraid of being eaten, but its hunger drives it forward anyway."

"And I told you it builds character. Simea will need a stiff backbone to stand up to those other young fools on the council," Eideron retorted, obviously forgetting that Aibhera, Simea's friend and confidant, was present.

The banter of the two old compatriots amused Aibhera. She tried to hide her smile behind her hand. She giggled, but mirth overpowered her, and explosive laughter sprayed the contents of her mouth across the table at Eideron and Himish.

Simea chose that exact moment to re-enter the room. If death from embarrassment was possible, Simea had one foot in the grave and another on a banana peel. For a moment, silence sat like a boulder teetering on the edge of a precipice.

The snicker began with Himish, expanded to Eideron as a giggle, and then crescendoed into a full-blown belly laugh from both the older men. In moments, everyone but Simea roared with laughter.

"That was the best…" Himish gasped, "the best way to end an argument…" *gasp* "…I have ever seen."

"Yes. You win the argument, Aibhera." Eideron struggled to regain his composure. "I am overcome by the explosive force of your persuasive power." Eideron guffawed, and his pun set them laughing again. Simea joined in the mirth, and it took some time before anyone could draw breath to speak.

❖

The atmosphere in the room had changed. It was more congenial than Simea had ever experienced. He realized he had never heard his master laugh, and the laughter transformed Eideron in Simea's eyes. He finally saw that Eideron was human, not just a revered figure who inspired fear and awe. He was not merely the Lion of the Synod, waiting to devour him for his mistakes. Eideron had a sense of humor and real feelings. Aibhera had demolished the invisible wall between him and his mentor, but Simea hesitated to step through the rubble of that boundary, fearful that it might trap him.

Himish was the first to speak. "That, my new young friend, is the best way I have seen to bring my pompous old crony back to earth. Simea, join us at the table if you please."

Himish invited Simea into their fellowship, and he stepped through onto new ground.

My world just changed in an instant because of Aibhera. Her mere presence brightens a room, and she transforms everything around her. Could we become more than just friends?

CHAPTER EIGHTEEN

HEMMED IN

Rehaak sat in the Dancing Dog Inn nursing his second drink after finishing his meal and avoided drawing attention to himself. The men dressed in hooded robes still sat at the table near the door. He held his beer mug before his face with shaky hands, nearly spilling the liquid on the tabletop. His seat against the inn's rear wall facing the doorway allowed him to observe the entrance. Rehaak, grateful for the dimness of the inn's interior, was about to order a third round of ale when the door opened and Dreynar entered.

Drey paused until his eyes adjusted to the Dancing Dog's gloomy interior. Rehaak was about to wave and invite Drey to join him, but before he could calm himself enough to set down his drink, Drey ambled over to the table occupied by the four grim strangers.

The hooded men shared handclasps with Drey, and once they had all greeted him, he took a seat at the head of the table. Rehaak could not overhear their conversation as they huddled over the table and plotted together. The way they reacted to Drey's presence marked him as their leader.

Rehaak gasped, slumped lower in his seat, and reached for his staff, his eyes almost level with the tabletop. *Thank the Creator I did not hail him before he saw me. I will*

continue my quest alone. The Creator has given me this
burden. It is my responsibility, and I will bear it unaided as
soon as I can exit the inn and slip out of the village.

The innkeeper brought a tankard of ale to Drey and
asked for his order, but Dreynar waved him off. Drey's
henchmen had fallen silent when Aert approached and did
not speak again until Aert was out of earshot.

Rehaak's heart hammered out a frenzied rhythm
against his ribcage. Aert approached Rehaak with another
mug of ale, although he had not asked for another. It would
have been his third, two more than his usual limit. When
Aert set the tankard on the table, he paused, leaned down,
and whispered to Rehaak.

"I knows who you are, Rehaak, and they be lookin'
for you. That fella' in the fancy clothes was braggin' that he
had some fella convinced to join him. They thinks my wits is
dull, and that may be, but my ear is as sharp as any man's. I
owes you a kindness for the herbs that cured my little'uns
when they got the fever last winter."

Rehaak started to whisper that he knew nothing of
this cure or the village, but Aert raised a forefinger to his
own lips and silenced Rehaak.

"I knows you don't, but my cousin what lives in
New Hope, he got the potion from you and sent it on to us.
Follow me, and I can repay my debt to you. If'n you waits
much longer, it might be too late unless you wants to go with
them. I wouldn't suggest it."

Rehaak slipped off the seat and followed Aert into
his private quarters attached to the rear of the inn. A quick
look back revealed that Dreynar and his friends remained
huddled over the table and had not taken notice of his
departure. Rehaak and Aert rushed through the kitchen. Aert
hushed his wife and children as they tried to greet Rehaak
and whisked him through the back door to the woodshed.

When they reached the shed, Aert said, "I wouldn't
stay hereabouts now if'n I was you. Rumor has it they got

Raamya's boys lookin' for you too. They been out to your place and found it empty. Mato, Raamya's youngest, has been 'specially curious 'bout your whereabouts, but none likes him, and none would tell him anythin'."

"I must get leather strips for a friend before I leave town. Is it safe?" Rehaak asked. He now realized his only way forward lay in completing his original mission and returning to his friends.

"Not less'n it be more important than your life. Tell you what…I'll send one o' the young'uns to fetch what you needs, and you hunker down here in the shed until dark. Then we can get you on your way without no fuss and bother."

"Thank you, Aert. I have gold for the leather."

"Never mind that foolishness. Ebrill, the tanner's girl, owes you too. You might'a heard tell 'bout how she fell in the lime pit and got burned bad as a youngster." Rehaak shook his head. Undeterred, Aert continued his explanation, "She suffered from itchin' and flakin' skin for most o' her life, but one o' your salves helped and eased her pain. She'll be more'n willin' to give you what you needs once we 'splain it to her. She'll be more'n willin' to give you what you needs once we 'splain it to her. The whole village is beholden to you in one way or another. Don't any of us want you to come to harm. 'Cept for that skunk Raamya and his boys, and I doubt even he'd wish you the kind o' misery what be waitin' back there." Aert nodded toward the inn's back door. "Most of us would eat our own slops rather than help him and his kind agin you. You lie low while we takes care of everythin'."

With that said, Aert turned and re-entered the inn. Within moments, his youngest daughter, Breisha, slipped out the door past the woodshed toward the alley. She was as silent as the shadows that deepened outside Rehaak's hiding place. She stopped, offering a smile and a wink at him where he hid among the hearth logs.

Rehaak shook his head in disbelief. *I am glad the villagers feel grateful for my remedies, but why hold me in such high regard that they risk their lives to save mine? Lately, everywhere I go, people risk their lives on my behalf. It seems I cannot escape people's loyalty. In Narragan, amid abundance, everyone hoards possessions for themselves, concerned only with their own success and prosperity. Here, on the rough edge of civilization where everything is in short supply, acts of kindness abound. It makes no sense that those who have the least should be the most generous.*

Rehaak had not given Drey his proper name, and his appearance had transformed. During Rehaak's time in the forge-house, he had shaved off his beard to escape the heat and put on several pounds of muscle from the arduous work. Now thanks to the earlier assassination attempt, he had a prominent strip of white in his hair. Rehaak assumed that anyone who did not know him well might not recognize him. He had hoped the changes allowed him a margin of safety, and yet Drey might identify him.

Raamya's sons certainly know me, and if Drey contacts them, my altered appearance will not protect me. I have somehow angered a powerful man. That mysterious character sent a young nobleman to find me, along with several groups of assassins. I am no longer safe here or anywhere if that man's influence extends to Baradon. What is happening in Baradon? I must discover what plans Drey's master has for the Eniila homeland. I want more than ever to know what happened to Aelfric, Laakea's father, and Voerkett, Isil's husband. It might almost be worth the risk to feign allegiance with Drey until I get answers.

Curiosity nearly got the better of Rehaak, but a chill ran down his spine when he thought of Drey's familiarity or outright leadership of the black-cloaked figures inside the Dancing Dog. He shuddered and shelved the idea of cooperation with Drey.

When he had left for the village this morning, he planned to abandon his companions to spare them certain death. If not for Aert's intervention, assassins could have ended his life today, or Drey's sweet words could have deceived him. Simple choices had become life and death decisions, and not for himself alone. People lived heedless of risk while the lives of those they loved hung on those choices. Life and death often hung on the toss of a coin.

Rehaak's previous decisions seemed unimportant, but many had landed him in serious trouble. When he believed nothing depended on the outcome, Rehaak had no difficulty deciding, but when the wrong choice spelled disaster, he dithered. Early this morning, he decided to leave his friends. Later in the day, Drey offered him another option, and he had almost taken the bait. Fortunately, he wriggled free of the hook that might have led to his demise.

Rehaak needed more information, but for every answer gained, he received three more questions. The choices made earlier today led him to a woodshed behind the Dancing Dog with only one alternative. He could not risk an alliance with Drey. He must return to the forge and then find his answers with Laakea and Isil.

They needed information from the Scriptorium in Narragan. Something he had read there haunted him like an ancient ghost. Drey had freed a faint memory of it when he mentioned his master's trip to the Eniila homeland. Possibly Baradon held the answers he needed to save Aarda from the ravages of the Nethera.

I wonder if I have been looking in the wrong place. Narragan is risky, and Baradon is even more perilous. The Eniila do not tolerate Abrhaani interlopers, but Laakea could pass for a young Eniila lordling with two Abrhaani slaves. It might work. In fact, Baradon might be safer for me than Narragan...or it might kill me.

CHAPTER NINETEEN

VOERKETT

Laakea and Isil prepared so they could leave once Rehaak returned with the leather strips Laakea needed for his breastplate. Isil packed provisions and blankets, while Laakea tested the balance and weight of his new weapons. Once satisfied with the rawhide-wrapped grips of his swords, he took some practice cuts at the tall stump he and his father had used for a practice pale. The weapons sliced gashes a hands-width deep into the dense wood with only light effort, and Laakea grinned as he examined the damage to the oaken stump.

Satisfied with the blades' effectiveness, he padded the backside of the breastplate with layers of woolen cloth and tied it in place with cords instead of leather straps. *Why am I wasting my time with string? Rehaak will return with the leather soon?* By midday, satisfied with the weapons and armor, Laakea set it all together and added his leather forearm guards to the pile. *The heavy leather protected me from sparks when I worked the forge, and it should protect me from weapons too.* "What's taking Rehaak so long?" Laakea dropped the bundle of gear near the table.

"We didn't 'spect him to return till early evening and we ain't leavin' till first light tomorrow. Come, sit a spell, and have somewhat to eat." Isil pushed a bowl of steaming stew toward him. "You must be hungry after all that pacin' you been doin', It bein midday and all."

Laakea had recovered from his ordeal in the Creator's forge, but his stomach ached with endless hunger.

"I still can't believe how much you eats—sees it, but I can't believe it—I expects you needs more fuel than us Abrhaani 'cause o' your big muscles."

I guess that makes sense. I only know that I get weak and dizzy when I'm hungry. Laakea picked up the spoon and shoveled the leek and lentil stew into his mouth. Between gulps he said, "Thank you for another delicious meal, Isil. You and Rehaak make every meal so tasty. I don't have the knack for cooking."

"That be a bit o' understatement, according to Rehaak, but you're welcome," Isil teased. Though she did not have firsthand knowledge of Laakea's infamous blacksmith cooking, she had heard Rehaak's description of Laakea's attempts at culinary prowess.

Laakea continued his assault on the bowl of stew in front of him and said, "Could you tell me more about your husband Voerkett, if you don't mind?"

"Sure, I'll tell you about him if you likes. I got most o' the hate out o' me now. What do you want to know?"

"Do you know much about his life before you met him?"

"Sure, he told me stuff about how he used to live in Baradon. Does that interest you, lad?"

"Yes, very much. Go ahead. I really want to hear what you know about Baradon."

"Voerkett's folk was rich merchants. He was born in Baradon, and he growed up in the port city o' Sethria. His kin was movers and shakers, high up on the social ladder."

"What caused them to leave?" Laakea mumbled through a mouthful of stew.

"That's the story I'll get to if you keeps your britches on."

"Sorry." Laakea shoveled the last spoonful into his mouth, wiped the bowl clean with a slice of bread, and when he had eaten that, he licked his spoon clean.

"The city was under siege by your pa's folk, and the gates of the city were about to fall. Young Voerkett's folks hid him in a secret room 'bove their mansion's portico to hide him from the invaders. He were a small boy, maybe eight or nine summers."

Laakea remembered the name of the city from the stories his mother told him. According to her, Sethria was the last of the Abrhaani towns in Baradon to fall. Aelfric fought in that ultimate battle for control of Baradon's coast and won Sethria from the Abrhaani. The Eniila forced the intruders out of Baradon and drove the Abrhaani back to Khel Braah. The victory set the Eniila free and left them in control of their homeland. Laakea's attention shifted back to Isil's story.

"While he was a-hidin', he spied the city below him from the window of his secret room. Voerkett watched them Eniila bust down them city gates. They flooded into the city like a wave, and blood flowed like water in their wake. Our people was fightin' to defend their homes and families, but they was no match for them bloodthirsty Eniila invaders."

Laakea always imagined the battle for Sethria was a glorious rebellion of the Eniila people to repel Abrhaani interlopers. The story, told from the Abrhaani viewpoint with Eniila forces described as bloodthirsty invaders of a peaceful and prosperous city, disturbed him. Laakea wanted to correct Isil's account, but he resisted out of loyalty to her. *Isil has earned the right to her opinions without argument from me, but I know she is wrong.*

"Our folk fell back to the city's center, and the fightin' flowed right up to the house where Voerkett was hid. The last o' the city's fightin' men stood firm at Voerkett's home, with Voerkett's pa and his bodyguards. The guards fought off a couple o' charges and held the steps o' the mansion till the Eniila king showed up."

Laakea slid to the edge of his seat and leaned forward, as his hunger for details forced him to interrupt. "Sorry, but what did he look like?"

"The king were a giant fella with a fearsome look in his eye, his armor, drenched in the blood o' his victims. He wore a great domed helmet and carried a big two-handed sword. There were a big gash down his left cheek, so's the side o' his face and chest were covered in blood. Voerkett tol' me he were a rampagin' demon escaped from the pit o' hell."

Isil's description awakened memories in Laakea. *Pa has battle scars covering his body, and he has a big scar on his left cheek and temple that glow like coals from the forge when he's angry, but many Eniila bear similar marks. He* said *the scar is "evidence of hard lessons learned, and bitter memories best forgotten."*

Isil went on. "Once he got there, things changed. The king organized the forces what had been skirmishin' with the household guard. He cut through the defenders like a hot knife through lard. His men followed him, fought their way up the blood-soaked stairs, tramplin' the bodies o' the fallen as they came.

"Voerkett's household guard surrounded his pa tryin' to protect him, but the king and his blood-crazed mob cut their way through 'em. When the guards was dead, he made Voerkett's pa kneel in front o' him while they brought the servants, the women, and Voerkett's ma out o' the house. He made 'em kneel beside Voerkett's pa while they looted the mansion.

"Once the valuables was hauled away, the king said to Voerkett's pa, 'You Abrhaani can expect more of this if you ever set foot in Baradon again. Baradon is our land, not yours. I suggests you go back to Khel Braah. The only way you stays in Baradon is dead or in chains as slaves. What's your choice? Give your answer to my men.' He walked away right through the bodies without waitin' for the answer.

"Voerkett said he would never forget that face as long as he lived. He swore to get vengeance on the Eniila and their king for what happened that day."

"Why was he so bitter when the king allowed them to leave?"

"But they wasn't allowed to leave, laddie. Them bastards stripped and raped the women, even Voerkett's ma. They forced his pa to watch it. Voerkett watched too, from the window 'bove the portico. Women died from repeated rapes. Once they done their worst to the women, they cut Voerkett's pa's head off and stuck it on a spear, a trophy they paraded around the city. Anyone what survived got took away in chains to be slaves."

Laakea no longer wanted to correct her version of the story. Bile stung the back of his throat. He swallowed rapidly, but the taste wouldn't go away. Laakea imagined his reaction if he saw his mother raped, and his father butchered like an animal in front of their home. *Those images could poison a person's life forever.* A lump in his throat formed as he tried to tell Isil how sorry he felt for Voerkett. "There is no honor or justice in such behavior, and I'm ashamed of my father's people if this is true." Afraid of the answer, he stopped himself from asking if Voerkett's mother had survived the rapes. The moment for asking passed when Isil continued. *Perhaps Voerkett never told her.*

"Once night fell, the Eniila got to celebratin' their great victory with more rapin' and burnin'. Voerkett slipped out o' his secret room. It took days o' hidin in the sewers, eatin' rats, lizards, and other filth before he found a small yacht anchored offshore. He swam out to it and climbed aboard the boat. The Eniila don't put much stock in ships, so they had left the boats alone. The harbor was nearly empty because most had sailed away to escape the butchery, but maybe this one's owner waited too long.

"Voerkett took more'n a tenday to sail across the Syn Gersuul by hisself to Khel Braah. He were almost starved to death, and he were sick from dehydration afore he got to Khel Braah. He used to wake up with nightmares from the memories."

CHAPTER TWENTY

AELFRIC AND KETT

Aelfric ignored the stiff postures, squared shoulders, and the hatred in the Abrhaani seamen's eyes while he climbed the gangplank. He'd had sixteen years' experience alone among men who loathed him, so their hostility was as familiar as the scars on his hands. Aelfric stalked up the narrow gangplank and stopped at the top long enough for Hermad to direct him to his berth. Once Hermad completed the errand, he left the ship again.

Aelfric found his place below, stowed his gear beneath his hammock, and lashed it in place like Hermad had instructed him. The other passenger the captain had booked was not in the cabin, but his gear, stowed below the other hammock, indicated he had sent his luggage ahead. The "fine gentleman" as the captain called him, had a significant pile of luggage, and the mound's size was evidence of the fellow's wealth and status. Aelfric stretched out in the hammock and waited for sleep to overtake him, but his mind chased schemes like a hunting dog pursuing a rabbit. It raced so fast slumber couldn't catch him.

The small window of the cabin dimly lit the cramped quarters. It was now just past noon. Slivers of sunlight, reflected from the water outside, played across the beams and planks of the deck above Aelfric's head. He ignored the noises of the deckhands and stevedores at work while he considered his options.

Once I arrive in Baradon, I see two courses I can pursue, but other possibilities might appear. The first and most direct way is to march to the front gate of the capital city, announce my identity, and challenge my brother to single combat. It's not a smart choice, but it's the most direct way to dispatch my underhanded brother, A tad shortsighted in the long term.

Whatever pleasure I derive from killing Aelrin, I must still get rid of Aelrin's fellow conspirators afterward. Unless I eliminate them at the start, they might push me out of power later, either by force, by subterfuge, or by assassination. Removing them singly will consume too much time and energy. Not an optimal solution.

Another troubling thought. Although I've practiced daily with Laakea, I spent the last sixteen years far from combat as a father and husband, not a warrior. Aelrin has doubtless fought many battles holding on to the kingdom he stole from me and forced me into exile. Pity I never grasped his jealousy of my growing political power, and the depths he could sink, just to have it for himself.

Aelrin will be hard to kill in single combat. Perhaps he is dead, either in a duel or by an assassin's hand. No, impossible. Aelrin is still alive. I sense it. I have a month or more to practice while aboard the Sea Witch, but training within the limited space onboard will make that near impossible.

He had not drilled since the night Laakea had fled from his anger. He had only three tendays to toughen up and hone his skills. But, if at the end of the voyage, he still felt unprepared, he could spend his silver on lodgings and wait until he felt ready or opt for plan number two.

Plan two will take longer, but it reaches farther, resolves more problems, and proves to everyone that I still have the charisma to lead. I'll have to find enough people sympathetic to my cause, raise a force, and begin a civil war. Mercenaries won't get the job done. I don't have enough silver to hire warriors for a large army. I've never trusted sell-swords since they have a nasty habit of switching sides if their opponents offer them a richer purse.

I must win the people's affection. The people will gladly face death with pride if they follow someone they love and respect. The people of Baradon are the army I need, not a pack of money-grubbing mercenaries. If the people put my brother's head on a pike for me, it's the ultimate proof of my right to rule and proves Aelrin is a pretender to the throne.

Plan two dealt with all the plotters who had helped Aelrin achieve power. The start was the most problematic part of his strategy. Aelfric needed to recruit a sizeable force to unseat Aelrin and his co-conspirators. Building an army large enough for a coup without attracting Aelrin's attention was problematic, but a coup dealt a deathblow to challengers. A purge of the elite would boost his morale and convince the people of his legitimacy. It provided Aelfric time to strengthen his hold on power and rebuild his reputation.

Aelfric smiled at the notion and let the problem remain unsolved. He would face the challenges when and if they arose. For now, he needed rest. He closed his eyes and drifted off to sleep, heedless of the hubbub occurring on the deck above him and the Abrhaani businessman's wintry smile and his veiled eyes staring at him through the hatchway.

CHAPTER TWENTY-ONE

SHARED DREAMS

Eideron scowled at both young people and said, "Begin. Tell us what you know."

Aibhera and Simea shared their identical dreams in a torrent of words that blended like water in a stream. They interrupted, clarified, and corrected one another. The barriers to friendship had evaporated like morning mist, only to be replaced by a feeling of dread. Himish, eyebrows raised, tapped his lips with his forefinger while Eideron leaned forward as they listened in solemn silence.

After Aibhera and Simea had finished their stories, Himish, white-faced, rubbed his chest while he spoke with Eideron. "You were correct, old friend. The Synod needs this information. Perhaps we can get their testimony onto the next meeting's agenda. If the Eniila and the Abrhaani work together again, it fulfills the old prophecy and means we must rejoin them and bolster their efforts."

Eideron nodded in agreement and looked at Aibhera. "Why aren't you apprenticed to someone? Anyone can see you are extremely gifted. What was your score when the Synod tested you?"

Both young people paled as though the room's temperature had fallen and frozen their faces into whitish masks.

"What is wrong?"

"The Synod has never tested Aibhera," Simea blurted.

Himish said, "I detect no falsehood in the statement but—"

Aibhera interrupted Himish by holding up her hand and then silenced Simea when it appeared he would speak again. "Don't say anything, Sim."

"All right then! Who assessed you? Simea's carefully worded half-truth means someone tested your talent." Eideron's voice rose in volume. "Moreover, why didn't we examine you? Every youngster must take the compulsory examination before puberty, by Synod law."

"It's not her fault, Master; they rejected her. They wouldn't let her take the exams."

"Who? Who prevented her from taking the test, and for what reason?" Eideron's volume increased again, and Simea trembled, but he wouldn't back down because of his loyalty to Aibhera.

"Enough! Eideron, remain calm!" said Himish. "Stop bellowing like a wounded mithun and listen to them."

"Aibhera, tell us what happened," Eideron said, as he took control of his passions.

"Simea told the truth. The Examination Committee refused to allow me to sit for the test. Simea felt the Synod treated me with contempt and smuggled the exam out of the exam room so I could take it under an assumed name. The council posted the scores, but they didn't know who the extra person was since the name wasn't on their roster for that session. They assumed it was a clerical error and posted my score along with the rest of the names."

"What reason did Councilor Herron and his bunch of legalistic nitwits give for barring you from the exam?"

"The Examination Committee said I was unfit because my mother had engaged in a morally questionable relationship."

"What do your mother's actions have to do with your status?" It was Himish's turn to raise his voice.

Aibhera continued despite the interruption. "My mother had remarried after my father died, instead of remaining single, and they said I was morally unfit because of it."

"They can't do that!" he spluttered. "The only reason for disallowing someone's application is for immorality."

"Yes, they said her *mother's* immorality disqualified Aibhera and her sister Kyonna," Simea interjected.

"What!" both men shouted in unison.

The older men's reaction baffled the youngsters, who had expected a scolding, at the least, for disobeying the direct edict of the Examination Committee. Eideron and Himish flew into a rage, but neither man was angry with *them*. The whirlwind of anger and outrage left Simea nervous and puzzled, but untouched at its center.

Himish was the first to relieve their bewilderment.

"The only reason for disqualification is a moral failure," he began.

"Have you had any personal moral failure, to your knowledge or Simea's?" Eideron asked.

"No," they both said, exchanging a glance that displayed their confusion.

Simea held up his hands. "Aibhera is the most scrupulously moral person I know."

Aibhera blushed, visibly embarrassed at his statement. "Sim, stop." Her eyes sparkled as she looked at Simea. She said, "Does this mean the Examination Committee had overstepped its authority, and I could serve as an apprentice?"

Eideron bristled, waved his arms, and veins stood out on his neck. "Yes! Of course it does. You may *only* be rejected for your *own* moral failure, *not* someone else's immorality. There is an excellent reason for that rule."

Eideron spoke slowly and with heavy emphasis. "Also, your mother's morality or lack thereof is not an established fact. Remarriage alone does not constitute a moral failure."

"As a matter of curiosity," Himish interrupted, "what was your score, Aibhera?"

"Aibhera scored ten points higher than I did," Simea boasted, proud of his friend's spiritual and mental prowess.

"Those idiots! Himish, we have before us the two highest test scores in at least eight generations, and that moron Herron has disallowed the better of the two from taking the exams!"

"I know," Himish agreed. "It's no wonder things are going to hell in Abalon."

"We must get her formally examined; otherwise, they will not allow her to testify before the council. Aibhera's ability is too important to let those pompous pinheads win. I believe our interpretation of what Simea and Aibhera told us is correct. For whatever reason, the Nethera are about to begin a new offensive.

"If the council does not act, we ensure Aarda's destruction while we cower here in our volcanic fortress. The Abrhaani and the Eniila fulfill the prophecy, while we, the supposed protectors of the truth, cower here in Abalon and ignore our responsibilities. The Eniila and Abrhaani are ready, and the Sokai must join them. They need us to combat the Nethera."

"Only a few of them have joined forces," Himish qualified.

"It's time for *us* to join those few before the Nethera gain strength."

Himish nodded. "I agree. The Nethera will destroy them without our help." He shook his head and bit his lip. "How can they win when they can't even see their enemies?"

"Or their friends," Simea added.

"I will talk to the men and women I trust on the council," Eideron said.

"As will I. I hope we can gain support."

"What can we do to help, Master?" Simea asked.

"Nothing for now. Aibhera, we will contact you with the time for your exam. Until then, both of you return to your duties and leave this matter to us. We have much to ponder before we act."

Himish said. "We have seen no Aethera since the Sundering, but it appears the Bright Host is active again. Their involvement with the three heroes is a momentous event."

"Yes, momentous indeed," Eideron seconded.

"Simea, escort your friend home. I will tend to your chores tonight. You have both done well, and I am proud of you."

Simea blushed again as he received those words of praise from Eideron. This time it was not embarrassment that caused his red face. He basked in the glow of Eideron's acceptance and approval.

Himish rose from the table. "I'm afraid I must leave you now, but I am so pleased to have met you youngsters. You have given hope to an old man's heart." They exchanged embraces, and Himish stepped out into the night.

After Himish left, Eideron removed the plates from the table. When Simea protested, Eideron said, "leave the cleanup to me. I am glad to do honest work again. The Sokai have been pampered and coddled long enough. It is past time for the Synod to hear the Lion roar. I doubt I will have many more opportunities given my age and the political climate in Abalon, but roar I will, and to hell with the consequences."

CHAPTER TWENTY-TWO

REJECTION

After hours of debate, the Synod had not reached a resolution, and the orderly meeting descended into chaos. Amoreya's lip curled, and her knuckles whitened from the grip on her staff of office—a long rod fashioned centuries before by unknown craftsmen. Whorls of leaves, nearly worn away by the hands of countless predecessors, decorated the long shaft of sea-green metal topped by a polished white crystal. She struck the staff on the dais. The impact of the rod, taller than the diminutive woman, thundered on the platform and echoed throughout the crowded room. The volume of a hundred voices dropped from a waterfall's roar to a brook's tinkle. She stared down the last few speakers until complete silence reigned.

"On the motion of examinations for the girl, Aibhera Liara, we *will* vote," she declared. "We will defer the vote on whether to allow her to give evidence to the Synod Council pending the outcome of the vote on the Examination Committee's ruling."

"It is unnecessary to vote on this matter," Herron waved his hand dismissively and shouted with contempt in his voice. "The Examination Committee found this young—" He paused as if searching for the proper word and sneered. "this young *woman* unfit." Herron looked at Eideron and

Himish with deliberate disdain. "And their judgment should be final. If you overrule them, you set a dangerous precedent."

"The Examination Committee already set the dangerous precedent, Herron." The muscles and veins of Eideron's neck stood out as he shook with rage. "Overruling that stupid mistake is simply a step in the right direction."

The noise level of the combined voices rose again as people shouted their agreement with one side or the other.

"Silence! All of you!" Amorcya's voice could carry across a crowded room no matter what competed with it. "There will be a vote! Right now! No further debate!"

"All in favor!" bellowed the Steward of the Chamber. He rose out of his seat beside the Speaker, counted the votes, and wrote the results on his tally sheet.

"Those opposed." The Steward counted again.

"Abstentions." He made the final tally.

Himish and Eideron saw it was a close call either way, but they never expected this result. They had prepared for weeks, cajoling their friends as they tried to convince them to correct the injustice done to Aibhera. Eideron sensed he was out of touch with the Synod when he realized how influential Herron had become. He cursed under his breath. "Damn it to hell!" *I should have noticed that Herron was busy accumulating favors, while I stood on principles. It has come to a vote, and they reached a decision based on popularity, not ethics and the rule of law.*

"If the Synod has descended to decision-making based on popularity," he whispered to Himish, "the Sokai are doomed."

Herron and his cronies used all their power to save face. They had slandered Aibhera, and her younger sister, who they claimed was a seductress. They brought several young men forward with testimonies against Kyonna. Eideron asked why they called Aibhera iniquitous and excluded her from testing when the young men, guilty of lust by their own admission, could testify and have their testimony accepted. Eideron asked how Herron allowed admitted lechers to take the examination when they had disqualified Aibhera, despite no proof of her moral failure. That caused a furor, which Amoreya quelled by shouting and pounding on the platform with her staff of office.

Herron and his cohorts slandered Simea for his association with Aibhera and her sister. They alleged there was indecency in their relationship but could not offer any proof of the allegation. They argued that based on those allegations, Simea's testimony was suspect and disallowed on the same grounds as Aibhera's.

Eideron had countered, "If you have witnesses to any moral failure by Simea or Aibhera, where are they? Unsubstantiated claims are not, nor have they ever been, proof of anything other than the accuser's prejudiced mind. If there was any failure, it was the failure of my colleague and the Examination Committee to treat every applicant with impartiality and fairness. Their failure is obvious to anyone who values truth and justice."

Those comments provoked the uproar, which led Amoreya to pound on the podium and call for the vote. The debate had concluded, and that was when the Steward counted the raised hands. The murmur of conversations subsided while everyone waited for the result.

"This has not gone well, old friend," Himish whispered.

Eideron nodded in agreement, but his mind constructed alternative plans. His gut told him they would lose this vote.

The Steward rose, walked to the podium, and handed the Speaker the tally sheet.

"On the motion to allow the girl Aibhera Liara, daughter of Riessa Liara, to sit and be assessed, the motion fails," she said. "The vote is forty-five in favor and fifty-one against, with four abstentions. The full council was present with no members missing, so a quorum was not in doubt."

Herron and his cronies had won, and sensing weakness, they went for the jugular. Herron suggested Eideron was too partial to his apprentice and moved that the Synod transfer Simea to another councilor's supervision forthwith.

When the debate ended and the shouting ceased, that motion passed too. For Himish and Eideron, it was like standing in the path of a rockslide as it picked up momentum. It swept them away and left them battered and bruised at the bottom of the slope. Eideron shook his head. His dull stare into the distance betrayed the sorrow in his heart. "I fear we can no longer work within this system." His hands shook, and his shoulders slumped as he led Himish from the council chamber. Behind them, people fawned over Herron, slapping him on the back and shaking his hand.

CHAPTER TWENTY-THREE

KETT'S PROPHECY

The sound of movement in the ship's cabin woke Aelfric. Sunlight streamed through the small window of the room and revealed his fellow passenger rummaging through his abundant belongings. Aelfric figured it was near evening if the sun was low enough in the sky to shine through the porthole.

Aelfric yawned and stretched, "Have we set sail?" He sized up the newcomer, an average-sized Abrhaani whose impeccable grooming and gaudy clothes demonstrated the fellow's vast wealth and a penchant to flaunt it. When the newcomer straightened and turned toward Aelfric, the sun highlighted his face. His smooth-shaven symmetrical features no doubt made him attractive to Abrhaani women, but his eyes contained a veiled ferocity.

"I am sorry if I woke you, I meant no harm, sir." The man's face smiled, but his eyes, devious and aloof, held no warmth in them. "We are about to cast off, so I wanted to check on my belongings in case we hit rough water. One cannot trust one's belongings to the care of servants and assume they have done a proper job."

"No harm done," Aelfric replied. "I wanted to wake up before we set sail."

"I travel to Baradon on business often," the man volunteered in an attempt to make conversation.

Aelfric slipped out of his hammock without comment and stood hunched over to avoid hitting his head on the ceiling. He found it hard to breathe inside the cramped cabin and craved the open sky on deck. Aelfric was less claustrophobic than other Eniila, but he still hated enclosed spaces.

"My, you are a big one," the man began. "In my line of work, I need someone like you. If you want a job, I will hire you."

Aelfric ignored him and climbed the narrow ladder to the deck. He watched the seamen cast off their lines and push off from the dock. Although he had been to sea before, the heaving water beneath the hull still made him uncomfortable.

The *Sea Witch* got underway.

Aelfric had nearly drowned when the small boat he used had foundered on the rocks before he reached Aeron Suul, and the experience heightened his apprehension as the gap between ship and dock widened. The green water stretched to the horizon on the seaward side, and the *Sea Witch* rose and dipped in the gentle swell.

His heart fluttered, and he broke into a cold sweat remembering the water closing over his head as he fought to reach the surface before the dark waters claimed him. The dinghy's loss, a mixed blessing, forced him to continue his journey on foot. Although his load was heavy and the way was hard, he preferred to struggle on soil with forces under his control. He shuddered. *The ocean is no place for an Eniila. The sooner I get solid ground beneath my feet again, the happier I will be.*

Sailors trimmed the sails and set the rudder in a flurry of activity that meant nothing to him. The helmsman bellowed out incomprehensible commands, and the sailors appeared to carry out the orders. Aelfric put his fate in their hands and hoped for the best. It was either trust them or jump overboard and swim to shore. The choice looked increasingly foolish as the gap between ship and shore enlarged. While Aelfric quelled his anxiety, his cabinmate strolled topside and leaned over the rail beside him.

"Excuse me for not doing so earlier, but I realized I neglected to introduce myself. People call me Kett." He waited for Aelfric to respond.

Aelfric smiled wryly while he eyed the man. "Well, I can call you Ketty," he said, using the childish form of the name. "And Ketty, when you call me, you can call me Al."

"That's better, Al," Kett responded, ignoring the slight. "As I said, I am bound for Baradon on business. Often people ask me what kind of business takes me to the land of my enemies." Kett paused and waited long moments while Aelfric, hands clutching the rail, stared back toward the wharf. "Good, you are a man who keeps information to himself and his nose out of other people's affairs. I am impressed."

"My heart skips in ecstasy like lambs in the springtime because I impress you, little man," Aelfric responded. "You'll have a delightful voyage if you are so easily enthralled. Now cease your chatter and leave me in peace before I wet myself in delight."

"In due time, my large, abrasive shipmate, but first, let me tell you what I see in you. I shall tell your fortune, for no charge, of course."

"I need no fortune-teller."

"You will require far more than a fortune-teller before your journey is over, and you will comprehend the reason once I begin."

Aelfric glared at the man. *What's this fop playing at?*

When Aelfric looked into the man's eyes, the hard edge in them mirrored his own wish for vengeance. An over-eager smile and attractive face masked a hunger for power

K. R. Schultz   Overture

and an iron will. This intrigued Aelfric more than any offer of fortune-telling. *Fine, I'll call this Abrhaani chiseler's bluff.* "Go on then. Tell me what you think you know."

"You are a veteran warrior who has suffered many reversals of fortune. Some setbacks happened long ago, but others are more recent. You are a man accustomed to power and authority, yet you travel back to your homeland with no possessions. I see a man who burns with passion for a mission at best, desperate, at worst, hopeless.

"I see a proud, noble, person, brought low by cruel fate and the treachery of those he trusted. You have run far to escape your destiny. You have squandered your youth in your flight from fate, but your true destiny still lies ahead of you. How am I doing so far?"

"Anyone with half a brain and eyes in his head could discern as much by looking at my scars. Someone who had a quick talk with Captain Harmish might do even better. It is a delightful story, as far as it goes.

"Tell me, charlatan, what destiny lies before me? Impress me with that, and I shall listen. If you cannot foretell my destiny, then disappear and trouble me no more. I warn you; I am not so easily impressed." Aelfric tried to stare the man down, but Kett never flinched. Kett's eyes glowed strangely in the setting sun when he answered Aelfric's challenge.

Kett answered so softly Aelfric had to strain to hear the words above the sounds of the wind, the waves, and the creaking of the ship.

"The rule of Baradon in your hands," Kett said, "or more precisely, the rule of Baradon *returned* to your hands, King Aelfric. If you are still strong enough to face your kin, I have considerable wealth and many contacts. I can help." Kett turned and went below.

Aelfric, wide-eyed and white-knuckled, gripped the rail and stared across the empty ocean toward Baradon as the sun sank below the horizon, and darkness fell.

CHAPTER TWENTY-FOUR

CENSURE

The next day brought yet another defeat for Himish and Eideron. The council had disallowed both Aibhera and Simea's testimony. Eideron and Himish had no other witnesses to prove any Nethera threat existed, nor could they confirm the Eniila and Abrhaani worked together. A clear majority voted against sending a delegation to support the people who fought the Nethera. No matter what Eideron and Himish said, the council reached a consensus. Any expedition outside the valley risked the safety of the Sokai people by exposing their location. The decision devastated Eideron since the vote had been almost unanimous. They narrowly defeated Herron's final motion to have Eideron censured and removed from his position on the council.

Himish tapped Eideron on the shoulder. "This entrenched mindset prevents our people from any role in Aarda's defense. The vote demonstrates and highlights our people's self-interest and disregard for everyone else. I wouldn't have believed it possible. How did we become like this?"

Eideron shook his head and rose to his feet. He stood silent with his hand raised until he captured Amoreya's attention, and she granted him permission to speak. *This will be my last address to these stubborn fools.* He spread his arms wide and turned in a circle to gaze at the entire gathering. "My beloved people and esteemed colleagues. Centuries ago, the Sokai avoided destruction and fled to Abalon, but our retreat from the world meant we abandoned the Creator's purposes for our lives. We ignored Aarda's needs and the needs of the Abrhaani and the Eniila. We decided the Eniila and Abrhaani were not worth saving." His voice quavered, and he lowered his head. "This council believes that since no one knows our location, the Sokai can live in peace and safety no matter what happens outside Abalon."

He raised his voice as he regained control of his emotions. "You shortsighted fools! You cling to a false hope! The annihilation of the Abrhaani and the Eniila spells our eventual destruction. Even if the Eniila and Abrhaani are not working in concert again, their mere existence diverts the Nethera's attention from us. If the Eniila and the Abrhaani perish, the Nethera will find Abalon. It is inevitable. When that happens, we stand alone and unaided. The Sokai cannot defend Abalon and its people without the help of the Eniila warriors and Abrhaani healers. There are no more rocks for us to crawl under, nowhere else to hide."

Herron leaped to his feet and countered Eideron's assertions. He repeated the refrain, "There is no evidence of a threat, and without conclusive evidence, we need not act. Eideron's proposed mission is lunacy. If Aarda remains unaware of our presence, we face no threat to Abalon's security. Any expedition outside Abalon exposes us and our location. It puts our entire species at needless risk and creates a problem where none exists…outside of Eideron's imagination."

Eideron slumped as people turned away from him, and a few waved their hands dismissively. *I have done my best to turn them aside from their foolishness, but they won't listen.*

Himish leaned toward Eideron. "The Lion of the Synod roared loud and long, but no one heeds your warning."

Amoreya stood following Herron's rebuttal. "It has grown late, and there is no point in further discussion. I dismiss the council for the day." She thumped the podium with her staff and councilors rose and left the great hall in pairs and small groups. Himish and Eideron stood watching the chamber empty until they stood alone in the Hall of Justice.

Eideron surveyed the empty amphitheater, with its ornate wall tapestries, basalt benches, and carved wooden doors. He ran his hand over the seat he and Himish had shared for decades. "Have we lived too long?" His voice bounced off the walls creating the illusion of a crowd as he spoke. "We are the only ones left since all our contemporaries are dead and gone. Do you remember how we used to come here as young councilors? We had such high hopes, so many brilliant ideas, and such magnificent dreams for our people. Have all our efforts been in vain?"

Himish pressed his lips together and clasped Eideron's shoulder. "Shall we head out?"

Eideron sighed, eyes downcast, and walked toward the enormous doors into the portico where a few stragglers lingered. Together the two old friends shuffled to the elevator across the Plaza of Justice.

Once they reached Eideron's quarters following the council's adjournment, he and Himish sat together and commiserated in the parlor.

"Well, that is that," Himish said, content to lick his figurative wounds.

"That is most definitely not that!" said Eideron.

"What do you mean? There's nothing else to do! If you try again, Herron will move to dismiss you again, and next time he and his cronies may win!"

"If a dismissal is the worst they can do, I can live with it. My position on the council is worthless anyway. We can no longer work with those ninnies."

"They think we are senile…" Himish paused to pick the correct words. "They have a point."

"Don't tell me you think we are senile too!"

"No, I want you to acknowledge they are right." Himish held up his hand to prevent Eideron from exploding in rage again. "Hear me out, damn you! They are right when they say that if anyone leaves the valley, we risk exposure to the Nethera."

"Do you think I am stupid as well as old? I know the risks, but if we do nothing and this joint effort of the Eniila and Abrhaani fails, the Dark Ones will swallow us too.

"The wasteland was expansive, and we depended on its protection for centuries. Things may have changed; it may not be as broad as it was. Aarda may have reclaimed it, so it does not guarantee our safety any longer. We have not scouted outside the caldera walls to gather information. Instead of keeping watch, we ignore everything outside Abalon.

"Although the wasteland is a barrier to the Eniila and Abrhaani, it is unlikely to deter spiritual beings like the Nethera. This valley is not immune to attack or discovery. Even if we obey the Synod's ruling and do nothing, Abalon is vulnerable. After the Nethera dispatch the Eniila and Abrhaani to work unhindered, how long can we survive on our own? The truth no one wants to face is that we don't know Aarda anymore. That is aside from the other problems looming on the horizon."

"What other problems?" Himish asked.

Eideron shook his head in dismay. "You must realize we are nearly out of room and resources here."

Himish scowled and said, "There will be plenty of housing. The caldera walls echo each time they blast more apartments into the cliff faces, and work proceeds well according to recent reports." As if to punctuate Himish's words, another explosion echoed across the Plaza of Justice.

Eideron flinched at the noise but refused to concede the argument. "And what will we feed them? Our land is nearly at capacity now. Each generation, our population grows larger, while our ability to produce food shrinks because of the need to expand our living quarters. I estimate that in two generations, we must look for more land outside this valley or face severe famine, even sooner if the crops fail." Eideron let the idea sink deep into Himish's mind.

"Even if we leave water supply out of the equation," he continued, "we cannot go on as we have for centuries. Our growing population, coupled with our limited resources, will force us to leave here soon and expose our position. If the Nethera eliminate the Eniila and Abrhaani, we will face the threat alone, and our species has produced damn few warriors, none who could dispatch a Dark One. We cannot avoid discovery and allow our population to grow. We can postpone our exodus from Abalon, but we cannot avoid it."

"What do you mean to do?"

"It is best if I say nothing further, my friend. Then you will not share my disgrace."

"No. Tell me what you plan. I can help."

"I cannot plan until I question Aibhera and Simea again. If you want to aid me after I meet with them, I will give you more details. Since they barred me from further contact with Simea, I need a favor from you."

CHAPTER TWENTY-FIVE

HERRON'S SECRET

Herron smirked as he marched down the broad hallway to his office with his apprentice Heysel beside him. He removed the key from his tunic and unlocked the wood-paneled door to his luxurious private workplace. Once inside his sanctuary, he turned toward his apprentice. "You know I rarely indulge, but it's time to celebrate our victory over those two pompous old twits, Himish and Eideron. You may join me if you wish." He waited for Heysel's response.

"Master Herron, I consider it an honor to share your celebration. They say vapor makes the darkness bright." Heysel's eyes glimmered and betrayed his eagerness to experience the rapture that vapor induced.

Herron unlocked a drawer in his desk and withdrew a small bottle and a vapor infuser. He set the stained ceramic bowl on its stand, lit the burner beneath it, poured the thick brown liquid into the container, and waited for the flame to boil the fluid. "You may have the honor of the first draft, young man." Herron beckoned Heysel to approach his desk and smiled when Heysel's haste betrayed his eagerness to experience the euphoria the vapor induced. Herron controlled his own desire for the ecstatic high, but Heysel had no control over his cravings. Vapor addiction provided

Herron with another level of power over his apprentice and allowed him to accept the young man into his inner circle.

Heysel drew a deep breath and flopped into a nearby chair, his eyes became glazed and unfocused. Herron leaned over the bowl and pulled the pungent steam into his lungs. It took only moments before the relaxation and euphoria took hold, and once it did, Herron staggered to a brocade couch beside his apprentice. He sprawled onto its cushioned seat. "It truly does make the darkness bright."

"Could I ask a question, Master?" Heysel drawled.

"Certainly. Ask me whatever you wish."

"Why are you so determined to destroy Himish and Eideron?"

"Let me tell you a story. Years ago, three brothers became orphaned by a foolish decision of the Synod Council. As orphans, they should have become wards of the council, but no one came to the older boys' aid as they struggled to care for their baby brother. Often their care caused them to do unsavory things to survive. For several years these boys lived in squalor on the verge of starvation. Then they attracted the Synod Council's attention when a young woman disappeared from the central park. The guardsmen spent many days looking for the little tease who had the same loose morals as all females.

"They found her and the boys in the volcanic vent caves below Abalon. Let us simply say she was no longer attractive or marriageable since she had suffered hard usage at the older brothers' hands. The brothers, now in their late teens, bore the blame for the girl's condition. The council, most of whom have died since that time, convicted and sentenced them to life imprisonment in the dungeon below us. Their younger brother, a mere child, was placed with caretakers who treated him as a servant, or on foul days, a target for abuse. The lad swore he would avenge his brothers and put women in their proper place, once he grew to manhood." Herron lurched to his feet and paced around the room.

"Despite the unfortunate circumstances of his life, the child grew into a talented youth, underwent the Synod exams, and achieved a score high enough to earn a Synod apprenticeship. By the time he became a councilor, only two members of the council that had imprisoned his brothers remained alive. All the others died of various misfortunes. I shall let you draw your own conclusions about the identity of the boy, but the only councilors left from that time are Eideron and Himish. Take another tug of the vapor if you wish." Herron gestured toward the bowl filling the room with fog that swirled around him. The mist gave Herron, the wooden furniture, and the wall-hung tapestries a ghostly aspect.

Heysel swayed as though the floor moved beneath him. He staggered over to the infuser, placed his hands on the table to steady himself, and inhaled another lungful of the white smoke. "I have noticed your eyes always rest on the Speaker's staff. Why do you covet it, and why is it significant to you?" Smoke swirled out of his mouth as he spoke.

"Two reasons: first—" Herron raised a forefinger. "I want the authority the rod confers upon its holder. Second—" He held up another finger. "It is more than a symbol of authority. The staff is a weapon if you know its secrets. The metal is unique, and there is an apparatus inside that draws power from the Aether, which a user can discharge in the form of lightning. It has other uses, but I haven't discovered them yet." Herron clapped Heysel on the shoulder and flashed a sly grin. "Since I have told you this much, tomorrow you will search the archives and look for references on the Staff of Escalus for me. Bring me any written material on the weapon and tell no one what you found."

Herron debated whether to take another breath of vapor from the bowl, since the room, already thick with fumes, made his head spin. *Another hit to celebrate my coming triumph couldn't hurt.* He struggled to his feet from the couch and tottered to the infuser. "May the darkness become bright," he murmured after he inhaled the mist rising from the vessel.

Although he had locked the door to prevent the discovery of his secret vice, he sensed another presence in the room when he lifted his head.

"You called?" A sibilant voice cut through the vapor fog in the room.

Herron turned toward Heysel, but the young man in the chair, incapable of speech or coherent thought, had passed out. To his left, a shimmering figure materialized. "Who are you?" Herron's mental fog lifted, the room's temperature plummeted, and Herron shivered from both fear and the frigid air.

"You asked for the darkness to become light after you inhaled. Your prayer allowed me to contact you. Surely you know that the vapor expands your mind and allows you to touch the Aetherial realm."

The being shimmered, pulling color from the room, and absorbing it as Herron watched. Herron hesitantly nodded, His voice quavered when he spoke." What is your name?"

"I have many names, some say I am the darkness, but I stood with the Creator when He formed Aarda, and I have come in answer to your call. We noted the prejudice you have endured. We will help you seek justice and achieve your vengeance."

Herron's teeth chattered from the cold. "You are an Aethera then."

"You have said it, and I will not deny it. No one must know of our meeting. Will you accept our aid to become the most powerful Sokai in all Aarda? You must affirm your statement with a blood oath. Be warned, you will forfeit your life and the lives of those you love if you do not obey us."

"Yes, I will do anything you ask," Herron said, excitement building. "If you help avenge my family, I shall willingly obey your every command, and if you guarantee my supremacy over my people, my life is yours."

CHAPTER TWENTY-SIX

SECRET MEETING

Himish handed a folded sheet of paper to Aibhera. "This note is from Eideron. I read it, and I don't think he overreacted. Herron is devious and deceitful, and he expects the same from others. He's no fool. He expects Eideron to disobey the Synod, and in this case, he is correct. My old friend has lost faith in our authorities and will scruple at nothing any longer. Eideron insists on the extreme precautions in this note so that no spies sent by that malicious upstart can report him to the council and stymie his plan."

Aibhera looked puzzled and opened her mouth to speak, but Himish held up a hand and said, "Before you ask, no, I don't know what the plan is. You'll find out when you meet him again." He laid a hand on her head. "May the Creator bless you with wisdom, young lady. Both you and your friend will need it in the days ahead." He started walking away, but after two steps, he turned and waved goodbye with tears in his eyes.

Aibhera unfolded the paper and read: *Meet me at my house after sunset tonight and don't speak of the encounter to anyone. My home will appear dark and deserted. Once you are both present, knock four times, in two sets of two knocks, and wait for me to let you in. Destroy this note once you have read it.*

Although Aibhera didn't understand the need for such secrecy, the prospect of a clandestine meeting excited them. It added spice and mystery to her otherwise ordinary evening.

After slinking along back streets and creeping up shadowy cargo ramps, Aibhera arrived at Eideron's home. *I'm pretty sure nobody saw me coming, and I didn't see anyone following me down any of those nasty back passageways. The garbage stink still clings to my clothes.*

While she waited for Simea, she hid in the shadows of Eideron's porch, a niche carved into the crater wall. Aibhera shivered in the semidarkness. *Is it the cold fog rising from the valley floor or nervous tension causing the shakes?* When Simea finally arrived by a separate roundabout route, her shivering decreased. *Well, that answers that question, definitely nervousness then.*

As Eideron had promised, the windows of his home were dark unlit holes in the wall of his dwelling. The light from the windows of nearby living quarters filtered through the mist and created bright halos around the openings, giving the street a ghostly atmosphere. Voices and sounds of family life drifted through the air and added to the eerie effect.

To casual observers, Master Eideron had turned in early after another disastrous defeat at Synod meetings. Simea grabbed Aibhera's wrist when she raised her hand to knock. He shook his head. "Let me do it." He knocked twice, paused for a moment, then rapped twice more, as Himish's note had instructed. It opened at once. Eideron must have been waiting in the foyer for their arrival.

Eideron held his finger to his lips when Sim tried to speak. "Enter. Hurry, before someone sees you," Eideron whispered, pulling them inside his darkened home. "Follow me. There are no windows in the pantry, so no one can see us or overhear our conversation."

Eideron led them through his darkened foyer and kitchen while he lit the way into the pantry with a candle shielded by his hand. He had set up cushions in the storage room, along with a low table on which he placed a lighted lamp. He closed the door and blew out the candle. Their shadows loomed large on the walls behind them. "We cannot be too careful," he said in a low voice. Eideron winced in pain as he lowered himself onto a cushion, looking suddenly older and frailer than Aibhera remembered. "Please seat yourselves so we can begin.

Simea spoke in a low voice. "Why have you called us together, Master?"

"Don't call me master. I am not your master anymore, Simea. Since you are not my apprentice, you no longer need to honor me with the title. Call me Eideron. I escaped disbarment from the Synod Council by a hair's breadth today. The council passed judgment on me and forbade further contact with you. What we decide tonight may determine the fate of Abalon and Aarda. I can't overemphasize the importance of this conversation and the danger if they discover us meeting like this."

"They are a pack of idiots," Simea said. Aibhera fidgeted and looked about to agree, but Eideron silenced her with a finger to his lips.

"The council has served our people for centuries." Eideron sighed and leaned across the table toward the youngsters. The wrinkles of his face formed grim shadows in the lamplight and made him look more stern than usual. "I will not tolerate contempt for the Synod Council, however much you or I disagree with their methods. They want to keep our people safe and happy. Although I believe they blundered in their recent decisions, they still deserve our respect. They are the custodians of this valley. They are doing their best, and they shall continue their roles long after we go."

Aibhera's face scrunched in puzzlement at Eideron's choice of words. *Long after we go? Is Eideron thinking of leaving Abalon?*

"Very well, mm…Eideron." Simea struggled to omit the honorific title.

Aibhera placed her hand on Simea's forearm. *This is hard for Sim. He's loyal, and he looks angry. He served Eideron for two years and then watched, helpless, as the Synod turned against Eideron despite decades of faithful service.*

After he and Aibby had read Eideron's note, he had told her how Herron and his cohorts engineered Eideron's humiliation. He explained that Heysel had cornered him before the meeting and said, "After today, Master Herron will control the Synod Council and drive all the old codgers out. My master will control Abalon from now on, so you'd better treat me with more respect because I will make life very unpleasant for people who don't."

Simea scowled, his lips a thin line, voice tight, and eyes flashing. "No matter what the Synod says, I will always honor you," he said. He bowed low before Eideron.

Eideron shrugged and shook his head. "Let's not waste time arguing. What's done is done. We cannot change the past. We can only move forward, and we have more important matters to discuss. I must learn how committed you are to acting on your visions since I have a plan that involves both of you. It poses grave risks and requires tremendous sacrifices."

"What is your plan?" Aibhera sat rigid in her seat, fingers toying with the fringe on the tablecloth. "Since we are meeting like this, I assume you want to keep it secret, and I imagine we are part of your strategy."

"You are a perceptive young lady. It's easy to understand why they should have tested you." Eideron's tone carried a bitter edge to it. "Our conversation may take some time. I will ask you some questions, and you must deliberate before you answer. If I receive the answers I expect and want, I will tell you my plan. If you answer otherwise, I will forget the whole idea, and this meeting never happened. Your lives will continue unchanged, and I will find ways to endure the changes in mine."

CHAPTER TWENTY-SEVEN

AELFRIC'S QUANDARY

Aelfric no longer knew how many days he had paced the *Sea Witch*'s heaving deck or how many nights he slept fitfully in the cramped quarters below deck. He awoke, queasy from the motion of the boat, and thanked the gods he had avoided full-blown seasickness.

Aelfric's fellow traveler, Kett, the Abrhaani businessman, slept on while Aelfric eased out of the hammock and avoided bashing his head on the low ceiling and lintel. Nothing the Abrhaani built suited Eniila's bodies, but the ship's tiny cabin heightened the problem. The Eniila, people of open spaces, often suffered from claustrophobia. Although edgy and unsettled, he avoided the frenzied terror other members of his race experienced.

Dreams of vengeance had awakened him early. Another tenday remained before they reached Baradon. That gave him enough time to ponder his options. Once out of the swaying hammock, Aelfric climbed the rungs of the small ladder, squeezed through the narrow hatch, and clambered to his feet on the wooden deck. Vertebrae snapped and popped as he stretched and straightened. Except for the sailors near the end of their night watch, he was alone on deck.

The endless skyline of the empty ocean would have relieved his claustrophobia, but the sky and sea appeared the color of lead. They blended, making the horizon impossible to distinguish. The heaving deck negated the benefits of the view and open air. Without a visual cue to anchor himself to the world, the rolling motion of the ship atop the swells caused a reciprocal movement in Aelfric's gut. He gripped the rail and bent over the side, expecting to vomit. After a moment, the feeling passed, but the cold sweat lingered.

He mopped his brow and sighed inwardly. *I'll never get used to this, but I'll survive. Sixteen years ago, Shelhera and I spent the whole voyage puking over the rail or into a bucket. What a nausea, vomit-filled nightmare! The smell of barf still makes me feel seasick. I had planned a pleasant life on Khel Braah, a way to make amends to a few of the Abrhaani, but when Shelhera died, my dreams died with her, and now Laakea is lost to me. My heart aches from my losses, but my new plan will ease it.*

Although he faced an uncertain welcome in Baradon, excitement built inside him. Aelfric squinted and hoped to make out a jagged blue line of mountains along the eastern horizon. No matter how he strained his eyes, the familiar peaks that formed the rocky spine of Baradon, his homeland refused to appear above the gray water. *The gods have favored this mission and blessed us with a storm-free journey, but until I stand on solid earth...best to think of other things.*

To combat his tension, Aelfric weighed Kett's promise of aid against his other options. *Although I dread entanglement with the little Abrhaani schemer; if I expect to regain my rightful place before old age or calamity claims me, I might need the little chiseler's help.*

Few Eniila men survived to old age. Combat, accidents, or duels ended the lives of the aged or even unskilled younger men. Eniila warriors preferred death on a sword point to the gradual descent into frailty. Oldsters often took on impossible duels to avoid decrepitude and senility. Shrewd tactics might extend one's life expectancy. An old campaigner once said, "Age and treachery will defeat youth and enthusiasm every time." However, time weakened the strongest arm and dulled the sharpest wit.

Aelfric was reluctant to test the veracity of that axiom. The vigor he retained, combined with stealth and treachery learned through experience, would have to carry him through the months of intrigue and struggle ahead.

Aelfric held few illusions about his Abrhaani shipmate's nature. *If only I could trust Kett...that is the heart of my problem. Kett is a slippery snake who masks deceit with feigned friendliness and has his own interests at heart. Kett's allegiance might turn deadly. Vigilance is the best protection from a dagger between the shoulder blades, but am I prepared for betrayal when it comes?*

Aelfric continued to ponder his options. Kett had hinted that Aelfric's twin brother Aelrin was still the War-Leader of the Eniila. A questionable third choice briefly held his attention. The Gray Brotherhood was a significant factor in Eniila politics, but they remained an unknown quantity. The Brotherhood followed its own mysterious purposes, so whose side they chose in a civil war was guesswork. Aelfric often wondered what they concealed in their Cities of Refuge.

I must win the people's affection. I need trustworthy and committed followers, not money-grubbing mercenaries. If the people put my brother's head on a pike, it vindicates me as war-leader and proves Aelrin is merely a pretender. That would solve my difficulties and prove that I am still worthy.

Despite Aelfric's mistrust of the Abrhaani merchant, Kett's financial and political influence, and his ability to recruit manpower, provided a way for Aelfric to square his account with Aelrin. A coup supported by the Abrhaani businessman dealt decisively with the men who had exiled him, leaving Aelfric in a position to strengthen his hold on power.

The longer Aelfric pondered the issues, the more he became convinced that Kett's help to unseat Aelrin and his co-conspirators presented the best solution.

Kett's network of contacts and fat moneybag guarantees a large army in the shortest time. Without Kett's aid, recruiting a large force risks Aelrin's notice too soon. The conclusion is inescapable. I need Kett. It's humiliating to beg an Abrhaani for help, but it's still the best way.

As the old warriors say, "Watch your back and prepare for the worst. Stay alert, and the Nethera take the hindmost."

He leaned over the rail and watched foam and bits of seaweed slide past the hull. *The ship's prow slices the gray-green water of the Syn Gersuul like a well-forged blade cleaves flesh and bone.* "I wish I had other options, but I don't." Aelfric felt suddenly hungry. He sighed and turned toward the galley. *An uncertain future awaits me, but this tiny sliver of wood must carry me home.*

CHAPTER TWENTY-EIGHT

EIDERON'S PLAN

Silence hung in the room like the mist outside, as the two youngsters waited for Eideron's questions. Eideron was no longer a threatening and forbidding presence, just a wise old man with more fire in his spirit than his frail body could contain. Out of respect, Aibhera and Simea waited for Eideron to speak.

Earlier that day, Simea had shared the debate details with Kyonna and Aibhera after the Synod meeting. He explained to Aibby and Kyonna how hard Eideron fought for Aibhera during the session, and that deepened her respect for Eideron. Kyonna wept when she heard the Synod's decision and blamed herself for Aibhera's difficulties. Simea assured her that Herron concocted the issue to divert attention from his own guilt, but Ky was inconsolable.

The Synod had ostracized Eideron and pushed him aside, but he remained unbroken. He was still vital in spirit, heart, and mind. Aibhera imagined that he was the grandfather she never knew. Her grandfathers, both councilors, had died together in an accident before her birth.

The determination to save his people glimmered in Eideron's eyes. "Do you still have the same dreams each night?"

.

They hesitated, glanced at each other, and then nodded.

"Things have changed," Aibhera said. "The dreams have become more vivid. We now hear their muffled conversations, and sometimes we can even smell what they are cooking. We stand beside them in our dreams, although they can't see us, and we *should* stand beside them before—"

Eideron interrupted her. "Are you convinced that we should do that despite the danger to Abalon and our people?"

"More now than ever, Master Eideron," said Simea.

Aibhera gave a curt nod. "Why do you ask?"

"I ask because, as I said before, I must gauge the depth of your commitment to your visions. I must ask you this too. Will you do whatever is necessary to help those who oppose the Nethera, no matter the personal cost?"

"Yes, Master Eideron," Aibhera looked at Simea.

He nodded and squeezed her hand. "I believe we are ready."

"Will you become outcasts, abandon your families, and cross the wasteland to find the ones you seek?"

So that is why he asks these questions. Eideron wants to send us to scout Aarda outside Abalon. Once Aibhera understood the full cost of the task ahead, it tore a gaping hole in her heart, and tears filled her eyes.

Sokai children grew up with stories of monsters and dangers outside the caldera. Stories of their ancestors' hardships and perils during the long trek across the wasteland, before they arrived in Abalon, filled volumes in the library. Aibhera brushed her cheek with her fingers to wipe away the tears, then put her doubts into words. "We have no experience outside this valley, and we know nothing of the outside world. Do you intend to send us out there?"

"You are not alone in your ignorance of what lies outside Abalon. Since I too lack knowledge of the world outside Abalon, I cannot help you with that." Eideron nodded, his voice becoming lower, and his tone soothing. "But I can help you in other ways. Think hard before you answer. Many lives may depend on your choices. You may discuss the issues now, or you may do so in private later. When we meet again, you may give me your answer."

Aibhera said, "With each meeting, we increase our risk of discovery. We will discuss this now and make our decision tonight. Do you agree, Sim?" *The visions are too compelling to ignore. I could not live free of shame if I do nothing to help the people who appear in our dreams.*

Simea began, "Aibby, since we have no experience outside Abalon, the council is right, we risk exposing our people to danger if we fail or if they capture us."

"Yes, the responsibility frightens me too, but consider this. Mother and the other planters say we must either stop having children or find new territory for crops outside Abalon. That will risk our exposure too. It may not happen next year, but at some point, we must leave Abalon. If the Nethera defeat the Eniila and the Abrhaani, we will face the Nethera alone when we leave."

"This decision is too big for young people," Simea protested.

"But Simea, the Creator has given *us* these visions. No one else has the information we do. Since the Synod has refused to act, what else can we do? I am terrified of leaving everything behind, but I am just as terrified of doing nothing. My heart tells me to stay, but my mind tells me that staying and doing nothing is an act of cowardice—or worse."

"You are right. I sense it too," Simea conceded. "We need the Eniila and Abrhaani as much as they need us. If we refuse to help them and they perish, no one will come to our aid later. Have we decided?"

"Yes, I have. Have you?" Aibhera asked.

"I don't see another choice." Simea shrugged and turned his palms upward above the table. "The Sokai must send someone to help the Abrhaani and the Eniila, who now fight alone against the darkness. We are afraid, but if you send us, we will go."

"The Synod will curse us and never allow us to return, even if we save the entire world," Aibhera joked, trying to lighten the mood. "Assuming we survive, if you'll pardon my gallows humor." Her shoulders slumped, and she looked down at her hands. *My departure will kill Kyonna. She has no one to confide in once I'm gone.*

After a lengthy silence, Eideron said, "I have heard your discussion. You covered issues the Synod ignored and reached a better conclusion. You both proved wise beyond your years, and although you fear the consequences, you will not flinch from your duty. No Synod councilor could do more, but I will not send you."

Both young people looked puzzled when he paused and sighed.

"No, I shall not send you," he repeated. "We shall go together."

Simea straightened in his seat and opened his mouth to protest, but Eideron held up his hand. "Hush. I know I am old. If you say one word about it, I shall beat you senseless. I can back that up with action. You must have heard the saying, 'Age and treachery will defeat youth and enthusiasm every time.'" Eideron smirked and winked at Aibhera, grew solemn again, and said, "I may not survive the journey. None of us may survive it, but you are too young and inexperienced to face this task alone. I still must teach you the Synod's secret knowledge, which may help you survive and contribute to the fight against the Nethera.

"You cannot learn those skills without my instruction. I must go along, if for no other reason than to complete your training. If I try to teach you in Abalon before we leave, we risk discovery and imprisonment or worse, and that ends any chance to aid the ones we seek. Besides, I would be a pitiful leader if I burdened you with a load *I* refused to bear."

Eideron hunched forward. "There is no one else, except Himish. He *is* younger than I am, and he might be more able to handle the physical rigors of the task, but Himish has family responsibilities. I have no one left here, no one who will miss me when I am gone. The Lion of the Synod will snarl one last time, but not within a cage devised by blind fools."

Both young people's eyes widened when he referred to himself by that nickname.

"Yes, they call me that, and I intend to live up to it. A lion is not a house cat. The wilderness is the only proper place for a lion to die. I am the only logical choice, and I will tolerate no argument from either of you. Is that understood?" Eideron said, looking far less stern than he sounded.

"Yes, Master," Simea and Aibhera replied in unison, contrite because of the reprimand.

"Now, it is past an old man's bedtime."

Eideron put out the lamp and guided his young guests through his darkened dwelling to the exit.

"Farewell," he whispered. "Aibhera, Himish will inform you of our next meeting time. I dare not send him to you, Simea, because I fear Herron will become suspicious if you have any contact with Himish or me. Come prepared to leave. I am sorry I cannot tell you what to pack, but I do not know what we need or what we face any more than you do.

"Creator, please guide us in our preparations," he prayed aloud. "Try to listen for the Creator's voice, children, since He alone knows what we need. Do not meet, for any reason, before we leave, and tell no one of our plans. I suspect that Herron may have us watched. Herron would love an excuse to impeach and imprison me. We must act before he anticipates our departure."

CHAPTER TWENTY-NINE

AIBBY'S STALKER

Aibhera and Simea shared a silent embrace before they parted. She took a different route home than the one she followed on her way to Eideron's clandestine meeting. Aibhera's mind raced as she glided along the deserted ramps and passageways toward her family's quarters, her heart a leaden lump in her chest. *Leaving Abalon is our only choice, but it's exciting, dangerous, and bold too. The Creator has a sense of humor. I can't believe He picked me, the cautious one, for a perilous adventure, while my impetuous sister will stay safe at home. I feel taller, and tougher just thinking about it.*

As she slipped through the shadows of the dimly lit alleys and passageways of the field hands' quarters, Aibhera got an eerie feeling of someone's eyes on her. At first, she dismissed the tingling skin and shortness of breath. *All the secrecy and skullduggery has made me skittish.* Then the scuffle of a footstep, out of place with normal nighttime sounds, made her flinch and jump. A dislodged pebble clattered down the alley behind her. Her heart raced, and her mouth became dry.

Aibhera wracked her brain for a solution. *Eideron was right. Herron's spy is following me. I could run home and outdistance him, or I could try to discover who Herron has tasked with the job. If I run homeward, I draw trouble to our household...a poor choice. My family has enough trouble. I want to see who it is.*

Aibhera descended one last ramp that ended on the caldera floor among the field hands' quarters near her home. *I know a place! A spot where I can avoid capture and spy on the spy.* She threw caution aside and sprinted forward.

Around the corner, a ladder led to a rooftop. The occupants and their neighbors used racks on the flat roof to dry herbs in the sun.

If I climb fast, I can go up the ladder, and once the stalker walks past, I can descend behind him. From up there, I can glimpse my pursuer as he passes. If he climbs the ladder after me, I can't escape from the roof, but I will risk it. I wonder if someone is following Simea too?

Aibhera dashed around the corner and scrambled up the ladder. A flurry of brief noises on the street below rewarded her caution. *So it's not my imagination.* Aibhera waited, every muscle tense as she peered over the parapet of the flat roof to catch sight of her stalker.

Clouds slid across the moon overhead and shrouded the street below in darkness. Aibhera cursed her luck. A figure in a hooded cloak hurried past the ladder. Her stalker was trying to pick up her trail. Darkness hid his face as he rounded the corner and disappeared. She waited until the noise of his footsteps faded away and then slid down the ladder into the shadows of the street.

More cautious now, Aibhera's ears strained to pick out unusual sounds from the background noises, but she heard only crickets and the occasional whir of moth wings. Once she neared her own house, she caught sight of the hooded figure again. It crept around the side of the residence to where her bedroom lay. She crouched low and crept after him.

Aibhera rounded the corner in time to see her pursuer trying to climb through her bedroom window.

Overhead, the clouds thinned and drifted away. Without the veil of clouds, the moon became a bright disk overhead and illuminated the prowler with its pale light.

Aibhera's stealth and patience paid off. The prowler's hood caught on the top of the window frame and uncovered its wearer. The moonlight rewarded Aibhera with a view of her mysterious stalker's profile. She sprinted forward and grasped the shadowy figure's cloak, yanking it backward. "Kyonna! Stop," she whispered as loud as she dared. "What are you doing?"

As Aibhera tugged on the cloak, Kyonna smacked her head on the lintel. Ky whimpered in pain but did not scream.

"Aibby, why did you do that?" Ky rubbed the sore spot on her head vigorously. "That hurt."

"Serves you right. Why did you follow me?"

"I wanted to understand why my honorable sister snuck out when she should be asleep."

"Well, what did you discover, nosy brat?"

"Let me go. Let's get inside before we get caught."

"Oh…right."

"I'm way better at this than you are," Kyonna bragged.

Once they were both inside and seated on their beds, Aibhera said, "All right, Ky, why were you following me?"

"I wanted to know why you snuck out of the house after you thought everyone was asleep. You never sneak out at night. *I* do, but *you*? *Never.* That was strange enough, but instead of meeting a boy or going to The Greenhouse dance club as I do, you went to old Eideron's house. Too weird. Then Simea showed up. I knew you were both in trouble after that huge fracas with the Synod. What is the big secret?"

"I can't tell you, Ky. I want to, the Creator knows I want to, but Eideron swore us to silence."

"Yeah, but we always share everything!" Ky complained. "First you go to a meeting with Eideron and don't invite me, now you sneak off to his house... Never mind. You know what? You don't want to tell me, and that's fine."

Kyonna stretched out on her bed and turned her face to the wall, resentment clear in her rigid posture.

"Don't be like that, Ky, I can't tell you."

"Fine, you don't have to tell me," she repeated, with an icy edge to her voice.

Ky's tone set off alarms inside Aibhera. It was unusual for Kyonna to drop an issue once she fixated on it. Aibby and Ky were sisters, but more than that, they were confidantes. They always shared their secrets, but this secret came between them, and it weakened the connection they shared. Aibby wanted to grab Kyonna's shoulder and confront her.

It breaks my heart, but I can't share this with her. It is hard enough to slip away with no farewells. Ky's unwelcome interference makes it even more difficult. Keeping this secret from Kyonna is the hardest thing I have done, but our mission could demand far worse of me before long. I am about to leave Abalon forever. I will never see Ky again, and Kyonna won't know where I've gone. Aibby stretched out on her bed, wept silent, bitter tears that burned trails across her face, and surrendered the outcome to the Creator.

CHAPTER THIRTY

DEPARTURE

An early riser might have noticed three silhouettes against the bright sky at the lip of the crater. Aibhera looked down into the caldera that had been her home. Abalon seemed small from this high on the rim. A network of canals and fields lay below her like a game board; the orchards and vineyards in neat rows faded off into the distance. Grain fields and gardens, at various stages of maturity, formed a patchwork pattern on the valley floor. Some patches were yellow and near harvest, others remained the bright green of new growth. Fruit trees blossomed in orderly rows and provided lines of blazing color between the fields.

They tried to capture Abalon, with all its technological complexity and natural beauty, in their memories. The central lake glistened in the caldera's center, but beyond Lake Selatan, the blue haze of the moist morning air obscured the caldera's opposite rim. Once they completed their wordless farewell to their home, Eideron and his young companions turned their backs on Abalon.

The three companions stood on the edge of a hostile and unfamiliar world. They stared down the slope of pitted and cratered rock, across an ocean of black sand and volcanic debris, which spread outward from where they stood on the volcano's lip. The lush greenery of Abalon formed a fragile island of vegetation behind them. Before them, an endless black desert danced shimmering in the heat.

Eideron broke the silence, ending their individual contemplations. "Now you know why no one has left Abalon for centuries. It is also why there are no guards or barriers to prevent anyone from leaving. The wasteland stretches as far as you can see in every direction. Well, shall we continue? This is our last chance to turn back." He waited for the youngsters' answers as they looked across the desolate wilderness that stretched to the far horizon and remembered the history. For those Sokai who survived, the first journey to Abalon was an arduous trek. For most of their people, it was a death march, and their bodies had littered the barren wilderness like a battlefield.

Since birth, all Sokai children heard horrific tales of the migration to Abalon as they carried the supplies and technology with them to make Abalon livable. Ten thousand Sokai began the trek, but only twenty-five-hundred lived through the ordeal. The march through the barren lands that surrounded Abalon had claimed thousands of lives.

The refugees abandoned equipment along the way when there were no longer enough hands to carry it. The wasteland destroyed most of the machines left behind. Stories and songs contained several versions of their trek, woven into the fabric of their culture, and once they settled in Abalon, no one left the valley. Eideron, Aibhera, and Simea were the first Sokai to abandon Abalon's security in over a thousand years.

The epic Sokai ballads "The Time of Sorrows" and "The March of the Ten Thousand" began with tales of attacks by creatures that prowled the edges of the wasteland. It told how the Sokai fought off those creatures before they straggled into the heat of the volcanic rubble field. Thirst and hunger took a continuous toll on their numbers until less than three thousand Sokai reached Abalon. As he viewed the vast wasteland below, those songs and legends struck fear in

Eideron's heart. *I wonder if any of us can survive this journey.*

The Sokai's numbers have increased since those days. Over a million Sokai now crowd a crater a mere eighty miles across. Over thirty generations of Sokai have lived out their lives in the caldera. In death, their flesh contributes to the land's fertility while their bones rest in the ossuaries beneath the cliff walls. My wife's bones rest there, and I expected mine to lie beside hers soon. If Aibhera and Simea survive, they will write a new history for our people outside this protected oasis, and who knows where their bones will lie at the end of their journey.

Now they know what lies ahead, I will not blame my two young companions if they turn back. If they stay, they might live long and uneventful lives. Aibhera and Simea are abandoning their families and their heritage. I am old. I have less to lose than they do, but the sight of the endless desert before us has me rethinking my commitment too. I wish we had the technology the original ten thousand had available to them.

Over the last thousand years, Sokai technology atrophied in some areas. The land speeders mentioned in the old books would have shortened the journey and increased our chances of survival. There was no way to bring the ancient land speeders over the caldera rim and down the cliff wall intact, and there was no reason for their use in Abalon. The refugees cannibalized them for parts, so they only exist as stories in the Annals of Abalon. For our return trip across the wasteland, we must walk.

Simea interrupted Eideron's extended reverie when he answered Eideron's question. "No, Master Eideron. We will not turn back. We only wanted to look and remember."

"I told you not to call me master."

"But you are our master, our teacher, no matter what the Synod said," Aibhera argued. "You are all we have left of our homes and our heritage." Tears trickled down her cheeks.

"I am sorry. I regret that neither of you could say proper goodbyes to your families, but we needed to leave before they miss us. The Synod will pursue us if they realize what we have done."

"I wish we could have taken three of the smaller gliders and loaded them with supplies," Simea said.

"I cannot fly one," Eideron confessed. "Can either of you pilot a glider?" Simea and Aibhera both shook their heads. "Besides, the council would suspect we took them if the gliders vanished when we did. Himish will keep them guessing where we have gone. The missing gliders would be harder for him to explain. Himish is a resourceful dissembler. He says misdirection is the most important prerequisite of a good councilor. You should have heard…oh, never mind. That's a story for another time. Shall we descend?"

They scrambled westward, down the slope of the ancient volcano, across basalt flows and obsidian outcrops. Gravel and fine sand had collected in the crevices of the rocks. By the time they reached the base of the cone and were on flat terrain, the noonday sun struck them like a hammer blow. The slight breeze brought no relief, and occasional gusts of wind blew dust that stung and burned their eyes.

"We had better ration our water since we have no idea when we will find more," Eideron cautioned.

The two youngsters nodded.

No doubt their throats are too dry and raw to argue, just like mine, and their thoughts are on the homes they left and the families they abandoned.

Simea and Aibhera trudged through the day's heat and suffered in silence. Despite all their precautions and their protective clothing, the dry air and the blistering heat caused their skin to flake and peel. Sunlight reflected off the bleak landscape, and the air rippled and shimmered above the black rock. Whirlwinds, swirling maelstroms of dust and debris, scoured their skin and blew sand into their eyes. They lurched and staggered like drunken men across the ancient lava field's uneven crust. Dust filtered into the cracks and crevices of the rock, and scrubby vegetation clung to life in those pockets. The lava had cracked in many places, creating irregular fissures and craters, which made walking perilous.

Eideron kept a steady pace without complaint and hid his frailty from Aibhera and Simea. Despite the need to watch his footing and his parched throat but driven to teach his two young companions as much as possible, Eideron maintained a steady monolog. He longed to train them in the Synod's secret knowledge, but that required concentration. The precarious footing out on the lava field made that impossible. Instead, he taught them the history of the Thousand Years War. The long war caused the Sokai to give up hope for peace and flee their only city, Berossus, near the mountains in northeastern Baradon.

By nightfall they were footsore, tired, and coated in a fine layer of black dust. The three Sokai looked like three man-shaped lumps of charcoal moving along the desert floor. They stopped for the night in a circular depression large enough for them and their gear. The temperature plummeted, and though the rocks retained heat, they cooled rapidly after sunset. Simea scrounged enough shriveled vegetation to build a small fire.

Eideron stopped them before they prepared the evening meal. "I have things I must teach you before we travel farther. We will eat after the lesson. Think of the meal as a reward for your efforts."

While Eideron rummaged through his pack, Simea whispered to Aibhera, "What can be more important than food and rest? I don't understand the urgency."

CHAPTER THIRTY-ONE

RETURN TO SETHRIA

"Fine, let's see what we can do together," Aelfric muttered to the waves, having reached his conclusion. He spat over the ship's rail and watched it arc into the *Sea Witch*'s wake as she surged through the waves toward Baradon. Reservations still niggled in the back of his mind, but only time could reveal whether he had chosen wisely.

"What was it you said?" a voice behind him asked.

Aelfric turned and faced Kett. His future benefactor and partner had awakened and slipped onto the deck to stand behind him.

I am getting soft...careless. How did the little fop approach me undetected? "I said, let's see what we can do together, you eavesdropping little sneak. Let's hear your plan."

"Ah, so you have made your decision. I suggest we postpone that conversation until we reach Baradon. These matters are best kept concealed, and privacy is impossible on board this ship."

"Agreed," Aelfric said, but the morning light shone strangely in Kett's dark eyes. His narrowed eyes and contrived smile reminded Aelfric of a forest adder coiled and about to strike. Aelfric pretended to watch the sun glinting off the swells but watched Kett with a sideways stare and suppressed the feeling that he was the adder's prey.

The creaking rigging, the hiss of the water against the hull, and the flapping sails filled the long silence that followed his statement. The mountains of Baradon lay ahead, visible on the horizon now. Soon he would nestle in the motherly embrace of those peaks rising from the ocean ahead.

"How long till we arrive?" he asked Kett, who leaned on the rail beside him.

"Three days, four at the outside, if I am any judge. Ask the captain if you want more than my educated guess."

Kett was right. At nightfall on the third day, the *Sea Witch* sailed into Sethria. The captain and first mate shouted orders from the helm while the crewmen tied off to the wharf in a bustle of activity and noise. By the time they had the ship secured and the gangplank extended, the sun had set, and lanterns lit the dock area in pale yellow halos of light.

Aelfric had a history with the port and the city. He and Shelhera had departed for Khel Braah from Sethria. They left behind everything he had fought hard to achieve. Baradon was free of the Greens' interference in Eniila affairs, but instead of honoring him, the council of barons repaid him with ultimatums and exile. The years changed both Aelfric and Sethria; neither of them had improved with age.

Seventeen years ago, he led the conquest of Sethria as the War Leader of the Eniila, an equivalent rank to an Abrhaani king. Once they broke the Abrhaani resistance, he left his commanders in the city to accept its surrender.

Aelfric had lost interest in the conquest because his heart lay elsewhere. Shelhcra was pregnant with their first child, and word reached him that she had fallen gravely ill. Aelfric left Sethria and raced to her bedside, but before he reached her, their baby daughter was stillborn. In his absence, the army succumbed to the bloodlust that sometimes overtook his people.

Aelfric had promised deportation to Khel Braah for the defeated Abrhaani if they surrendered the city. Against his orders and in thrall to their violent passions, the warriors butchered the male inhabitants of Sethria, then raped and pillaged for two days until their bloodlust abated.

Deaths were by-products of war and did not bother Aelfric, but the warriors had dishonored him when they ignored his orders. The slaughter was not his fault, but it was his responsibility. His word bound him to the promise of clemency for the Abrhaani. As Aelfric's second in command, Aelrin should have reigned in the army, but instead of stopping the rampage, Aelrin joined them in their brutal acts, and because of it, Aelfric blamed Aelrin for the failure.

Aelrin and the other commanders seized the opportunity presented by Aelfric abandoning his post. They declared Aelfric a traitor to the Eniila people and an Abrhaani sympathizer because of his offer of clemency to Sethria's citizens. Instead of gratitude for his years of leadership, they offered him three choices.

Their ultimatum left Aelfric with three alternatives: he could die at the hands of Aelrin's co-conspirators; live in exile on Khel Braah, the home of the Abrhaani and Abrhaani sympathizers; or join the Gray Brotherhood in a City of Refuge.

Aelfric knew little of the Brotherhood or its purposes and goals. Despite the Gray Brotherhood's reputation as fearless warriors, Aelfric and many other Eniila men branded them effeminate because when they ventured outside their Cities of Refuge, they busied themselves with alms-giving and charitable acts in the service of their mysterious, unnamed god.

Aelfric refused to abandon Shelhera, and he refused to allow them to browbeat him into submission. He had chosen exile on Khel Braah, not because he loved the Abrhaani. He picked it because he loved Shelhera and would not abandon her. He hoped to atone for his failure in some small way by helping the Abrhaani in their homeland. Wary of assassination attempts, they left Baradon for Khel Braah later that year.

Aelfric had wanted to live out his life with Shelhera, atone for Sethria, and raise their unborn children in peace, away from the intrigues endemic in Baradon. He expected no favors from the Abrhaani, and he was not disappointed.

Now he had returned to his homeland, and he no longer cared what the gods thought of him. Shelhera's ashes lay in a cold heap on the other side of the Syn Gersuul, and he suspected his son's bones lay somewhere in the forest of Khel Braah. His sorrows left a void that nothing filled, and thoughts of revenge served as a poor substitute for his missing child and his dead wife. The lust for vengeance had drawn him back to Baradon, but his rage provided no comfort or peace.

The bustle of the deckhands, while they prepared to unload cargo and passengers, interrupted Aelfric's reminiscences. Longshoremen filed up and down the gangplank, unburdened the vessel, and stacked bundles and crates on the wharf.

I must keep a cool head and find cover before the guardsmen recognize me. Given my size, remaining inconspicuous among these Abrhaani is a tall order. Aelfric smiled at the pun. *The dim lantern light on the dock helps my cause, and the cloak and mantle conceal my identity.*

Aelfric never asked and didn't want to know where Kett found the distinctive light gray garments that passed for a Brotherhood uniform for Aelfric. He focused on a distant point ahead as if he were on a critical mission, avoided eye contact, and feigned disinterest. The guards noticed him before he had gone halfway down the dock. *Both guards look just old enough to grow beards. Not much older than Laakea.*

"Hold, stranger. What's your name and business in Sethria," the guard challenged.

I feel like a wolf with a mongrel pup yapping at me. "Relax, guardsmen. You can see by my clothes, I am a traveler of the Gray Brotherhood," Aelfric lied. "I am on a pilgrimage to Harthang, where I will pay my respects to my family's honored dead and give alms there."

"Then why are you in Sethria?" the second guard asked. "Harthang is far inland. Why travel by boat to Sethria?"

"If you knew where I started, my method of transport and my route make perfect sense," Aelfric added a touch of annoyance to his tone. He did not offer more information and mimicked the arrogance and secretiveness of a Gray Brotherhood pilgrim.

"Do you wish to detain me?" Aelfric asked, his lip curled in annoyance as he looked directly into their eyes. He stepped closer to the two guards and closed the gap between them. It was a near insult to approach another man without an invitation, let alone make eye contact. They would either yield or challenge him. *Inexperience and stupidity can be a deadly combination for all of us, but this too may help me.*

The risky gambit worked. The young guardsmen hesitated and broke eye contact while they considered a response to the unspoken challenge from this battle-scarred veteran. Aelfric noted their indecision and pressed his advantage. He thrust out his chest and raised his chin just enough to signal aggression but not enough for an outright threat. "I asked you a question, guardsman. Do you wish to detain me?"

Before they could answer, Kett and his porters arrived with their luggage. The guardsmen, grateful for the distraction and the ability to save face, motioned Aelfric away while they searched Kett, tore apart his baggage, and rifled through his belongings. Aelfric's heartbeat slowed, and the tension ebbed as he turned and walked up the street toward the inn where Kett had arranged rooms for them. With the immediate crisis past, Aelfric peered down the dark garbage-strewn street ahead, feeling out of place in the land he called home. "I hope I haven't made a mistake coming here."

CHAPTER THIRTY-TWO

WASTELAND NIGHT

Shadows created by the firelight flickered and danced across the rocks behind them as Eideron, voice cracking, hoarse with exhaustion and dehydration, began the lesson. "Fatigue is no excuse for any of us, you must learn about Quickenings, and sooner is better than later. The concept of Quickenings is an important part of the Synod's secret knowledge. We teach only those students of the highest moral character about Quickenings."

"Is that why the Synod tests every young person, Master?" asked Aibhera.

"The tests reveal a candidate's spiritual potential, but during their time of service to their appointed mentors, we gauge the apprentices' moral standards. Apprentices may score high marks on the exams, but we have no reliable test for morals and ethics. The extended apprenticeship, where we guide our apprentices' moral and ethical development, establishes character, and prepares them for the next phase of training.

"Since we are out of options and beyond the Synod's control, its rules no longer bind us. What I am about to say is meant to give you confidence, not inflate your egos. You both scored higher than anyone in recorded history." Eideron looked stern. "You will need confidence and courage for the tasks ahead. I hope my teaching helps you overcome the incredible challenges you will face alone.

Aibhera frowned at Eideron's use of the word 'alone' and elbowed Simea, who shifted his position because of it. He raised his eyebrows and glanced at her, but Eideron continued his lecture without pausing. He shifted his attention back to his master.

"Once the apprentice's master judges an individual has enough strength of character, the second phase of their education begins."

"What's that?" Aibhera asked.

"The second phase is the development of gifted students' Quickenings. Quickenings pose hazards to the user and those around them. If its users have not mastered their egos, power can twist and corrupt those who wield it. Simea, you worked for me for two years, and it was already time to teach you about Quickenings. In your case, Aibhera, we bypass that first phase and skip straight to instruction on the Quickenings. I will take a calculated risk to teach you this.

"Through a Quickening, the Creator pours an extra measure of His power into an individual for a brief time. When the Creator Quickens us, we can become conduits or agents of His will."

"Aibby and I understand," said Simea, as somber as his mentor. "This is a special circumstance."

Eideron nodded, his halo of silver hair gleamed golden in the firelight. "Quickening is the term we use to describe how the Creator endues us with extraordinary power when needed. The Sokai believe everything alive in Aarda exists because the Creator gave it life. His power also holds creation together and keeps it from disintegrating into nothingness.

"Each species has unique ways to receive and direct this power. Individuals within a species may display greater or lesser capabilities with any gifts. You showed the highest levels of potential ability, and you already have a high level of integrity and moral development. Perhaps you can tap skills our people lost millennia ago. That is my fervent hope.

"In recent times, Quickenings rarely manifest among our people. Although we teach the theory, very few have experienced the power of the Creator acting through them. In my opinion, it is because we no longer serve the other species as He intended.

"We are unfaithful to Him, for He designed us to be seers and prophets for Aarda's other species. The Creator responds to needs. He does not answer selfish demands or display His power to flaunt it; He empowers people to do His will. I suspect your impressive abilities manifested now because the Creator prepares to intervene, and you have a role in His plan. He has created you with a purpose and a destiny."

"What abilities might we expect, Master?" Aibhera asked.

"That is an excellent question. The dreams you experienced are prophetic Quickenings. Prophecy is the ability to view future events or distant activities. Sometimes prophecy is foreknowledge, knowing things in advance; at other times, it's the ability to discern between truth and illusion."

"Are there other abilities available to us?"

"Yes, Simea, the possibilities are limitless, since the Creator's power is immeasurable. We have legends from the Battle of the Three Kings. In those legends, we Sokai protected people with walls of light, attacked the Nethera with javelins of blinding light, or *Shifting,* traveling incredible distances in an eyeblink."

Simea's brow wrinkled. "Then why must we stumble through this desert? Many Sokai perished during The March the Ten Thousand. Why not just *Shift* to Abalon?"

"Excellent questions. A partial answer lies in how much knowledge we have lost during our centuries of isolation. Let us not get bogged down in regret; instead, let me explain what we still know. Aarda is the part of the universe we experience, the Aether is another part, and both are only fragments of creation. Both the Aethera and the Nethera can move at will between Aarda and their planes, which exist at different energy levels than Aarda. Does this make sense to you?"

"Yes, my stepfather, Leoned, is an engineer. Leoned often talks about energy states," Aibhera said. "He told me liquid water and steam are different states of water. But he says it takes energy to change water into steam."

"Leoned has provided a perfect analogy. The natural state of water in Abalon is liquid. When we heat water, it gains energy and becomes steam, or it loses energy and becomes ice, water's solid form. The natural state of humankind is what we experience now. The natural state of the Aethera and the Nethera is the Aetherial form. To interact with them, either we must gain energy to reach their level, or they must lose it to enter ours."

"How can we gain energy and rise to the Aetheric level?" asked Simea.

"Without the Creator's power, we cannot. He must pour energy into us, just like we must heat water to turn it into steam. Be aware we risk our physical bodies when we stay at that higher level. Sokai bodies cannot survive for long on the Aetherial plane. Think of it this way. If you had a piece of thread and a piece of rope and you tried to lift a rock with each of them, which one would break?"

"The thread, of course," said Aibhera.

"That is correct. The Creator designed each of His creatures with different capabilities. Each one can cope with different energy or stress levels. Man cannot live for long on the Aetherial plane, nor are the Aethera designed to live at our level."

"The rope can lift both light objects and heavy ones, but why not just use the rope for every task?" asked Simea.

"That is fine if you only intend to lift things. Imagine threading a needle with a rope or stitching your torn clothes with it," Aibhera responded.

"Exactly," said Eideron, pleased with the young woman's quick mind. "Each of the Creator's beings has a special purpose and role. Aetheric beings can discard energy to interact with the physical world. Once they shed energy, they cannot leave this world unless they replenish their power. Without gaining energy again, they cannot return to the Aether."

"If they became trapped, would Aarda destroy them as the Aether would destroy us?"

"We presume so, but we are uncertain. It may take longer for the Aethera and Nethera to perish here than for us to die in the Aether. A body designed to exist at a higher energy level probably finds it easier to live at a lower energy state than the reverse. Remember the rope and thread analogy. The rope can lift lighter objects while the thread can't lift heavier ones. Another analogy you may find useful is that of a log and a twig on the fire. The fire consumes twigs in moments while logs burn long."

"So, the Aether is fire, and we are twigs," said Aibhera.

"Almost, but not really. The Creator is the fire, and the Aether is a manifestation of His energy or power."

"Is there an energy state below ours, or are we at the lowest level, like ice is the lowest form of water?" Simea asked.

"The Sokai always believed Aarda is alive. If that is true, that is the lowest level imaginable."

"Master, tell us how to travel, Shift, the way you mentioned. I am tired of walking," said Simea with a wry grin.

Aibhera elbowed him and shot him a fierce look.

Eideron croaked with laughter at the byplay. "That is just one of many things I hope you can manage."

"You?" Aibhera's eyes widened. "Do you mean we must do this alone?"

"I fear you are correct, my observant youngster. The attempt would kill me. I am too old."

"Pardon me, Master, but walking will kill you." Aibhera shifted to a more comfortable position on the rock beneath her. "I can see how this journey depletes your strength, although you hide it. *Shifting* must be easier."

"Creator preserve us from sharp-eyed children," Eideron slumped, sighed, and gave up his pretense of strength. "To answer your earlier question, Sokai can only Shift to a place we have seen, and not every Sokai has the ability. I never expected to return—"

Aibhera interrupted, "Return is not the issue, Master, the survival and success of this mission are."

"We do as we must fulfill the will of Him who made us, dear girl. Our future is in His hands, not our own. Let us continue, shall we? Without the interruptions, if you please."

"Yes, Master," they both chorused, chastised by his gruff words.

"Let me cover the Quickenings common to the three species, but understand the list is not exhaustive. To recap, the Creator quickens the Sokai for prophecy, Shifting, and protection. Battlefury is an Eniila Quickening, as are justice and Voice of Command. He quickens the Abrhaani for healing, compassion, and mercy.

"Besides their spiritual abilities, the Eniila have prodigious physical power and regenerative capabilities, but without copious amounts of food, the Eniila grow weak. The Eniila have an affinity with fire and a talent for working and shaping metal, but they cannot read and have no written language. Unfortunately, they are also belligerent, short-tempered, and prone to violence.

"The Abrhaani understand agriculture, the arts, and herbal healing, and they can sense the emotional states of individuals. They have an affinity with plants and water.

Sailing and agriculture, for example, are two of their strengths."

"What is the downside for the Abrhaani?"

"The Abrhaani become sick in prolonged darkness, and despite their creativity, they lack concentration. They flit from one interest to the next without completing the tasks they start.

"The Sokai are builders and engineers and can master wind and earth. We see the Aetherial realm better than the others, and we can dispel the Dark Ones' illusions. We have kept and protected more history and lore than the other two species because we fled the conflict and took much of Berossus' library with us."

"Do we have weaknesses too?" Simea asked.

"We do. The Sokai are prone to legalism and rigidity of thought. We seek and enjoy stability, routine, tradition, and comfort. We are often prisoners of those things because we refuse new methods and fresh ideas. We obsess over details at the expense of compassion and mercy. The other species say the Sokai cannot see the mountain for the pebbles."

"That explains a great deal, doesn't it, Sim?"

CHAPTER THIRTY-THREE

SHIFTING

Eideron continued his teaching. "When we abandoned Berossus, our city in eastern Baradon, and traversed the eastern wasteland in search of a refuge from the fighting, we took much of our knowledge with us. Education was paramount in our culture. However, the Abrhaani and the Eniila have descended into barbarism because of their constant warfare.

"There is one artifact of enormous value that we no longer possess, a book called *The Chronicles of Aarda,* also called *The Aetheriad.* We lost it long before the Thousand Years War. An Aethera named Naom'han wrote it. The Aetheriad might contain knowledge useful to help stem the dark tide, but enough about the book, since we do not have it.

"There is a myth of a faithful remnant of Eniila who follow the Creator. The story, an unsubstantiated legend, alleges that our ancestors entrusted them with the book since they believed the Eniila warriors could best protect the precious volume. After so many years, the Eniila may have lost the book, or they may have used it for kindling. The Eniila cannot read and might not have valued *The Aetheriad* enough to preserve it. I doubt our forebears expected millennia to elapse before someone looked for it.

"Tomorrow night, I will teach you what I know about Shifting, instantaneous travel between two points. Of all the Quickenings, this one should be most useful to us. You must prepare and concentrate. We are too exhausted and hungry to walk farther today. I have shared enough for a first lesson and laid a foundation for what must follow."

After a meager ration of water and a scanty meal, they rolled themselves in their bedrolls. Aibhera soon fell asleep. Simea remembered what Eideron had said about Shifting and memorized his reference points for Shifting tomorrow. Simea placed a medallion, a birthday gift from his mother, in a crack in the rock. He felt it might help him find his location better than the landscape alone. When he was satisfied, he joined Aibhera in sleep.

Simea roused and shifted position when Eideron fed the fire before dawn and thought he heard the rustling of parchment before he faded back to a night of restless sleep.

❖

At dawn, Aibhera awoke to the sound of her teeth chattering. "How can it be so blasted cold," she muttered. "We broiled all day, and now I am frozen half to death."

"The March of the Ten Thousand says scorching days and icy nights are common here." Eideron's muffled voice issued from beneath his blankets, only the top of his head protruded from under the bedroll. "It's part of the wasteland's charm, I'm afraid."

"I'm sorry I woke you."

"I was awake. It's too cold to sleep," Eideron said. "We should get started; the activity will warm us." Eideron stood and wrapped his blankets around his shoulders while he coaxed the campfire back to life.

Aibhera shook Simea awake.

By the time they finished a sparse meal of dried fruit and bread and repacked their gear, the sun painted the wasteland in golden light. Long black shadows lay in the hollows and crevices to the east where Abalon's black volcanic cone rose high above the plain.

"Which way are we headed?" Simea asked.

"The ancient records say our people took several routes to Abalon. Most survivors came from that direction." Eideron pointed directly away from the sun's bright disk hanging above the horizon. "I hope the sunrise bodes well for our success."

"We estimated we brought enough water to last us five or six days. Can we find water before it runs out?" Aibhera asked.

"The last week was the toughest. By then, our ancestors were afoot with little water left. Most of the deaths occurred that week. There should be a canyon ahead with pools of drinkable water. If we find the canyon, we should be fine," Eideron replied.

"And if we can't?" asked Simea.

"In that case, we shall depend on the mercy of the Creator or your abilities to Shift."

"We must either find water soon, turn back, or learn to Shift? Glad we have options. Sounds easy enough. No pressure, right, Aibby?"

They set out in the direction Eideron chose and picked their way through the broken lava and the scrubby brush that grew in cracks and crevices. The sun was a merciless burning eye that stared down on them out of a pale blue sky. They stopped to eat at midday in the shade of a boulder.

"Master, we must rest here until the heat of the day passes. We are using up the water too fast when we exert ourselves in this heat." Simea stowed their rations in their packs,

"I agree, Sim. We did not sleep enough either. We should nap before we continue." In response to Eideron's suggestion, they unpacked their blankets.

"Master Eideron, you look worn out." Aibhera scooted over to help Eideron smooth out a sandy spot and adjust his bedroll.

Eideron smiled a weak smile as he stretched out on the bedding. "I will agree to nap if you try to Shift while I rest."

To the youngsters, Eideron's easy acquiescence highlighted his failing strength.

"Yes, it's an excellent idea," Aibhera said, and Sim nodded in agreement. "What do we need to know?"

"It is difficult. If you focus on your breath, it should help. Then call upon the Creator and hold a memory of the location in your mind. I know the theory, although no one has Shifted in centuries."

"But Master, we know only one other place—Abalon. We can't go back there." The task overwhelmed Aibhera, who pulled her knees up to her chest and circled them with her arms.

"That is true. You might Shift home, but your dreams of late are vivid. You could Shift to their location if they are vivid enough, but you should try something more modest. Last night's campsite is enough."

Aibhera sat on a big slab of stone, closed her eyes, and concentrated on a uniquely shaped rock that fixed last night's campsite in her mind. She slowed her breathing and reached toward it with her mind. Before long, her concentration faded, and her head nodded as she nearly drifted off to sleep. She jerked upright.

"I can do this." *Not sure if I'm trying to convince them or myself.*

"Try again." Eideron placed a hand on her head. "Creator of all, give her strength."

"Maybe I should try it," Simea said.

"No, it's fine. I'll keep trying." Aibhera shifted position. "I'm having trouble picturing the campsite. It keeps slipping from my mind." She rolled her shoulders and tried to find a more comfortable position. Panic knotted her stomach. *If I can't focus, we could all die out here. Failure is not an option.*

The rustle of windblown sand, the crackling fire, and her companions' breathing suddenly drew her attention. "Could you two move away from me or stop breathing so loud. I can't concentrate with all the noise you're making."

She shook out her arms and took a deep breath to calm herself as Simea and Eideron moved to the far side of the fire. *Here goes nothing.* After several minutes which seemed like hours, she had still not succeeded. This is not working. I need to try something else.

"Do you think I'm focusing on the wrong thing? Eideron, you said that our Quickening's come from the Creator. Perhaps I should focus on Him instead of on the campsite."

The old man's face looked haggard and wan. "As good an idea as any I'd say."

This is harder than anything I've ever done. Aibhera wiped her clammy hand on her thighs, took a deep breath, and tried again. She suddenly remembered the cradle song her father sang to her when nightmares plagued her. It reminded her of home and always calmed her. To calm herself, she hummed the melody.

> Let the trumpets sound.
> And songs of joy break forth
> The mighty King is coming
> As we proclaim his worth
> The King of glory
>
> He comes in blazing virtue
> With fire in his eyes
> He tears apart the heavens
> Descending through the skies
> The King of glory

The enemy's defeated
And you shall fear no more
Let all mankind embrace him
Praise worship and adore
The King of glory

Lightnings flash and thunders roar
The King of glory
Who was and is forevermore
The King of glory
Stretch out your hand and touch his face
Creator, King of glory

As she reached the last line, her surroundings changed. She connected to a powerful ancient creature while she floated in a sea of ever-changing colors.

When the being spoke, the rumble of its voice sounded both noble and sad. "Be careful, little sister. You fell short of your goal. Fortunately, you reached me and not one of the Dark Ones. I am Shel'gharim of Naom'han's cohort."

Aibhera shook like a leaf in a windstorm. She broke her connection to the Aether and plummeted back to the campsite below, gasping like a winded runner.

"What happened? Aibby, what just happened?" asked Simea in a panic. "You disappeared for a moment and then popped back again."

"I reached up like Eideron told us to, and I contacted someone named Shel'gharim. I panicked, and I shot back here."

"Shel'gharim of Naom'han's cohort?" Eideron's mouth gaped in disbelief.

"Yes. Why?"

"Shel'gharim was the Aethera ally of the Sokai in ancient times. He can help us. You must try again when you are ready."

"Shel'gharim warned me to be careful. He said I must avoid meeting the Dark Ones," she answered, afraid to try again.

"Well, we will rest and continue when the heat diminishes. Sleep now, while Simea watches over us."

Aibhera awoke to the sound of Simea's and Eideron's voices.

"Is it time to continue?" she asked.

"Yes, we debated whether to wake you. Have a drink, and we will leave."

The day continued as it had begun. They stumbled across the plain's broken crust, the sun burned their skin, and sweat stung their eyes. They discussed and dissected Aibhera's experience while they walked. Simea suggested he try next. Sim explained his plan to Shift back to last night's campsite, where he left his medallion. When nightfall approached, they gathered brushwood for fire and took shelter in one of the small craters that dotted the wasteland.

While Eideron huddled by the fire, he had abandoned the pretense of vitality, Simea and Aibhera prepared the meal.

"I don't know which will give out first, Eideron, or the water. Both are depleting faster than I expected. I thought we had brought enough to last for five or six days." Simea leaned close to Aibhera and lowered his voice to a whisper, "Two days into this desert, we are over halfway through our supply. We have enough if we turn back now, but if we walk one more day, we cannot return to Abalon."

Aibhera managed a weak smile and joked, "Unless we master Shifting. No pressure. Right, Simea?"

"None. Let's eat. I'll try Shifting while the master rests. Even if we turned around now, he wouldn't survive the return trip. This is harder than he expected. Eideron should have stayed in Abalon and lived out his life in comfort. It's hard to remember that a tenday ago, I feared him. Now I fear *for* him."

They ate in silence while Simea prepared for his Shift to their previous campsite.

After he finished his food, Eideron broke the silence. "You should leave me here and continue alone. Take the supplies with you. You will get farther without me. I use up your resources and slow your progress."

Simea said, "We will discuss this in the morning once you have rested, Master, but not before I find out if I can Shift." Eideron failed to argue with Simea, which exposed how exhausted he was. With that settled, Simea began the process Aibhera described. He reached up for the Creator and contemplated his medallion.

Although Aibhera was unsure what she should watch for, she stared at him for signs of distress. Aibhera, more tired than usual, observed the regular rise and fall of Simea's chest. Her eyelids drooped as she fought to remain alert. The short trip into the Aether earlier, combined with the day's exertions, tired her more than she expected.

The master had warned them not to linger in the Aether. If her brief experience sapped her, she feared the exhaustion involved in an extended visit. Aibhera's eyes closed, her head dropping forward onto her chest. A pop followed by a slight puff of air shocked her back to wakefulness. Aibhera opened her eyes and expected to see Simea in front of her, but he had disappeared.

CHAPTER THIRTY-FOUR

VANISHED

In the first moments after lurching awake, Aibhera thought Simea had given up the attempt to Shift, and wandered off to relieve himself. A careful search proved he was nowhere nearby. Aibhera returned to the fire, hugged her knees, and tried to quell the fear and the sickly ache in her stomach. "It will be fine. Simea will find his way back," became her mantra.

As moments passed, she found it more difficult to convince herself that nothing was wrong. Aibhera considered waking Eideron, who still slept in front of the fire, but she discarded the idea. *Eideron is exhausted. Simea must find his own way.*

More time passed, and fear took hold of her mind. *Without Simea, I'll fail. We did everything together, even shared the same prophetic dreams. We're doomed. Eideron's old. I'm alone. I'll die out here alone, and no one will know.*

In desperation, she prepared to search for him in the only way that stood any chance of success. Aibhera reached for Shel'gharim again with her mind, as she had earlier in the day. Aibby's thoughts scattered like clouds before a mighty wind, and she couldn't control them. The tempest of fear overcame her, and she failed.

Miserable and driven by desperation, Aibhera tried again. She hummed the tune that her father sang to calm her after a nightmare. Under the familiar melody's influence, the storm inside subsided, enabling Aibby to reach up and outside herself again. Within moments she drifted in the place of shifting colors where Shel'gharim, a gigantic ethereal creature of light, met her.

Her fear of him had vanished or merely lay buried beneath the more deep-seated fear of losing Simea. A profound power and calm dignity emanated from him. *If an Aethera, a created being, radiates such splendor, the Creator must be blindingly beautiful.* She bowed before him in worship.

"Rise! Do not commit blasphemy! Only our Creator is worthy of our worship. Your ignorance can be pardoned this time, but never repeat your mistake," Shel'gharim thundered as he pointed an accusing finger at her.

Aibhera rose, trembling, on wobbly knees. "I'm sorry. I promise it won't happen again, but your presence overwhelmed me."

Shel'gharim held out his hand to steady her. "Be at ease. You are forgiven because you acted innocently. For what purpose have you returned, little sister?"

Aibhera's words came out in a torrent. "My friend got lost, and I need help. Simea tried Shifting to our last campsite. I fear for his safety. Please help us."

"It has been almost a thousand of your years since your kind has ventured here. Longer still since one of you tried to use the Aether to travel. I shall find him and bring him to you if I am able. Your kind is too fragile to survive here."

"Master Eideron warned us, but may I stay longer to search with you?"

"You are not safe here. The region under my guardianship has limits, and you are near the border of the Nether." Shel'gharim pointed out the dark region at the edge of her sight. "Stay here, if you must, and call out to Simea with your heart. Do not enter the Nether. The enemies of light and life who travel there will consume you." Shel'gharim's spirit shrank and vanished. Without his presence, the area darkened, and the utter blackness of the Nether appeared closer.

Aibhera noted her surroundings. Music so vibrant it formed clouds of brilliant colors filled the space around her. The Aether sang with life, pulsed with energy, and infused her with strength. Vitality cascaded through her body in ecstatic waves. All her fears and insecurities vanished under the influence of the Aether's energy. In the distance, the dark border Shel'gharim pointed out earlier blotted out everything beyond it. The impenetrable darkness devoured light and life. It tugged at her and tried to absorb her power, but she resisted its pull and searched for Simea instead.

Aibhera looked downward to see what supported her in this place. Her feet stood on an energy barrier like translucent quartz, and below her, the shadowy shapes of the landscape appeared.

Eideron and their previous campsites became vague distorted images below her. Even Abalon became visible, although other locations remained concealed by the barrier. *I could step from the Aether anywhere on Aarda. This is how we Sokai Shift. We zip into the Aetherial Realm and then step into Aarda again somewhere else. If we can find it, we can go there.*

Aibhera focused her mind on home and sang the song "Aamori's House" from her childhood, and Abalon grew closer. *I could go home… right now.* She shook her head and hugged herself. *I can't abandon Simea and Eideron or our quest.*

Aibhera called to Eideron and watched as the old man roused from sleep. He scrambled across the blackened rocks around their campsite, hunting for her and Simea. "Eideron. Help me find Simea. He is lost. I need your help," she shouted and thought of Eideron standing beside her, and suddenly he was there, wide-eyed and confused at his new surroundings.

Eideron gaped and turned in a circle. "What happened? Where are we, and how did I get here?" his hands fluttered and shook.

"We are in the Aether. It fills me with power, so when I called you came, but I can't find Sim."

"You brought me! Impossible."

Aibhera tilted her head and threw back her shoulders. "Not impossible. You are here, aren't you?"

"Be careful that you do not become drunk with power, it can twist one's thoughts. Fire provides warmth, but if you stick your hand in it, it will burn you."

Aibhera gave a quick disgusted snort. "Nonsense, I have never felt better."

Eideron's forehead furrowed, and his eyes narrowed as he listened.

She began, "I'm stronger tha—"

Eideron raised his voice. "Remember your analogy, fire consumes the twig. The Aether will destroy you if you aren't careful." He pointed at the black barrier. "Have you looked there in the darkness?"

"No, Shel'gharim said to avoid it. It marks the boundary of his protection. It's called the Nether, and it's unsafe."

"I sense a powerful evil beyond the wall. Let us call out together to Simea," Eideron said. Aibhera and Eideron joined hands. Their voices floated off into the distance in all directions without an echo. Aibhera was ready to give up when a faint cry attracted her attention.

"Help me. I am trapped," Simea's voice called out from the darkness.

"I hear him, Eideron, he's trapped in the Nether. We must rescue him." Aibhera strode toward the dark barrier. "I can't leave Simea trapped and alone in that evil place."

"Stop! Aibhera, I sense nothing but evil from that direction. Don't," Eideron shouted. As Aibhera approached the wall, he raced to catch up to her. "Wait. Do not enter. For the Creator's sake, go no farther."

Aibhera paused and turned to Eideron. "I can see him now, Eideron. Help me. He is hurt and can't escape without help. We must not fail him."

"It is a deception, Aibhera. Simea is not there. If you enter, you will never return. It is a trick of the Dark Ones." Eideron grasped her arm and spun her around. "Please believe me."

"Can't you see Simea is injured? We can help him. Don't you care? How dare a man who professes to be our guide and teacher ignore Simea's pain."

Old fool! He may refuse to rescue Simea, but I will not succumb to fear like he has. Aibhera's anger became stony resolve. "You aren't strong enough to stop me, you feeble old coward. I dare you to try." Aibhera tore free of his grip and turned toward the barrier; her eyes blazed red, and shadows played across her face.

Eideron stepped between Aibhera and the barrier, but she knocked him aside with the back of her hand like she was swatting an insect. Eideron struggled to his feet and grappled with her. Aibhera easily cast him aside again, but this time she stomped after him. When she reached him, Aibhera picked Eideron up as if he were a toy and threw him toward the black barrier. Eideron fell and lay still for a moment. His chest heaved, and his breath came in gasps. He struggled to his feet to face her again.

She stalked toward him like a predatory beast, and snarled, "Get out of my way, old man,"

"I shall." Eideron backed toward the barrier behind him. Black tendrils reached out from beyond the wall as he approached, wrapping him in their greasy coils and draining life from his body. His eyes rolled, and he grimaced in agony.

"Watch," he croaked as the life drained from his body. Aibhera stumbled backward. "See what they'll do to you. Do you believe me now? No one can live beyond that wall." Eideron's voice quavered and cracked. The last of his strength vanished. His body turned to ash and drifted down to settle in a heap at the sharp edge of the darkness.

Sacrifice accomplished what his feeble strength could not. Shock broke Aibhera free of the compulsion that held her captive. Sobbing openly, she dropped to her knees in despair, alone, among the blackened rocks of their campsite once more. *I killed him. I lost control to the darkness, and it's my fault.*

Aibhera sat alone in the dark beside the embers of the dying fire. Guilt etched and burned her soul like acid and left the bitter taste of bile in her mouth. The moon and stars, Aibhera's only companions, seemed farther away than usual. *I'm so arrogant and naïve, the Nethera deceived me. I'll never be free of the stain on my soul. I killed Eideron as surely as if I sucked the life from him myself. Perhaps Simea is dead too. How can I go on?*

CHAPTER THIRTY-FIVE

RETURN

I have been so stupid—spent my entire life doing the right thing. I was the dutiful daughter. Kyonna is the rebel, but Kyonna wouldn't—I took pride in my virtue, but today I discovered how shallow my integrity runs. I'm doomed to die alone in the darkness, and I deserve my fate. Aibhera, lost in recrimination and flushed with shame, wrapped herself in her bedroll, too exhausted to feed the fire.

After what seemed like moments of fitful slumber, she awoke to a hand on her shoulder and the sound of Simea's voice. *Surely wishful thinking.* Aibhera bolted upright, momentarily blinded by the sun in her eyes, and stared at a silhouette formed against the bright sky. The broken black surface of the lava plain already shimmered with the sun's heat, creating a gleaming ocean of wavering light. "Is…that you, Sim? Am I dreaming?"

Simea touched her again. "I'm as real as you are. Where's Eideron?"

"You *are* real.' Aibhera leaped to her feet and threw her arms around him. "I feared I would die alone out here. "Thank you, Shel'gharim. Thank you, Creator," Aibhera wept into Simea's shoulder in a tangled muddle of joy and sorrow. She soaked Simea's shirt-front with the flood of grief she had held at bay all night.

Once her sobbing subsided, Simea pushed her away, holding her by the shoulders. "Where's Eideron?"

Aibhera crumpled to the ground. She howled and moaned as she had at her father's death long ago. "Simea… I… killed Eideron!" Simea towered over her. His shadow fell across her face as she looked up at him through her tears. "Please don't hate me."

Simea stiffened and said nothing for a moment. "How? What happened?"

"When you didn't return, I got scared. I went into the Aether to look…and when I couldn't find you…I panicked and pulled Eideron up there with—" Aibhera's voice broke.

Simea sat beside her and put his arm around her shoulder. "Eideron wasn't strong enough." The boy gouged a groove in the gravel with his heel.

"No. It's worse than that." Aibhera leaned forward, hid her face with her hands, and shook her head.

Simea pulled her toward him. "Aibby. It's my fault—if I hadn't gotten lost, you wouldn't have taken Eideron into the Aether with you. I played the hero…tried to travel too far. I should have known…I'm such a useless failure." He let go of Aibhera. Head hanging, he scuffed the gravel with his boot heel again. "I wanted to get supplies from Abalon, but once inside the Aether, I got distracted by the colors, the music, and the power flowing through me. Then I couldn't find Abalon, and I couldn't find my way back either. His voice broke, and tears ran down his cheek. "I'm stupid, arrogant, and weak, just like my mother says."

Simea's shoulders heaved as he drew breath between sobs while he told the rest of his story. "I saw the black barrier, and the darkness drew me toward it. Although I resisted, I couldn't move. The evil beyond that wall paralyzed me with fear." He sniffled, wiped his nose on his sleeve, and turned toward Aibhera. "If Shel'gharim hadn't found me, I would have died frozen in fear, either burned to a cinder by the Aether or consumed by the evil that lurks in the darkness. Shel'gharim called it the Nether."

"You *saw* it, but it got *inside* me." I *know* what lives on the other side of that wall of darkness." She wailed and hammered her thighs with her fists to emphasize her words and her guilt. "I threw Eideron into the darkness. I killed him!"

Simea's jaw dropped, and his eyes widened. "You didn't—"

She glared at Simea and raised her voice. "*I* did it! *I* was stupid, and because of my pride and stupidity, the darkness overpowered me. *I tell you*, *I* killed him!" Aibby pulled her legs into the fetal position, then dissolved into wracking sobs, her arms wrapped tight around her knees with her head resting on them.

Simea wept beside her until his grief subsided. He rose first and pulled Aibhera to her feet. "We can't stay here. Let's pack up our gear and move." Neither of them spoke while they packed up Eideron's things. As they broke camp, a folded parchment and a scroll tumbled out of his bedroll. The folded paper bore their names in Eideron's flowing script. Shaking hands unfolded the letter, followed by fresh tears, which stained the paper while they read:

To Simea and Aibhera:

It is time for your Synod initiation. I feel a mixture of sorrow and pride for you. If you are reading this, it means I cannot carry out a ceremony, ancient before the Time of Sorrows. Our people practiced it before the Sundering when all the species of humankind lived together in peace. I had looked forward to this day, but now I shall never see you take your rightful place in the Synod.

Tradition requires that the master perform the ceremony with the apprentice in front of the entire Sokai Synod. Once complete, the Synod should welcome the initiates into their fellowship and honor the apprentices with a banquet. It is heartbreaking when one old man and two children are the only Sokai available for your solemn and sacred rite of passage. I regret we are incapable of so small a recognition for you. Even in this barren place, I had planned to complete the ceremony, minus the banquet in your honor. Since my stomach grumbles as I write this message, I confess I miss the feast more than the ritual.

You are the best and bravest of our species. Farewell. Be strong and courageous when you face adversity. Trust the Creator and trust each other. You have accomplished more in your short lives than I dreamed possible, and I am beyond proud of you.

I knew I would not survive this mission. I hope I ended well and with dignity. Think well of a feeble old man. I loved you both like I would my own children.

Use your abilities to protect yourselves and contact the Aethera if possible. Find *the Aetheriad*. I pray that you discover how to receive the Creator's power to fight the Nethera, and I hope you find the scroll useful.

With pride,

Eideron

I have included the map of the route to Baradon. I hope it guides you better than I did.

Simea refolded the note, and a torrent of tears burst open the floodgates of their grief. "I can't read anymore. We'll read Eideron's scroll, later, okay, Aibby?"

Aibhera's sobs indicated her assent.

They packed up the rest of their gear and began another march across the bleak plain, picking their way across the ancient lava flow in the direction Eideron had chosen. They plodded forward, their eyes fixed on the ground at their feet itched and burned, parched as the dusty plain around them. Their canteens felt perilously light., but they had encountered none of the dangerous creatures of Sokai legend. Other than scrubby plants, they were the only life forms braving the stinging dust and blistering heat of the wasteland, but then an enormous shadow passed over them.

CHAPTER THIRTY-SIX

RESCUE

When the shadow of a large airborne object sped past them, Simea ducked and cowered in a crater behind a large rock, pulling Aibhera down with him. They had seen no wildlife other than insects since they entered the desert, so his first thoughts ran to the ancient stories of predatory creatures in the lava field.

Aibhera jumped up, waving and shouting, "It's a Windrider, Sim. It's one of the big freight gliders. We are saved. Hey! Down here, we're down here!"

Simea pulled Aibby down behind the boulder again. "Are you insane? It might be a Synod scout. Remember Eideron's warning. He said they would pursue and capture us if they figured out where we went."

"That's no Synod scout," she said. "It's Ky. Kyonna followed us. Don't you recognize the style? The way she shifts her body when she banks to maintain lift through the turn."

The glider circled and swooped lower, and now Simea recognized the pilot. The wind blew through Kyonna's hair, and a satisfied smile lit her face. Kyonna banked once more to lose airspeed before she turned for her final approach with the big supply-laden glider. She swooped low over them, pushed the control bar forward, and caused the craft to stall with her feet just inches from the ground.

"Ky always times that move just right in any wind condition. I'd wager she could land on a branch like a songbird." Aibhera raced toward her sister's landing spot. "Ky, I'm so glad you're here." Aibhera and Simea swarmed the younger girl and attempted to hug her while Kyonna removed her harness.

"Get off me. Let me get out of my gear before you properly and humbly thank me for rescuing your sorry tails. Where's the old man? Won't Eideron want to thank me too?" Simea and Aibhera's faces fell at the mention of Eideron. "Something bad happened, am I right?"

"Eideron is dead," Simea said. He had no strength left for tact or diplomacy.

Kyonna studied them both before she spoke. "I am sorry I never got to meet him," Kyonna continued unloading the glider. "The wasteland appears too harsh for an old man, but your expressions tell me, there's more to this story. We don't have time to listen right now." Kyonna embraced them once she was free of her harness.

"I brought supplies, but I didn't know how long I had to stay aloft to find you, so I brought less than I wanted to carry. I saw a canyon farther west, and water gleamed at its bottom. If we make it there, water should be no problem, unless you want to turn back. Let me tell you, that's not the best idea. I'd rather face the unknown than what waits for you in Abalon if you ever return."

"I guess the Synod Council is upset," Simea said.

"The council members are so far beyond upset…even enraged is too mild a word for it. But we need to get moving. So, my daring darlings, I suggest we grab as much as we can carry, then hustle our backsides into that canyon as fast as our feet can take us. The next glider will carry presents you won't want. I'll explain later."

Kyonna unhooked packages from the glider, then turned and looked at Simea and her sister. "Did I forget to mention the time constraints? Why are you both standing still? Move it, people!" Her shout shook Aibhera and Simea out of their daze, and they helped unload the supplies Kyonna brought. "Come help me strip the glider down to its frame. If searchers spot the glider, they will figure out which way we went, and that's a bad thing." Kyonna disassembled the frame and stowed the pieces in crevices in the ancient lava flow, but stuffed the fabric of the wings into a sack. "We can use the cloth to shade us from the sun. I'm already sweating like a lava-raker."

With the glider frame concealed, Kyonna loaded supplies into Eideron's pack and slid the harness over her own shoulders. Once they hid everything they could not carry and did not need, they set a brisk pace toward the gorge.

"I hope Eideron's map is right," Simea said.

Kyonna chattered like a small bird while she led the way across the rubble field. "I wish we could have stayed longer and had a feast with all the extra food I brought. It's a shame we had to leave so much behind." Simea and Aibhera, too heartbroken to carry on a coherent conversation, stumbled along in her wake while Kyonna filled the silence with enough words for them all. "Without Eideron to help carry it—well—we've got enough to last for several more days anyway." Aibhera and Simea too numb to care or listen, regardless of how comforting Kyonna might have believed her prattle was, cast an occasional look at each other.

Before long, Kyonna found a gully that looked like it might lead into the canyon, and grateful for the limited shade it offered, they descended into it. Exhaustion brought them to a halt in the ravine long before they reached the chasm Kyonna had seen from the air.

"We shouldn't light a fire. Windriders might spot it." Ky took off her pack and set it on the broken stone of the ravine's floor. "Windriders rarely fly at night, but the full moon and the sky full of stars make night flying possible. Besides, there's no spiderweb of big ugly cables to dodge out here in the wasteland like we have in Abalon."

They made camp for the night using a tent made from the glider's fabric in a vain attempt to stay warm. As they sat wrapped in blankets, shivering in the dark, Kyonna shared news of home. "Abalon is like an anthill someone kicked over. The Synod has everyone scurrying around looking for you, and Herron has incited the entire population of the valley against you. They arrested poor Councilor Himish. His wife Leela languishes in the widows' barracks, but no one knows where they are holding Himish prisoner.

"They hauled our parents in for interrogation several times." The only reason Mom and Leoned aren't imprisoned with Himish is that they need Leoned's expertise to keep the trams operating. Leoned refused to work if they detained him and Mom. He kept Simea's mother out of prison with that threat too." She nodded to Simea. "Our stepdad has a backbone of steel, and I'm so proud of him. They suspended me from duty, but I have friends in high places." Kyonna grinned at the pun and punched the air with her fist.

"Spies watch our house day and night. Synod guards have turned Abalon upside down and inside out in their search for you, and Synod Council was desperate enough to send Windriders out over the wasteland after you. That was their mistake since Rais snuck me up to fly in his place.

"The council is terrified you'll reveal our location to the Nethera. They've stopped denying the Dark Ones exist. Call it progress if you wish, but it's propaganda to whip up more fear and exercise more control over our people. If you return, they will hang, draw, and quarter you, then feed you to the crows, but only after they have pissed on you, both figuratively and literally. It's not my idea of a proper welcome home party. They won't give *me* any medals either since I *borrowed* their best freight glider to hunt for you."

Aibhera raised an eyebrow. "If they suspended you from duty, how did you wrangle the big glider to bring us those supplies?"

Kyonna giggled. "Like I said, I have friends in high places. Rais made it happen. He smuggled me into the hangar before work early this morning. Windriders hate to be told what to do, and we stick together. Aiyo, Loran, and a couple of others stashed the supplies ahead of time. My friend Boon," she paused, searching for the word. "The dispatcher has always tried to catch her eye." A broad grin displayed her amusement. "Let's just say he was somewhat distracted while I loaded, strapped in, and launched Rais's glider." She threw off her blanket and rummaged through a bundle. "Let's get some of this food into our bellies. Is it always this cold at night?"

"No. Sometimes it's even colder, but then we've built a fire." Simea put a hand on the rock behind them. "Thankfully, the ravine's walls are still warm. If we huddle together against them, we should be fine."

Kyonna winked at her sister. "Cuddling, just the thing for a chilly night."

Simea glared at her, his eyes glistening in the moonlight. "I'd like to Shift to somewhere warmer that's for certain."

"What's he talking about, Sis?

"We'll explain it tomorrow," Aibhera tore a portion from a loaf of bread. "Eideron taught us about Quickenings before he died. I'm too tired and hungry to explain it now." She bit off a chunk of the loaf and chewed in silence.

"Fine, till tomorrow." Ky unwrapped a round of cheese, cut three sections with her belt knife, and passed them to her sister and Simea. "You'd better fill me in though. You've kept me in the dark long enough."

After they had shared their meager meal, they huddled together with Aibhera between her and Simea and slept fitfully.

Once the sun crested the horizon, and the three young Sokai shook off the torpor of a cold night, they were on the move again by midmorning. They continued along the gully's gravel-strewn bottom.

Aibhera stopped to take a drink and passed her canteen to Simea. "Water eroded this defile to create this gravelly bottom. It makes walking simpler than the lava plain. We don't have to watch every step for fear of twisting an ankle."

Kyonna took the canteen from Simea's hand after he finished drinking. "Even more important, it will lead us into the canyon where we'll find shade and water." She took a few swallows and passed the container back to her sister.

Until the sun reached its zenith, the walls of the gully provided shade and shelter from the blistering heat; however, at noon, the ravine became a furnace. Heat shimmered and radiated off the rock walls, which became too hot to touch. Sweat poured off the youngsters, dripping into their eyes and soaking their clothes.

Aibhera said, "We've got to get out of this crevice before the heat kills us."

"How? The walls are too hot and too steep. Ky, you led us into a death trap," Simea wiped the perspiration from his face with a shirtsleeve already soaked with sweat.

"Right, it's all my fault as usual," Kyonna snapped.

"Stop fighting. No one is to blame, but we have to find a place to take shelter, or we'll char like loaves left too long in the oven."

CHAPTER THIRTY-SEVEN

THE BOOK OF SONGS

Nearly blinded by the blazing heat, they followed the twists and turns of the dry wash, slipping and stumbling across the black-pebbled streambed. The sun had sunk in the sky, but the heat had not abated. They rounded a bend, and Kyonna, who led the way, spotted an inky shadow ahead. "Look. There's shade ahead. Not much farther to go," she panted. She led the way forward and discovered a place where water had eroded part of the gully wall, leaving a large outcrop of stone overhanging the ravine. The recess penetrated deep enough to provide a cool place to rest and recover. "Saved your ass again, didn't I, Simea?"

Simea glowered at Kyonna but remained silent.

Aibhera slipped off her pack's shoulder straps and let it fall to the ground. "Let's stop here for a meal and rest until things cool down. Hopefully, we can reach the canyon soon."

Kyonna slumped to the ground beside her sister. "I could use a break. My feet are sore. Even my blisters have blisters. I don't know how you managed to walk so far."

"Simea and I walked everywhere in Abalon, while you made loop de loops overhead with your glider. You never walked across the caldera like we did."

"Okay. I get it. I've led a pampered existence." Kyonna winced as she removed her boots, flexed her bare toes, and examined the blisters on the soles of her feet.

Once they finished eating, Simea said, "Let's read the scroll Eideron left while we wait."

Ky curled her lip. "That should be interesting."

As Simea unrolled the scroll, a scrap of paper fell onto the gully's gravel floor. Aibhera picked it up and unfolded it. "It's a note from Eideron." She read it aloud, although her tears soaked the paper and blurred the words on the page.

If you are reading this note before I have read the enclosed scroll to you, I am no longer with you. This is one of my favorite stories. I have always liked it, and I hope you find it useful. It is a condensed version of The Book of Songs. *Please take the time to read it. Although it ends on an ominous note, it may provide helpful insight.*

Kyonna wrapped her arms around Aibhera. "Sim, why don't you read the scroll."

Simea wiped hot tears from his own cheeks and read:

The One existed, and He was alone in the vast and empty void. He sang forth His songs. The melody flowed out of the abundance of joy in His heart. It filled the darkness with bliss.

"It is good, but let Us create with Our song."

He sang the universe into existence. Thus, He became the Creator. Its brilliance glittered and shone in the void. Pleased by His work, He sang to the stars, and although they gave light to the darkness, He sought to create further splendor. The Creator sang Aarda into existence that it might be the choice jewel of His creation.

The Creator spoke again. "Let Us create living beings to share in Our song and sing with Us." He sang the Aethera into existence. They were brilliant creatures of light and power. The Aethera shone like the stars, but they were living beings, able to harmonize with Him and share His pleasure. The Aethera loved their Creator while they journeyed among the stars and added their songs to His. Their harmonies filled the universe with a chorus of sound and color, beautiful, incredible, and intricate. Creator and creature sang together for uncountable ages in sweetness and harmony.

The Creator gave names to the Aethera and loved them like a father loves his children. He loved them and the beauty of their harmonies. In time, S'ek'zekaar, one of their number, became discontent to sing harmonies to the Creator's tune. He composed a melody of his own, loud and strident, a song of power and purpose. It captivated him, and he contemplated rebellion against the Creator.

S'ek'zekaar rejoiced in his own strength, for he knew his song would free him from the Creator's control. The notes were discordant, but the power within them was seductive and beautiful to him. S'ek'zekaar's melody seduced some of the Aethera, and they sang this new song with him. Discord arose among the Aethera. For the first time, chaos threatened creation.

The Creator heard S'ek'zekaar's song. He paused to decide where this new song led, and His silence filled the universe with an immense and awful emptiness. The Aethera wept in sorrow, and they tried to compensate with their own songs, but without the Creator's power, their songs faltered, and discord deepened.

S'ek'zekaar reveled in his power when the Creator stopped singing. The growing discord thrilled him. In his heart, he said, "Now I can make the universe as I wish. I will be its god, and all that exists shall be mine to rule. I shall set them free like I am free." S'ek'zekaar became known as The Defiler since he brought chaos into the cosmos and defiled the purity of creation.

The Creator commanded Naom'han, chief of the Aethera, to summon all the Aethera for a council. He commanded him to record this council for all time and for all creation. The Defiler and his followers demanded freedom from the Creator's presence so they might do as they wished in the universe. The Creator granted their demands and allowed them to sever their connection to Him. They were free, but once they severed the connection to Him, they no longer had access to His power.

Since they no longer shared the Creator's life-sustaining power, their glory dimmed, and they became the creatures of darkness known as the Nethera or Dark Ones. For the first time since their creation, they experienced hunger. Since they no longer received power from the Creator, they drew energy from nature, consuming whatever they touched to satisfy their hunger, and it twisted them into grotesque forms.

The loyal Aethera requested help tending Aarda and the rest of creation since the rebellion among them reduced their numbers, and the task was enormous. The Creator spoke again and said, "Let us sing together once more and bring forth more life, for it will balance the discord in creation. Let us sing mankind into existence."

The Divine melody took root in the water, earth, and air of Aarda, and the Abrhaani, the Eniila, and the Sokai ancestors became living beings.

The Creator gave mankind charge over Aarda to tend it and care for it. The Creator gave the rest of the universe to the Aethera to manage. Aethera helped mankind to care for Aarda, watched over humanity, and helped all the species create and sing their own songs. Aarda flourished under their care.

Mankind's new chant of life upon Aarda restored harmony to the universe. The Creator rested and said, "Continue, my beloved ones, sing as you please. Sing well, for I will judge what you create with your songs and your lives."

Mankind multiplied and grew powerful. Men built cities, wondrous machines, and devices and gloried in their creations.

S'ek'zekaar became angry with mankind because men had restored harmony in creation. His ominous tune, filled with a hunger for power, gave him an appetite for men. Once the Nethera discovered that human life provided superior nourishment, they seduced humanity with S'ek'zekaar's melody and its promise of freedom and personal power. So men desired power for themselves, as S'ek'zekaar did. Men strove against each other. In their pursuit of power, mankind learned warfare, and the Nethera feasted on the lives of multitudes.

Simea looked at the girls, who waited expectantly for him to continue reading. "That's all. There's nothing else written here." He passed the document to the sisters so they could see for themselves.

The sun had sunk low in the sky outside their protected shelter. Even in the waning light, they could see there was nothing else written there.

"I'm too tired to walk any farther today," Kyonna said. "Let's camp here for the night; we can have a fire since the overhang will keep any glider scouts from spotting it."

No one argued. The heat had sapped their strength.

"Why don't you girls gather brush and twigs while I set up camp. "A fire tonight sounds appealing." Simea set about building a ring of stones to contain the fire and leveling spots for their bedrolls. The sisters' voices, chatting as they worked, echoed, and lent an air of homey calm to the evening until chittering squeaks and the sound of falling pebbles farther ahead made Simea stop and listen. He strained to hear, but when he heard nothing more, he shook his head and unrolled their bedding. *Must have imagined it.*

CHAPTER THIRTY-EIGHT

PRAYER-SONGS

"That's all it says," Simea rolled the document and re-tied the thong around the scroll. "Why would Eideron leave us this useless legend? It's no good to us?"

Aibhera's forehead wrinkled as she searched for an answer. "I have no idea." Suddenly she brightened, and her hands fluttered in her lap. "When I tried to rescue you from the Aether, I panicked and couldn't focus until I sang Papa's song." She nudged her sister. "Remember…the one he sang for us…before bedtime. It calmed me and anchored—"

"It's like when I… Never mind." Kyonna gave a quick shake of her head.

"It's like what, Ky?" Simea asked.

"Forget about it. Go on, Aibby. Finish what you were about to say," Kyonna said.

"What if songs help us connect to the Creator, like a prayer. What if they open a doorway to Him? The song reminded me of home, so the prayer-song anchored me and allowed me to reach out, wake Eideron, and transport him to the Aether. If you had done something similar, Simea, you might not have become stranded."

"I suppose it's possible," Simea said. He stared blankly into the distance while he tried to recall the details of his time spent in the Aether.

"What did Eideron tell you about Quickenings? You still haven't explained them to me as you promised." Kyonna frowned. "What other magic can we do?"

Simea said, "Not magic, Ky. We present ourselves to the Creator, and once His power flows through us, we become capable of the incredible feats recorded in our legends and histories. We must reach beyond the Aetherial plane to the Creator of all. He is the source of all power in the universe.

"Even the Aethera receive their strength from Him. I have learned, to my shame and regret, that we become more susceptible to the Nethera's influence when we reach the Aetherial plane. The Nethera exist beyond the dark barrier, which separates the Aether from the Nether. The Nethera's presence paralyzed me with fear and would have killed me, if not for Shel'gharim's intervention. That is why the Synod Council trains apprentices in moral and ethical development before they attempt to teach Quickenings."

Aibhera stared at the ground while Simea confessed his weakness and explained Eideron's teachings. His explanation saved her from repeating her own story of guilt and shame, the result of Nethera influence.

"Ah, I see," Kyonna said.

"Eideron mentioned prophecy, discernment, travel, and protection, but he said the possibilities were limitless," Aibhera said.

"What was the song you used, Aibby?" Simea asked.

"The one Papa sang to us at home when we were little, 'Aamori's House.'"

"Oh! I know that one too," Simea brightened and slapped his knee.

"That might be the song's purpose. The words describe the things Aamori misses in her house and lists them until she realizes that she misses her family more than anything." Aibhera laid a hand on Kyonna's shoulder. "I'm sorry I couldn't tell you we were leaving. I missed you most of all." Aibhera's voice quavered, so Kyonna took her sister's hand, encouraging her to continue. "The lyrics remind you of familiar things and focus you on home and family, and they express a longing to return—"

Simea bounded to his feet. "Hey! What if 'Dragan's Wall' was like 'Aamori's House'? The words of the song ask the Creator for protection against threats, for example, in the chorus, it says:

> Hide us in the safety of Your presence.
> Hedge us from the wicked schemes of all.
> Save us from the evil and the darkness.
> Surround us, save us, build us a strong wall.

A prayer-song that builds a wall of protection around us sounds super useful."

"Yes, an invisible wall, remember the line from the second verse, 'To keep the beasts at bay.' If the Creator could make an invisible barrier, the prayer-song might work that way. Let's try it now. We might need protection soon. We should test our theory before we need it. Help us sing it now, Ky."

The sound of their voices blended and flowed, echoing off the ravine's walls. The vibrations cut through Aarda's atmosphere, penetrated the Aether, and traveled upward. The youngsters' bodies tingled with energy that flowed down a pathway their song had opened. Once they made the connection, a wall of light formed and thickened as they continued. When the barrier shimmered and stabilized, Ky stopped singing, but the wall held.

"Stop, Aibby, but Sim, keep on singing."

Aibby fell silent while Simea held the wall alone. The sisters shared a grin, and their eyes sparkled with triumph in the waning light.

"Remember the second chorus about the gate in the wall, Aibby? We always sang it as a round with the song."

"Let's."

The sisters began the second chorus; the wall shimmered and faded in one place just before the entire wall winked out.

"Forgive me. I can't continue." Simea's shoulders sagged, and his arms hung loosely at his sides. "I'm so tired I can barely stand, and my throat is raw from breathing dust all day."

"It's okay, Sim, besides, it's late." Aibhera unpacked their provisions for an evening meal while the shadows changed from gray to black., Simea lit the brushwood Ky had collected. The oily wood sent a plume of black smoke skyward while the flames cut through the chill air of the canyon bottom and cast flickering shadows on the rough rock surfaces around them.

Night fell like an ax and chopped off the light, except for a tiny strip of stars overhead that glimmered cold and distant in the black sky above them. The firelight formed a bright haven from the utter darkness around them. The dancing shadows and the echoes of their voices gave an ominous chill to the evening that the fire did not dispel.

They ate their ration of dried fruit and bread huddled around the campfire while wrapped in their blankets. They discussed the potential and value of other ancient songs. After they had exhausted all the possibilities, the youngsters curled up around the circle of warmth the fire provided.

"What was that? Simea stiffened and sat up wide-eyed, trying to peer through the darkness. "I thought I heard squeaking noises last night, too…but it's louder tonight."

"Probably rats." Aibhera elbowed him and smiled.

"No, I heard it too." Kyonna stood and stared into the darkness. "Not rats…something bigger than rats.

CHAPTER THIRTY-NINE

DARK CANYON

The young Sokai awoke and emerged from their bedrolls chilled and tired. After a cold breakfast from the provisions Ky brought with her, they began their trek anew. Above them, the sun seared the lava plain into a blazing furnace. While they descended, the walls of the depression gradually grew taller around them as the ravine wound and twisted downward. Until the sun reached its zenith, the narrow declivity shielded them from the blistering sun. At midday, the defile became an oven again. Heat pummeled them from all sides as the black stone absorbed the sun's energy and reflected it in shimmery waves.

Kyonna, clothes soaked in sweat, struggled under the weight of her pack. *If not for my boots, the ground would burn the skin off my feet. My mouth feels as dry as the gravel underfoot, and water doesn't quench this thirst.* She glanced at her sister and Simea. *Sim and Aibby aren't any better off than I am.* "I doubt the lava beneath Abalon is hotter than this," Ky said, flushed from exertion and red-eyed from the glare. "How long until nightfall?"

"Hang on, sis, once the sun sinks below this gully's rim, you'll long for warmth. This barren hellhole is either too hot or too cold, never comfortable."

"It's no wonder nothing lives here," Ky said.

"Are you sure you saw water in the canyon when you flew over it? I hope you're not leading us to our deaths. At this rate, our canteens will run dry before tomorrow night." Sim shook his canteen in Ky's face to emphasize his point. "You hear that? It's almost half empty."

"Yes, I definitely saw water in a canyon ahead. I circled several times to make certain before I set the glider down next to you on the plain. This ravine leads into a gorge, and we're nearly there. It's probably around the next bend or two."

They plodded on. Rocks and gravel crunched and rattled beneath their feet, echoing off the stone around them. The two bends Kyonna predicted became a distant memory. They trudged farther, and when two more twists in the channel did not lead them into the gorge, Simea turned on Kyonna once more. "You will get us killed. We should turn back."

"Simea, why would we go back?" She put her hands on her hips and glared at him. "We're almost there. You'll die on the plain. When your water and supplies run out, your bones will bleach in the sun."

"Look." Simea raised his voice and pointed ahead. "This gully ends in a solid rock wall. If we don't go back, we'll have to climb out anyway. We'll die, and it's your fault."

"Are you joking? The heat has cooked your brain," Kyonna stiffened and stepped toward him. "If not for the supplies I brought, you'd be a pile of roasted meat out on that plain by tomorrow. I saved you, but you want to blame me? The wrong direction? We're following Eideron's map! I say we keep going, and if we must scale the wall ahead, then we'll scale the wall. I haven't bitched about my blisters, so stop whining and walk." She shoved him forward.

Aibhera stepped between them and pushed them apart. "We are all tired and irritable from this heat. If Kyonna says the canyon lies ahead, I believe her." She clenched her fists. "I am tired of you sniping at each other. Simea, you can stay here or go back, but Kyonna and I are headed forward." Aibhera stomped toward the rock face that sealed the far end of the ravine while Kyonna and Simea glared at each other.

Before Aibhera neared the ravine's end, the west side became bathed in shadows, and the air had cooled noticeably. She stood in front of the wall at the end of the ravine and shouted, "Are you coming, or will you glare at each other until dark when you freeze to death?" She beckoned them forward. "You must see this. Come on and follow me."

Kyonna and Simea ended their standoff and trudged toward Aibhera but threw angry glares at each other every few steps as they moved forward. Before they had gone far, Aibby disappeared. Simea and Kyonna stopped, baffled by Aibhera's disappearance, exchanged a puzzled look, and forced their leaden legs into a trot.

Once they reached the wall, Aibhera's disappearance remained a mystery no more. A narrow cleft, barely wide enough for them to squeeze through, branched off and angled left. Kyonna went first, and Simea followed. Once through the gap, the cleft widened and plunged steeply downward. They stumbled and fell on stones worn smooth and slippery by ages of erosion and arrived bruised, battered, and rubbery legged at the gorge Kyonna had seen from the air.

Even in the early afternoon, the sun no longer penetrated to the canyon floor, and most of the ravine lay in shadow. Sunlight only reached partway down the rock face on the east side. Scrubby vegetation clung to the canyon walls in clumps, and small shrubs sprouted on the vertical rock faces on either side. The air in the gorge seemed frigid by comparison to the heat of the ravine.

Around a sharp bend, they spotted Aibhera kneeling beside a pool of water. "I don't think we can drink this water. It smells awful, but other pools ahead might be drinkable." She stood and brushed sand from her knees. "Let's go farther before we stop for the night." Her voice filled the air with sonic ghosts as it echoed off the stone walls.

The young Sokai shivered, enervated by the chill air, as they picked their way through the broken stone and gravel. Aibhera stopped and looked back. "It must be late afternoon. We should stop for a meal."

"And a rest." Kyonna rubbed her hands together. "A fire would be nice too. I'm so cold I can't feel my fingers."

Simea had brought up the rear but heard Kyonna's complaint. "Most of the chasm is already in deep shadows, and it's getting colder by the moment. I hear squeaks and chirps coming from the canyon walls occasionally, but I still haven't seen anything."

"I'll gather the wood this time," Aibhera said.

"Keep alert though, we still don't know what's making the racket." Kyonna dropped her pack and sat on it.

After Aibhera had scrounged enough brush for a small fire and the youngsters had eaten, they resumed their journey among the scattered boulders. The clatter of pebbles tumbling from the heights kept them on edge.

Eerie echoes bounced off the rocks, so they remained silent and hoped to avoid whatever predators lurked in this gloomy fissure. When night approached, they made camp and lit another fire. The small fire lifted their spirits and warmed their bodies. Once darkness fell, loud squeaks and grunts echoed up and down the gorge, but Simea and the girls couldn't see anything outside the circle of firelight.

The next day's journey proved as grim as the previous days. The shade in the canyon was welcome after the heat of the lava plain, but uncertainty dampened their spirits, and bitter cold at night sapped their strength. Without

Kyonna's supplies, they would have run out of water by nightfall of the day she arrived. There were pools of water in the canyon, but most smelled like the underground sewage treatment facilities in Abalon and looked unsafe to drink. On the third day, Kyonna found a spring trickling from the canyon wall. It took a long time to fill their canteens with the cold, clear liquid, and after they drank their fill, they moved on.

After six days in the gorge, the three youngsters grew accustomed to the nightly chorus of unseen animals. On the seventh morning, Aibhera awoke with a shriek. A stampede of furry creatures raced away from the campsite. The canyon exploded with their high-pitched squeals as they streaked across the canyon floor and scurried up the walls.

Simea shot out of his bedroll and scrambled to his feet. "Aibhera, what's wrong? Why did you scream?"

"Something fuzzy brushed my face. When I awoke, eyes the size of my fist stared at me. When the little beast bared its fangs at me, I screamed. You would too. Look at them covering the walls."

The little animals had reached safety. They clung to the rock face and scolded the Sokai with a cacophony of echoing barks and squeals. Finally satisfied they had berated the Sokai interlopers long enough, the skittish little creatures swarmed over the rocks and nibbled plants on the rock wall as if nothing happened.

"Well, you scared them off, so let's have breakfast," Kyonna said. She yawned, stretched, and walked over to where their packs lay near the embers of the fire. She picked up her bag. *It's lighter than it should be.* Her fingers found a tattered hole in the canvas. She unfastened the top flap, turned the pack upside down, and shook it vigorously.

"Well, I have good news and bad news. The good news is my pack is lighter. The bad news is those evil little bastards have eaten everything in my bag. You'd better check yours. If they stole your food too, we won't have breakfast, lunch, or any other meals unless we catch and eat a few of them." She pointed at the creatures clinging to the rocks around them. "I wonder how they'd taste roasted over an open fire."

CHAPTER FORTY

CAPTURED

Rehaak awoke with an aching head. *It is blacker than midnight in a mineshaft here. I do not remember how I arrived here, wherever here is.*

All Abrhaani avoided the darkness. If deprived of sunlight for too long, they weakened and became ill. Darkness bothered Rehaak more than most Abrhaani. He had feared it since childhood—that, and rats.

Rehaak lay on his side, the musty mineral scent of soil wafted up from beneath him. When he tried to move, he discovered that someone had bound him hand and foot. His arms fastened at the wrists, and securely tied behind his back, sent pain shooting through his neck and shoulders. Because of the awkward placement of his arms, he could only roll onto his face to relieve the discomfort in his neck and shoulders. Rehaak's change in position did nothing to ease the pain in his ankles, which were also bound, nor did it stop the throbbing in his head.

Footsteps approached. A faint glow brightened as the steps came nearer. The flickering light allowed Rehaak a closeup view of a dirt floor and rough rock walls. Stalactites hung like monstrous teeth overhead, and stalagmites poked up from the cave floor, evoking the image of a creature holding him in its jaws. He now knew where here was—a cavern. Unseen hands seized him, wrenched his overstressed shoulders, and forced him to sit upright.

One of his captors untied Rehaak's ankles and wrists. "Get on your feet, the master wishes to see you now."

Rehaak wobbled to his feet like a newborn lamb and staggered a single step before he fell to his knees. His feet were numb and refused to obey him, and his hands prickled and stung as his circulation returned. His captors dragged him to his feet, pushed him forward, and cuffed him whenever he stumbled.

Their flickering shadows preceded them, and rocks of all sizes, barely visible in the dim torchlight, tripped Rehaak several times as the two men pushed him forward down a dark hall.

The passage ended in a chamber lit by many torches. Many men knelt, stripped to the waist, facing forward. Rehaak lost count of the number of men bearing the familiar Odium tattoos across their shoulders. There were many.

His guards pushed him through the kneeling crowd. He raised his eyes from the crowded floor to notice what held their attention. Dreynar Asan, the young nobleman he met on his way to Dun Dale, stood over an altar fashioned from a truncated stalagmite. Drey wore a black ceremonial cloak covered in embroidered silver runes, like the tattoos on the other men's backs. In his hands, he held one of the long knives with which Rehaak had gained an unwelcome familiarity.

Isil was right, they use the knives to offer sacrifices to their Nethera gods. On the altar, a lamb, its legs bound, awaited the knife stroke to end its life.

Rehaak stumbled again and fell to his knees. Neither the uneven floor nor the sight of the impending sacrifice caused his fall. What sapped his strength was the sight of the entity behind the altar. The nightmare creature from his childhood lurked there while the tattooed men worshiped it. Rehaak wanted to rise and run, but fear paralyzed him as it had in his nightmares. *Even if my legs obeyed me...I am surrounded...I could not escape. Unless I am mistaken, I will be next on that bloody altar.*

The Dark One loomed over the altar. Its form was total darkness that flowed and shifted so his eyes could not focus on it. It reflected no light; it devoured the illumination. The torches near the altar shone dimmer than the ones farther from where it hung motionless behind the slab. While the Nethera awaited the knife stroke ending the innocent creature's life, Rehaak sensed its hunger and hatred.

The men's chanting built to a frenzied crescendo, anticipating the sacrifice. The knife in Dreynar's hands descended, and blood spurted from the lamb's severed throat while Drey caught the flow in a chalice. Once the last of its lifeblood dribbled into the goblet., the lamb twitched and became still.

The men shouted as though they had accomplished a magnificent victory instead of an act of depraved butchery. The Dark One moaned in ecstasy and expectation. Rehaak suspected it received sustenance both from the debauchery of the men and the sacrifice on the altar.

The Nethera gains strength from them because it demeans and twists them into the opposite of what the Creator intended. They do not realize the creature draws nourishment from them, nor do they know that their participation in this sacrifice weakens them while it strengthens the Nethera. They believe it feeds on the lamb's blood, but their corruption gives it more power than any animal sacrifice. I feel the Nethera's pull on my life force too, but the Creator shields me from the Nethera's hunger. It can't draw strength from me because I do not serve it.

Drey stepped from behind the altar and raised the chalice of blood overhead. He chanted in an unknown language, and the men joined him. Their voices built to a crescendo of incoherent rage and hatred. When the noise of their voices peaked, Dreynar lowered the chalice to his lips and gulped the warm lamb's blood. When he finished, he extended his arms and held the goblet out, offering the contents to the assembled crowd. "My brothers, drink deeply. This offering is blessed by Ashd'eravaak's presence today. We are the Odium, chosen to rule Aarda under the benevolent gaze of our god."

The men jostled each other to be first to drink as if it were an honor rather than a disgrace. Dreynar passed the cup to them. He turned, lips bloodstained, eyes unfocused, and approached Rehaak where he knelt on the gallery's floor. The Nethera followed Dreynar. It rent the air and left a void in its wake. Rehaak grew faint from the horrific stench of rotten flesh that emanated from it. He did not know how any man tolerated its company without vomiting. Although the Nethera was still halfway across the underground chamber, Rehaak's gorge rose, his vision blurred, and bile burned his throat. His stomach spasmed, and he spewed its contents onto the cavern floor.

CHAPTER FORTY-ONE

WELCOME TO SETHRIA

The Swordsman and Swallow Inn, like the rest of Sethria, had seen hard use over the last sixteen years. A thick coating of soot, dirt, and grease covered the stone facade. Aelfric had seen the building's former glory, but it would take years of scrubbing and scraping to expose the flawless white marble underneath the thick layer of grime. Aelfric pulled open the door and found the interior only slightly less grubby than its exterior. Patrons in various stages of drunkenness lounged at the tables while harlots flogged their wares to the customers.

Aelfric wrinkled his nose at the stench of unwashed bodies and stale beer. He made his way to the bar where the bald, hairy-chested innkeeper in a greasy apron wiped the bar with a dirty rag. "I have rooms reserved under the name of Kett," Aelfric said.

"Oh, *do* you now? You are not one of Kett's regulars. How do I know the room is yours? We are swamped this time of year." The fellow's eyes narrowed as he took Aelfric's measure. "The hotel is fully booked. Perhaps we could come to some arrangement." He rubbed his thumb and forefinger together and licked his lips, anticipating a payoff.

Aelfric scanned the room before he turned back toward the innkeeper. "I'm certain that hogs stand in line outside the door to rent rooms in this pigsty. Let's negotiate an arrangement now." He reached across the bar and grabbed the innkeeper's tunic and a handful of chest hair with it. The innkeeper squealed like a stuck pig.

"Perhaps you misheard the name. I have rooms reserved under the name of Kett," Aelfric growled, shaking the innkeeper like a dog shakes a rat. The threadbare tunic tore, and Aelfric ended up with a handful of cloth and greasy chest hair. "Is our arrangement satisfactory?" His hand drifted toward his knife, and his lip curled in a sneer. "If not, we can negotiate at greater length."

"Oh, aye, sir. More than adequate. The boy will show you to your room immediately, sir." He rubbed his wounded chest with a filthy paw. "Vim, show this fine gentleman to his room." He waved his free hand at a young fellow who sprawled on a bench behind the bar, cleaning his nails with the tines of a dinner fork. The motion, intended to motivate the youngster, took effect only after the innkeeper added a hiss and a curse to his gesture.

By his appearance, the youngster, who looked about Laakea's age, was one of the innkeeper's offspring. *Vim indeed. Glaciers move faster than this dolt.* "I believe this belongs to you." Aelfric placed the torn cloth on the bar, wiped his hand on his thigh to rid himself of the fellow's chest hair, then followed the young man. The youngster slouched up the broad stone stairway ahead of Aelfric. When the boy reached the top landing, he grunted and pointed at the door to his left.

Aelfric pushed the door open with his shoulder, and rusty hinges emitted a squeal that set his teeth on edge. Beyond the open door lay a simple room containing an Eniila-sized bed, a small table, and two shabby wooden chairs. Rusted pieces of decorative metalwork, festooned with cobwebs, hung above the bed. Light-colored rectangles on the walls indicated where tapestries had hung during its Abrhaani occupation. *Thank the gods I can sleep in comfort tonight if the place isn't bedbug infested.* "This is acceptable." Aelfric sent the innkeeper's boy away with a dismissive wave. *Have I spent so much time among the Abrhaani that I no longer am at home among my own people? If I feel so out of place in my homeland, how can I expect to rule it?* He shrugged and threw his gear onto the table in the middle of the room.

Sethria had changed, and he no longer recognized the city. Remnants of many Abrhaani buildings lay where they had fallen, forming blackened piles of stone. Wherever there was space among the ruins, shacks had sprung up like dilapidated wooden mushrooms feeding on the decay. The well-ordered streets of the Sethria Aelfric knew had become a chaotic maze of alleys and passageways, choked with rubble and stinking garbage.

Did we conquer Sethria to replace it with this? Is this stinking cesspool of shacks and shanties the best we Eniila can manage? May the gods help us if this slum is the best my people can salvage from my most significant victory, or is this a portent of some sort? A tap on his door interrupted his morose thoughts.

"It's me, Kett." Aelfric opened the door, and Kett sauntered into the room. "What do you think of our beautiful city, friend Aelfric?" Kett closed the door behind him. "Are you fond of what they've done with Sethria? Are you impressed with the improvements?" Sarcasm tainted the words. Kett flopped into a rickety chair near the table, while Aelfric stood by the window overlooking the dirty street below.

"Not exactly." He turned away from the scene of disorder and decay and faced the Abrhaani lounging in the chair. Aelfric couldn't identify the emotion in Kett's eyes and hesitated before he chose an honest answer. He hoped it cemented their relationship.

"My blood burns to see how they have misused this city. Is that what you wanted to hear? I am disgusted by the filth and poverty. Does that answer your question?"

"More than adequately, my friend."

"So—what's next?"

"Here is what we'll do."

CHAPTER FORTY-TWO

NEW OFFER

"We meet again, Rehaak, scholar, troublemaker, and heretic," Dreynar sidestepped the pool of vomit in front of Rehaak and lifted his chin with a bloody hand. "It would have been easier on both of us if you accepted my offer and came with me." He squeezed Rehaak's jaw and shook it before letting go. "Instead, you forced me to send Odium's disciples to bring you here."

Dreynar's words refreshed Rehaak's memory. He had remained hidden in the Dancing Dog's woodshed until Breisha approached with the leather straps for Laakea's breastplate. When he slunk out of the shed, someone put a sack over his head and grabbed his arms. Rehaak remembered nothing more until he awoke on the cavern floor. An ache in his temple confirmed they had clubbed him unconscious.

Behind Dreynar, the disciples renewed their chanting after they emptied the chalice.

"What do you want with me, Dreynar?" Rehaak spoke loudly to be heard above the voices chanting Ashd'eravaak's praises.

"We wish to convince you of the error of your beliefs. My master's master, Ashd'eravaak." He nodded toward the evil creature behind him, "Ashd'eravaak, our rightful master and god, hoped a demonstration of his power would convince you to serve him."

Rehaak shuddered at the idea of serving the abomination before him. His eyes bulged. He could not blink, nor could he look away from the blazing red eyes of the Nethera who lurked behind the young nobleman. This was his childhood nightmare made real.

"Now that we have your attention, we would like to reason with you and lead you to the correct path. The Odium wishes to free the last remnants of mankind from its bondage to the Nameless One. We will achieve our goal once we reunite mankind under the benevolent leadership of Ashd'eravaak and his brethren. Ashd'eravaak and his kind, under the guidance of S'ek'zekaar, have fought tirelessly for our freedom for countless millennia.

"We seek to bring the Eniila and the Abrhaani together, so we might enjoy harmony and fruitfulness as we did in ancient times. Surely that is a noble goal and one you would support. Isn't that your wish for mankind?" Dreynar stopped and waited for Rehaak's answer.

Who is this Nameless One? If I play along, I might satisfy my curiosity. "How will you and your fellow Odium members carry out such an ambitious goal, friend Dreynar?" Rehaak asked, hoping his sarcasm did not show through his words.

"We will send our brothers, gathered here, to inform our people of our god's return," he said, pointing to the men behind him. "Our apostle has made inroads in Baradon. I told you, my master has gone ahead of us to complete the arrangements to spread the word further still."

"And if the Eniila will not listen to reason?" Rehaak asked.

"Then we shall compel them by every means at our disposal, friend Rehaak. This mission is far too important to allow a few stubborn, misguided men to frustrate us."

"You said 'every means.' What methods of persuasion will work against the Eniila?"

"What does that matter, once mankind unites and gains freedom from the Nameless One's oppression?"

"Do you mean the Creator?" Rehaak asked. "Where does He fit into your plans?"

The Nethera hissed and spat like water dropped onto hot iron at the mention of the Creator's name.

"The Nameless One deserted mankind and left Ashd'eravaak and his kind in charge of Aarda. They are few, and their strength has ebbed because the task is far too massive for them alone. That is why they have enlisted our aid to help them reunite the species. We, the members of Odium, help them to become dominant again, so we might profit from their benevolence and leadership.

"Do you not wish for mankind to rediscover the knowledge it lost in the Sundering? Do you, a scholar, not value, even long for such knowledge? Is knowledge not the reason you seek *The Aetheriad*?" Dreynar prodded Rehaak's chest with the forefinger.

"I value knowledge a great deal," Rehaak replied, shaken to the core. *They know everything about my desires and my quest.*

"Then join with us, and Ashd'eravaak will give you all the knowledge you seek and much more."

"Friend Dreynar, what will such profound knowledge cost?"

"It costs you nothing but allegiance to our true god, the only god with the power and determination to act on our behalf. Ashd'eravaak and his kind require that all men serve them so that their strength is enough for the task. The followers of the Nameless One, who remain, hinder their efforts."

Rehaak struggled to his feet. "A true god does not need power from its creations; it supplies power *to* them instead. What true god would need our pathetic help? You must see…and smell…that this vile creature you worship is no god. Tell me, Drey, how the few remaining followers of the Creator can thwart your plans. You boast that you have far greater numbers. If your god is so powerful, he should easily triumph over so few."

Drey's nostrils flared, and his eyes blazed, incensed by Rehaak's comments. "The Nameless One's followers received jurisdiction over Aarda by decree. If a single follower remains, that decree is in effect, and our gods cannot exercise complete and proper control over the world, so chaos reigns among us."

Aha. At last, we come to the meat of Odium's problem. The Creator ceded control to us by divine fiat. It has stymied their efforts and explains why they try to eradicate the Creator's followers. He omitted who issued that decree. Maybe Ashd'eravaak has not seen fit to share this information with them. Only the Creator could issue such a declaration. Rehaak remained silent. *I could never convert these fanatics by pointing out Ashd'eravaak's fundamental weakness.*

"Now that I have answered your question, join us and rule Aarda with—"

"And if I decline this beneficent offer?"

"We cannot allow it. If you are stubborn and resist, it puts Aarda's reunification at risk. We have endeavored to convince you of the nobility and correctness of our path, but if you persist in your rebellion, our relationship will end unpleasantly for you. However, you will reap enormous benefits if you accept our offer.

"Look around you, Rehaak; this is the best way for us. We know how many times you have compromised your so-called principles for far less value. Are you foolish enough to believe you can resist our methods of persuasion?"

Rehaak shouted, "I am sure of one thing. I cannot abide the stench of your pathetic false god any longer." He spat on the cave's dusty floor to emphasize his disgust.

I will not capitulate. The consequences of taking this stand will cost me my life, but death has not claimed me yet. Rehaak quoted Laakea to his captors, "Better to fight and die with dignity than to live on in disgrace."

"Take him, and teach him the error of his choice," Dreynar snarled.

Two men rose and dragged Rehaak down a dark passageway. "You will beg for death to embrace you and end your suffering," Dreynar shouted as Rehaak, pulled forward between Odium's thugs, disappeared into the darkness.

CHAPTER FORTY-THREE

TORTURE

Rehaak writhed and fought his captors, but his efforts only exhausted him. The journey ended in a torch-lit cavern beneath the earth. They dragged him kicking and cursing to a stone slab set atop a truncated stalagmite, which formed a table in the grotto's center. The men tore off Rehaak's clothing and tied him, spread-eagled, to four steel rings pinned to the corners of the slab. Once they tightened the ropes around his wrists and ankles, they began their bloody work.

Bathed in flickering torchlight, Rehaak's tormentors took him to new heights and depths of pain. Time passed slowly on the table. The length of each heartbeat became an eternity of agony. The smell of his blood mingled with the musty odors of the cavern floor and walls. Rehaak focused his thoughts on the torches and tried to ignore the pain. He fought the urge to scream. He failed, and his throat grew as raw as the rest of his body until he lost consciousness.

Odium's torturers were masters of their craft. Each time Rehaak passed out, he believed it was the end. Then he awakened again to an ocean of agony so deep, that he thought he would never break the surface again. Only death's merciful hands could end his torment, so Rehaak proved the truth of Dreynar's words and prayed for death to release him.

When Rehaak thought he could endure no more, he slipped free of his body. He hovered above the mangled mess of his mortal shell in a cloud of light, and the pain vanished. *Am I dead? Is this the afterlife? Have I suffered enough to earn my release?* He reached out to the Faithful One. A blinding brilliance enfolded him. Power flowed like a river around him and through him.

Whenever Rehaak fainted before, he had escaped into the black well of unconsciousness, but this was different. Disconnected from the brutality they inflicted on his flesh, Rehaak watched his tormentors mutilate his body while the loving presence of his god surrounded and sustained him. *I will die from the abuse if it continues. I have always considered death a problem, but now I see death is the solution. Life is the problem—I have not learned how to live.*

The Creator's whispered encouragement permeated the glowing fog surrounding him. *"Every man dies. Isil and Laakea will die someday. You cannot prevent their demise any more than you can prevent your own, but I can save you if you surrender to me. I can convert horror into beauty if you trust me. Your choices have brought you to this place, but my plan for you remains in effect. The life you live matters more than your death. Wouldn't you rather come to death nobly having accomplished everything I chose for you? Few people can change the world through their choices. You are one of those few. Instead of a humiliating death, at the hands of your persecutors, wouldn't you rather save your world?"*

Rehaak looked at the bloody mess below him. *I have nothing left to lose. Both my friends are ready to give up their lives for me and my quest. It is their choice, not mine to make. In cowardice, I convinced myself that running away was a noble act of self-sacrifice, but that decision dishonors their choice and their gift of friendship. I was ready to desert them, but I came to my senses before Drey's henchmen captured me. I wish I could tell Isil and Laakea I have not abandoned them. Since childhood, I have run from the things I feared. I fled my duty to my family, forsook my obligation to You, my god, and deserted the only people who loved me. I will run no farther.*

He surrendered himself to his duty, and in surrender, he found peace and freedom amid the bondage and pain. His soul returned to his body. Cuts and burns marked his flesh, but cuts did not excise his faith, and burns did not obliterate it. Instead, they inscribed faith deep into his soul, and the burns ignited a fire inside him. The pain engulfed him again, but now every shriek of Rehaak's agony declared, "I will not give in to evil! Not this time!"

The torment stopped.

Dreynar arrived and asked, "Have you repented of your foolishness?"

"I have repented entirely of all my foolishness," Rehaak slurred through the spittle and blood in his broken mouth and swollen lips.

"Excellent. Release Rehaak from his bonds."

Rehaak laughed. Pain shot through his chest from broken ribs. He said, "I have repented of abandoning my Creator and my mission to end your influence. No matter what you do to me, I will never surrender. Whether the Creator delivers me from your clutches, or I die here, I will not follow your perverted ways or worship your false god. You have broken my body, but you cannot conquer my spirit. So yes, I have repented of the foolishness of running from my destiny and the Creator's purposes for me."

Drey spat in Rehaak's face and snarled, "Bring him to the great hall. We will remove his skin, one piece at a time, as an offering to our god since he refuses to listen to reason."

I will die now, and failure to complete my mission is my only regret.

They dragged his mutilated body down the rocky passageway to the main cavern toward their blood-soaked altar.

CHAPTER FORTY-FOUR

BAD NEWS

The door to the house burst open and interrupted Isil and Laakea's morning meal. Laakea leaped from the chair, snatched his weapons from the sideboard, and in an eyeblink, he held them to the neck of a breathless villager.

"Don't slay me, young sir," he panted. "I brings you a word 'bout your friend."

"What word?" Laakea glared at the fellow, swords in hand.

"Easy, lad." Isil stepped between Laakea and the villager and put her hands on Laakea's forearms. "This be Arak from Dun Dale. I knows him. You can see he be frightened out o' his wits."

Laakea bit his lip, red-faced at the violent image he projected to the little Abrhaani villager, and lowered his weapons.

"That I is, and the whole village is too," Arak admitted. "I brings news about your friend. He were took prisoner by them vile men what has been hangin' about of late. They calls themselves the Odium."

Laakea returned the swords to the sideboard and listened.

"Tell us what you knows. We be mighty interested if you can tell us where Odium took Rehaak," Isil said, inviting the man to sit.

"That I can, 'cause Aert's little 'un spied on 'em and followed 'em to their lair. Soon as she tol' us, I come straight here to tell you, 'cause it near scared the liver out o' her and ever'one else. Breisha were gettin' leather for him from Ebrill, the tanner's daughter. Breisha were just about to give Rehaak the leather when 'em fellas whacked him on the head and drug him away.

"Them fellas carried Rehaak to a cave near the waterfall on the crick what runs out o' the mountains just this side o' Dun Dale. I can lead you there if'n you needs a guide."

Laakea shook his head. "I've been fishing there many times, so I know where it is. We can get there on our own. No need for you to risk your life."

The fellow breathed a relieved sigh.

Isil scooped up the remnants of their meal from the table and bundled them in a cloth. "Here, take these vittles for your trip home. I don't 'spect you had time for a decent meal afore you came a-runnin' to warn us."

"I thanks you mightily." Arak bowed and hustled out the door leaving it swinging open in his rush to depart.

Laakea gathered up the rest of his gear. "We had best move quickly if we want to reach Rehaak before dark."

Isil, already busy stowing food, dressings, and medicines into packs, merely nodded.

Laakea paced around the room. "This is my fault. If I hadn't sent Rehaak to fetch the leather, Odium wouldn't have caught him."

"That be utter nonsense. You has no control over Rehaak. He can't hardly control hisself. Like as not, he got hisself into this fix by doin' somethin' stupid. It ain't the first time neither."

Laakea put on his breastplate, fastening it with rope instead of the leather straps Rehaak had gone to buy. "I can't help feeling responsible." Laakea smacked the tabletop with his fist.

"Ready when you is." Isil held out a pack to Laakea.

Laakea took it, slipped the swords into the carry loops on the pack's sides, then slung it over his shoulder.

"Let's go."

The sun was high above the western treetops when they set out, but Laakea assumed they could reach the cavern before nightfall if they jogged double-time and followed the trail Laakea knew well. When Isil became winded, they slowed to a walk along the path.

Isil had recovered her breath, and they were about to resume their pace when men leaped from the shadows of the forest. They encircled Isil and Laakea, and a contorted shadowy entity emerged from the woodland behind the men.

Laakea drew both swords, the Battlefury coursing through his veins again. *The black thing behind them must be a Nethera.* That was Laakea's last coherent thought before the Battlefury took control of his body.

Laakea skewered the first man as the hideous shape closed in on him. He disemboweled a second man, spitted a third, and hamstrung the fourth combatant before the Dark One sank its misshapen claws into his back. The Nethera's touch paralyzed him and pulled at his soul like someone sucking an egg through a hole in its shell. His swords fell from his nerveless fingers. He knew he must break free or become an empty husk like the miller's son. The pain of the spiritual attack burned in his blood like molten metal, but he couldn't scream. Colors faded from his vision as Laakea mentally defended himself against the assault.

As consciousness began slipping away, the creature turned him around so he was facing it. It drew Laakea's life force up from the center of his being and out through his mouth. Laakea had lost sight of Isil and didn't know if she still fought on or if she had fallen to their attackers.

This was his battle to fight alone. Laakea stared into the bottomless darkness of the Nethera's soul and heard its voice boast in his mind, *"You are mine. You are young and strong. Your soul will satisfy my hunger for many days to come."*

Nothing prepared Laakea for this. His father's drills, Rehaak's knowledge, and Isil's wisdom were no help in this battle. If he lost this fight, there would never be another. Laakea refused to surrender. His spirit rallied, fought back, and clung to consciousness while he dangled over the edge of a spiritual precipice.

Laakea summoned his outrage at the injustice of the Nethera's attack and used his anger as a shield. *This is a different sort of battle than the kind my father prepared me for. Skill at arms can't save me. Although my will to live keeps the malevolent creature at bay, I can't survive by determination alone. This is a spiritual battle. My resolve and anger, as potent as they are, cannot confound this hate-filled horror forever. I need help. Rehaak and Isil told me that the Creator responds if those in need call upon Him, and my need is dire.* His shield of righteous anger buckled and warped from the Nethera's assault as he composed his prayer to the Creator.

Laakea was desperate, not eloquent; his fear and panic formed a single-word plea. "Help!" he prayed toward the place where he imagined his god lived. The prayer traveled upward like a shaft of light, a beacon of desperate need streaked up from him into the bright and infinite sky. Calm and peace shielded him where before there was anger, pain, and terror.

In a heartbeat, his plea for help opened a conduit to the heavens. Laakea sensed divine energy flowing down that channel, a trickle in a streambed that grew to a raging torrent. A barrier exploded inside Laakea, and a brilliant pillar of power extended downward to him and increased to blinding brightness. If he had looked directly at the light with his eyes, it would have left charred cinders in his eye sockets.

The energy surged brighter still and flowed into his anger. Laakea's shield of rage thickened and flared more glorious than the sun. It exploded outward, and the melodic words that formed the explosion had the power to shatter mountains and kindle forests into flame. The authority in those words humbled him. Laakea recognized the golden voice, but it didn't speak to reassure him. It spoke through him with a mountainous anger that dwarfed his own.

"Let my servant be!"

The words blasted his attacker backward, and the thunderous voice left Laakea and his assailant both stunned. The sound slammed the Nethera onto the forest floor so hard that the ground beneath it cracked and shuddered. Laakea recovered before the Nethera since he was the channel of the power and not its target. Color returned to his sight, and his limbs regained their strength. Laakea recovered one of his swords from where it lay beside him and advanced toward the demon crumpled on the ground. Holy rage burned within him as he raised his weapon.

"You have overstepped your bounds, Ak'eldemea, brother to Ashd'eravaak," Laakea thundered in a voice that shook the creature like a leaf in the wind. "I know your name and your deeds. You and two more of your kind tried to butcher my servant Rehaak at his cabin, and when you failed, you fled and took the life of an innocent child to feed your hunger. Your wickedness ends today!"

Once Laakea raised his swords, he and his weapons blazed fury-bright. The thing cringed until Laakea plunged his swords into the center of the ugly evil form. Power flowed through Laakea and surrounded him in an explosion of brilliance as the incandescent sword pierced the demon.

The Nethera hissed, shrieked, and writhed like a worm stuck on a fishhook.

"You are judged guilty and condemned," Laakea said. The demon dissolved into a light gray mist and vanished.

With the death of the creature, the glow around Laakea faded from white to red and then disappeared, leaving him weak and wobbly as he sank to his knees. He felt a hand upon his shoulder and found Isil looking at him, eyes filled with awe. It took a long time before either of them found the strength to speak.

"I s'pose you just answered the question you asked Rehaak," Isil said with a wry grin.

"What question?"

"The one you asked him, you 'member? The one 'bout if'n you might be able to kill these things. I remembers him askin' me if I knew summat 'bout it."

"Ah, that question," Laakea murmured. He slipped into unconsciousness and fell facedown onto the crumpled and bloodstained grass beside the trail.

Isil knelt beside him, rolled him onto his back, and supported his head in her lap. She checked him over, concerned for her young friend, but he was in the capable hands of her god. Instead, she offered a prayer of thanks to the Creator.

When Laakea's breath became regular again, and his heart thumped out a slow, steady rhythm, she rose to retrieve their belongings. On her return, Isil attempted to move Laakea, but he was too heavy. After she failed to budge him from where he lay, she stretched by arching her back, then covered the boy with their blankets. "It be hard for me to remember that you, half a head taller than Rehaak and solid as yonder tree trunks, be just a young'un. I reckon we stays where we is till you recovers. I dunno if'n battle left you weak, or if'n you just burned out like the time you spent in the Creator's forge. I doesn't understand; perhaps Rehaak could…but Rehaak ain't here. It be plain as anythin'—

"Odium knowed me and Laakea was comin' to rescue Rehaak, and they done used him for bait to lure us into this here ambush."

Isil shook her head and cast a sidelong glance at Laakea. After tucking his blankets around him, she gathered firewood from the forest's edge and lit a fire. Shadows deepened around them, as the sun sank below the treetops. She wrapped her blanket around her shoulders, prodded the fire with a stick, and never noticed the eyes watching from among the trees or the silent shapes slipping through the shadows.

CHAPTER FORTY-FIVE

THE CAVE

The smells of woodsmoke and cooking food awakened Laakea. Although stiff from his battle last night and sore from sleeping on the cold earth, he felt fine otherwise. Steam rose from the pot Isil tended beside a small campfire, and the breeze carried the mouthwatering aroma of spiced porridge to where he lay. "Good morning, Isil."

"Good mornin' to you as well, lad," she replied. "I suspected vittles would rouse you from your beauty sleep."

"I hope you made plenty because, for some reason, I'm starving." Laakea threw his blankets aside.

"Yer always starvin' for any reason or for no reason at all from what I seen," she shot back.

Laakea got to his feet and stretched the kinks from his muscles with the conditioning routines his father had taught him. Once he completed his stretches, he said, "We'd best eat and be off as soon as possible. I fear we sprang a trap set for us by Rehaak's captors yesterday. They used him as bait to lure us into an ambush, and they will kill him since the trap failed."

"Yup, I been thinkin' the same thing myself, lad."

"I'm sorry, Isil, I should have been more observant. If I had, we might have been able to avoid that bit of unpleasantness."

"Nah, look at it this way, yesterday we whittled down their numbers summat. Today we likely be havin' an easier time 'cause o' it."

"I hope you're right, because I don't know if I can survive another fight like that one. If more Nethera are—" Laakea shook his head but didn't finish the sentence.

Isil shrugged and remained silent as she handed Laakea a spoon. While seated on their bedrolls, they shared the contents of the pot. Isil wrestled the container away from Laakea several times to stop him from devouring the vessel's entire contents.

Isil and Laakea broke camp under the brightening sky and continued on their way. Laakea urged more caution than the previous day, so they traveled carefully toward the falls, alert for any danger. Once the roar of the waterfall reached them, they crouched low to avoid making silhouettes that sentries could recognize. Laakea scanned ahead for guards while they moved from one patch of cover to the next. The roaring water drowned out every other noise, so he relied on sight alone to find the sentries.

Laakea's keen eyes spotted movement near boulders along the stream bank. He warned Isil of the sentries with a hand signal and motioned for her to hold her position as he analyzed the sentries' routine. *I won't rush headlong into another ambush—won't push my luck again. The gods don't abide repeated stupidity. A wise man learns from his mistakes if he outlives them.* Laakea shrugged and shook his head. *I've begun to think like my father; his proverbs echo through my mind, but I never thought I would find them useful.*

Three guards hid in cover among the rocks. The watchmen had spread out in a semicircle, well in front of the cave mouth. The interior of the cavern was too dark for Laakea to see inside the cavity. He couldn't tell the passage's length or how many men it held in its depths. By dusk, the guards had changed three times. That meant there were over a dozen men inside the cave. The odds were terrible unless he evened them.

Once night fell, they crept toward the sentries. The guards had lit a fire to ward off the chill, and five more men exited the cavern and sat around the flames. The firelight illuminated the sentries for Laakea and ruined the lookouts' night vision. He smiled at Isil and pointed out their respective targets. They eliminated the two guards on the flanks first. Isil used a rope to choke her victim, while Laakea slit the other man's throat. Neither made a sound.

Isil worked her way toward the last guard, while Laakea readied an arrow and crept as close as he dared to the four men gathered at the fire. He stuck four more bolts in the dirt so he could draw and release them quickly. Isil moved into position, and when she throttled the last guard, she edged toward the fire and acted as bait.

Laakea cued Isil, and she rustled the bush she hid behind. The men had been talking but fell silent when they heard twigs snapping and bushes rustling. Two of them motioned, picked up their weapons, and advanced toward the shrub where Isil waited. Once they were more than halfway to Isil's location, Laakea targeted a man near the fire and sent an arrow through his throat. The fellow beside him barely realized what had happened before death claimed him too.

Laakea released another arrow, and a man headed toward Isil's position stopped to stare at his chest, a look of surprise on his face as he saw two feet of wood ending in black crow feathers sprouting from his ribcage. He cried out before he collapsed. The last man heard his cry above the sound of the water and turned to look.

That act made him Laakea's next victim. When he fell, the last guard turned to investigate the disturbance. Isil dashed toward him, swinging her staff, but before she got there, he too sported an arrow in his chest. Isil clubbed him for good measure as he fell.

Laakea dragged the bodies into cover while Isil stood guard and watched for newcomers exiting the cave. It was nearly midnight before they began a cautious entrance into the cliff's darkened mouth Torches lit the stone corridor, but no additional enemies lurked there. Once they entered, chanting, punctuated by screams, echoed off the passageway's walls from somewhere ahead.

"That'll more'n likely be our friend Rehaak joinin' in that sing-along. It sounds like there still be a whack o' them crazies though," Isil said in a faint voice.

"Let's hope we whittled them down enough to survive." Torchlight gave Laakea's face and grim smile, an eerie appearance.

They followed the sounds through a narrow rock-strewn passageway to the altar chamber. Over two dozen men chanted and pranced in front of the altar to the rhythm of a drumbeat. Rehaak lay on the slab, bleeding from many wounds. A man in a black robe held a knife to Rehaak's skin. When Isil saw Rehaak tied to the stone altar, she moved as if to dive into the crowd. Laakea grasped her shoulder, pulled her backward, and forced her to stand beside him.

He removed the last of his arrows from his quiver.

"Me first, greedy, you can have them when I'm done. Hold these arrows for me and put one in my hand each time I release," Laakea said, unconcerned about the men overhearing his words. The noise inside the chamber was so loud, that he almost had to shout for Isil to hear him.

Three men fell to Laakea's arrows before anyone noticed. Two more before anyone reacted. The next one died with his warning shout still in his throat. The chants stopped, and the drums fell silent. Two more fell. The men in the chamber realized their peril and began their charge.

Laakea threw down his bow, drawing Justice and Truth from his belt. His swords gleamed blue-green in the torchlight of the narrow passageway that limited their attackers' mobility. Isil and Laakea fell back slowly under pressure from their opponents and made them pay for every inch of ground. Four more fell to Laakea's swords and three to Isil's staff before she hooked her heel on a rock and landed on her backside.

Laakea saw her fall and moved to protect her. He fought with all the skills Aelfric had drilled into him, but the berserker rage that overcame him at other times failed him tonight. Laakea knew that without Battlefury, he would never withstand the onslaught of these crazed minions of the Dark Ones. The previous night's battle had drained him too much.

He drew a ragged breath and shouted, "Creator, help us!"

Laakea pushed them back with a flurry of blows long enough for Isil to rise, but she had twisted her ankle in the fall and struggled to stand.

"Creator help us!" he bellowed again, and this time Isil joined him in his shouted prayer.

Their shouts enraged their attackers to new heights of bloodlust. They shrieked incoherent syllables and pressed Laakea even harder. Isil did what she could while she hobbled backward toward the cave entrance.

Laakea felled two more men before a hard blow struck him in the midsection. His breastplate stopped the weapon from disemboweling him, but it knocked the wind out of him. The spasm in his diaphragm doubled him over, and black spots marred his vision.

Isil stood on her uninjured leg and fended off blows until Laakea's breath returned. Laakea's arms and hands, leaden with exhaustion, kept a tenuous grip on his swords, but blood made the rawhide grips slippery. He blocked a blow from an opponent, but his sword clanged off the wall in a shower of sparks and rock chips, as he lost his grip on the blood-soaked handle. He sidestepped the fellow's counterstroke and felled the attacker with his remaining sword.

It won't be long until they overwhelm Isil and me. We can't hold out long enough to reach the cavern entrance. At least we've halted the activities at the altar…the screams have stopped…either that…or Rehaak is dead, in which case we're about to join him in the afterlife.

CHAPTER FORTY-SIX

KETT'S REVEAL

Kett lounged in the chair while Aelfric, the scarred warrior, stared out the window of the Swordsman and Swallow Inn. "Our arrival in Baradon is both fortuitous and timely, Aelfric. Today I received word my plans are about to bear fruit. This is my gift to you," Kett pulled a map from a pocket of his embroidered waistcoat and smoothed the edges to flatten it on the worn tabletop.

"And what do you expect in return for this 'gift'? That is what I want to know." Aelfric crossed the room and bent over the map Kett displayed.

"A gift requires no repayment, my friend. My offer carries no obligation to you. My agents have organized cells among the Abrhaani slaves who work throughout Baradon. At the proper moment, all the slaves will turn on their masters. The slave revolt will bring the economy of southern Baradon to a halt. The mines, the farms, and the workshops will halt production, and in a matter of a few tendays, southern Baradon's discontented citizens will be hungry and angry."

"You are mad if you expect the slaves can unseat the nobles and vault me to power. It will never work."

"Ah, but first, we must fan the coals of unrest among the Eniila into flame. I contacted those Eniila who are loyal to our cause through my operatives in Baradon. They know you are here and will stand with you against your brother and the other nobles and draw Aelrin to battle. With the troops removed from the south, the success of the slaves' revolt is guaranteed. The uprising will cut Aelrin's supply lines while weakening and demoralizing his forces. Then we crush Aelrin and his confederates between the hammer of your Eniila and the anvil of my Abrhaani."

Aelfric pondered the statement. Kett's foresight shocked him. If Kett had organized the Abrhaani war effort, the Eniila might have ended in chains instead of the Abrhaani. *Thank the gods for that mercy.*

"You call it our cause, Kett, but your cause and mine may diverge."

"How so? I fervently desire you to become the war leader again. Is that not your wish?"

"True enough, but what of afterward? What happens once we unseat Aelrin and his cronies?"

"Did you not express regret at the enslavement of the Abrhaani in Baradon, and did you not promise they could return to Khel Braah?"

"True…"

"My cause is my people's freedom; you want to regain your honor and keep your word to the Abrhaani. We are of one mind unless you wish to dishonor your promise to the Abrhaani in Sethria."

The little bastard has me there. How dare this little ferret—I would never break an oath. I wonder how he knows …unless he was…there…impossible. Aelrin put every male in Sethria to the sword. No one survived.

"Let us prepare to return you to your rightful place and stop quibbling. Your cause and my cause are similar. Set aside your paranoia and listen to my offer."

"Very well, tell me your plan," Aelfric said.

"Lords Aldwynan, Torquil, and Sveinn are ready now to revolt. Lords Undalis, Kellain, and Addae need proof of your return before committing their forces. Their holds are in the far north of Baradon."

"Yes, I am familiar with some of those names, but others must have risen to their estates in my absence, and I don't know them. The northerners were always restive, even when I was the war leader. Why would they support me now?"

"They perceive you as the lesser of evils. Aelrin and the southern lords have made life burdensome for them with extra levies for roads and other improvements."

"Roads? In the north? No wonder they are riled. To northern isolationists, roads are symbols of invasion and subjugation by the South. They never wanted close connections to the southern lands. If Aelrin forced roads upon them, that alone would rankle, and if he forced them to pay for those roads, the smoke must be curling out of their ears. I never understood their foot-dragging. Trade is a necessity, and roads make trade possible. I suspect the northern lords fear losing people to the South once their subjects see the variety and richness there. The northern climate is harsh. Only tough, pigheaded bastards survive there. 'Poor but proud' is how they put it."

"There is more, Aelfric. They paid levies, but the roads were never built. There are other reasons for their antagonism." Kett smirked and picked a piece of lint from his pantleg.

"The northern lords resent the southern lords. Well then, if Aelrin has pissed in the pristine water of their frigid lakes, they will not stand for it. I can't believe Aelrin was stupid enough to poke a stick into that hornet's nest," Aelfric rambled, undeterred by Kett's hint at secret knowledge.

"But he has, and that stick shall become the club you use to shatter your brother and win the title of Supreme War Leader."

Kett grinned wolfishly at Aelfric's shock when he heard the title.

"There has not been a Supreme War Leader since the Sundering. You believe we can unite the Eniila of the north, south, east, and west into a unified empire again? Impossible!" Aelfric shook his head and scowled at Kett.

"We can, and more. Have you heard the prophecy of how the Eniila and Abrhaani must work together in the last days to bring peace to Aarda?"

"That campfire tale?" Aelfric dismissed Kett's statement with a flick of his hand. "You accept that fable as fact? Have you lost your mind?" He bit his cheek, then pursed his lips in thought.

"You and I are proof of its authenticity. Are we not working together? Are not your northerners and Abrhaani slaves both ready to unite against a common foe? Is that not enough proof?" Kett leaned forward in the chair, eyebrows raised, arms out wide. "This is a sacred cause, my friend, ordained by the gods. The prophecy's fulfillment is at hand, we cannot fail."

"So… what is our first step?"

"You go north to meet your loyal supporters and to convince the few remaining holdouts to join our cause. I will meet with my agents throughout the rest of Baradon and oversee our other preparations. Incidentally, I arranged mounts…horses for you once you reach Fort Pathar." A sly smile appeared on Kett's face.

"Horses? There are no horses…they're extinct. Where…how—?"

"You said the northerners were secretive, as indeed they are. Horses are their best-kept secret. Their generations-long breeding program is one reason they do not want the southern lords involved in their affairs."

"How many horses?"

"Enough to mount a sizeable cavalry force."

"That changes everything. With cavalry, we can raid and flee. Aelrin's infantry and mithun carts can't move fast enough to overtake us. We can harass them deep in their own territories and melt away like snow under the spring sun."

   If we can draw Aelrin's forces north, Kett's plan might succeed. Possibilities flooded Aelfric's mind. *The Eniila have not seen cavalry for a millennium, and they are a massive tactical advantage for an army—my army. No wonder the northerners were secretive. The seeds of this revolt have taken generations to germinate. Only the gods plan with such foresight.*

CHAPTER FORTY-SEVEN

DOUBTS

Simea and the girls now understood how the ancient nursery songs contained prayers meant to focus their concentration and enable them to connect with the Creator in specific ways. They practiced every evening. With each practice session, they gained strength and confidence and could do more. Kyonna suggested it was like manual labor—the harder they worked, the stronger they got.

When their food ran low, and the water ran out, Aibhera Shifted to Abalon after dark, when the risk of discovery was slim and filled their canteens from lake Seletan. She also pilfered food from a storehouse to replenish their supplies.

While Simea and Kyonna waited for Aibhera to return, they sang as many of the ancient prayer-songs as they could remember, with varied and sometimes unexpected results. "Light of the World" became Kyonna's favorite since it dispelled the canyon's gloom and surrounded them with light.

The furry little quadrupeds with sharp teeth who had stolen their food shrieked and scurried for cover whenever she sang it to create light around the campsite. They clung to the canyon walls with long claws and furry prehensile tails while their large yellow eyes gleamed from the shadows.

Kyonna would allow them to creep close to her pack, then sing the blazing light into existence. After she tormented them with several repeat performances, they kept a safe distance. Ky considered that an excellent benefit.

Once Aibhera returned, they trudged through the gorge's dank gloom again. Three more days of effort brought the three Sokai out of the canyon and onto a flat gravelly plain. Scrub brush and short spiky yellow grass stretched westward to the horizon. The canyon was the only gap in a wall of black lava several meters high, too high, and smooth to climb. The wall of lava looked like a giant black cake sliced by an enormous knife. Far to the north, purple mountains raised their jagged profiles against the pale blue sky, and forests cast their hazy outline along the foothills.

Once out on the plain, they checked Eideron's charts frequently while they traveled but soon realized his maps were useless. A thousand years of wind and rain had obliterated the landmarks mentioned on the map. The Sokai abandoned the other species and slipped unnoticed into Abalon, and it appeared a vengeful Baradon had erased them from its memory.

The plain's flat sunlit surface was a welcome contrast to their trek through the cold, gloomy canyon. The sere grass crunched underfoot as they trudged tired and footsore toward an uncertain future. Aibhera and her party flushed clouds of large flies from cover as they walked. Small yellow birds with red breasts flying overhead swooped low and snatched the insects from the air as they flew.

The sun, their only guide, still rose in the east and set in the west. At least that much remained unchanged. They walked toward its orange glow in the western sky and hoped to find the narrow river shown on Eideron's map. It had either dried up, or they had much farther to walk before they reached it and followed it to the abandoned metropolis of Berossus in the foothills. Centuries ago, the Sokai, fleeing Eniila oppression, left Berossus and set out across the barrens to Abalon. Before they abandoned the city, they sealed it hoping to return someday to reclaim it and the trove of technological wonders they left behind.

Doubts assailed Aibhera, who felt responsible for Eideron's death. Shame weighed more than the pack she carried. To atone for her failure, she pushed herself hard each day and insisted she was okay.

Aibhera, at the lead, heard Simea whisper to Kyonna, *"It's her fault. She killed Eideron. We can't trust her."* When she turned to face them, Simea lagged far behind her and Kyonna. They couldn't have whispered together. The moment she turned forward; the whispers began again. *"She's under the influence of the Dark Ones." "She's evil. She will kill us all like she killed Eideron."* Aibhera wheeled around and shouted, "Stop that. I couldn't help it, and I feel bad enough already. Just shut up!"

Kyonna looked puzzled. "Stop what? I haven't said anything. I am too tired and hungry to waste energy talking."

❖

Farther behind, Simea stared at the ground and plodded behind the girls. Simea either hadn't heard the girls' exchange or was too lost in his own misery to respond. The voice in his head said, *"You wasted the time spent with your master—-afraid of your own shadow— responsible for Eideron's death. Your people need a hero, but you're a clumsy clown who trips over his own feet—inept— incompetent. Eideron should have left you behind. The girls have a better chance without you."*

Simea looked around and waved his arms, "Shut up and leave me alone. I've heard it all before, from my mother. I can't help it. After Father died, Mom expected too much of me. I was just a small boy. I wasn't strong enough or smart enough—

"You're not a small boy anymore, but you're still weak and stupid. You haven't changed at all—loser— crybaby. You think Aibhera loves you, but you're too foolish

to see the truth. She only puts up with you because there's no one else. Blind—blind—blind, just wait and see. She could never love a clumsy fool like you, so someone else will win her heart. Maybe if you had the guts to tell her how you feel you might stand a chance—but you won't—you're afraid of hearing the truth—you're so pathetic—she could never love you.

Simea stumbled on a rock. *"See—you can't even walk like a man—tripping over a pebble—disgusting.*

"Shut up." He raised his voice. "I said, shut up!" He whirled around and nearly fell.

His shout caused Kyonna to turn and look at him. "We never said anything. What's the matter with you? Are you losing your mind?"

"Yes—you are. Don't worry—you'll die soon anyway." The whispers grew louder, and Simea fell farther and farther back as the voice tormented him.

Kyonna kept pace with Aibhera, noticed the dark circles under her sister's eyes, and wondered at the source of her companions' foul moods and strange behavior, but kept silent. *I won't poke the bear.*

The sun sank lower in the western sky, and shadows lengthened across the plain. Aibhera led Kyonna and Simea through the grassy plain and up a gentle slope. Once they reached the hilltop, they surveyed the area. Sunlight glinted off the water of a wide river that divided the plain ahead of them.

Simea pulled out Eideron's map. "Finally, something that *is* on the map, but it's supposed to be a small stream, not *that*. It's huge. No way we can cross *that*." He lowered the map and pointed at the expanse of shining water. "We were stupid to think we could do this."

"We must rest soon," Kyonna said. "Once we reach the river, we might find a place to ford it."

"We can get to the river before dark, camp there, refill our canteens, and look for a place to cross," Aibhera put her arm around Simea's shoulders to comfort him and stem his negativity.

Simea shook off her arm and stepped away from her. "We should Shift back to Abalon and forget the whole thing while we still have enough strength. We can beg the Synod's forgiveness and blame Eideron for leading us astray."

"What? Blame Eideron—you must be insane. You always want to quit when things are difficult," Aibhera retorted.

"Oh, and you are always perfect," Simea snapped at her.

"Stop it! Both of you! You know we can't return to Abalon. The Synod will flog us or burn us at the stake if we go back! Besides, our dreams showed us what we must do." Kyonna stopped when Aibhera and Simea stared at her.

"Don't look at me like that. Yes, *our* dreams. I had the same dreams you had. Those three people fighting the Nethera have plagued my sleep for months now. The two of you needn't think you're special or that you're the only ones who can have nighttime visions. You both made a big issue of your dreams, but I just wanted them to stop.

"You shared them with Eideron before you talked to me because I'm your brainless little sister. You thought I wasn't important like you, Simea, or smart like you, Aibhera. I didn't want prophetic visions. I only wanted to live my life, enjoy my job, and hang out with my friends, but the dreams wouldn't go away.

"That is why I wanted to meet Eideron, Aibby. I had to come along with you, don't you see…they need us so badly!" Tears spilled from Kyonna's eyes and left wet trails through the dust on her cheeks.

Simea had never seen Ky cry, and Aibhera could tally those times easily, their father's funeral being the most memorable.

"It will be fine, Ky. We're sorry, please don't cry," Simea said.

"Let's stop here," Aibhera dropped her pack on the grassy knoll and wrapped her arms around her sister.

After they had prepared a meal, they sat around a fire wrapped in their blankets and ate in silence. Both Aibhera and Simea barely looked up from their food.

Kyonna said, "What's the matter with you two? We crossed the wasteland and lived. We made it to Baradon. Nobody's done that in a thousand years, so why the long faces? And why did you shout at me to shut up earlier when nobody was talking?"

"I thought you and Simea were saying nasty things about me," Aibhera said.

"What nasty things?"

"You and Simea said I killed Eideron and that I was evil."

"I said nothing like that, and neither did Simea. We weren't talking at all, were we, Sim? I don't know whose voices you heard, but they weren't ours. You imagined it. What about you, Simea? Did you hear voices too?" Kyonna asked.

"Yes, I did."

"What did the voices say to you?" Aibhera asked.

"Never mind. It's not important. The important thing is we will never find the people from our dreams. Look around. There's nothing but endless prairie in front of us, and a river we can't cross blocks our path. Our mission is hopeless." Simea stirred the fire and avoided eye contact with the girls.

Kyonna leaped up. Her eyes blazed, and she shook her fist at Simea. "So what do you propose we do, curl up in the fetal position and die in the middle of nowhere? The Creator gave us dreams for a reason. We survived the wasteland for a reason. He didn't lead us out here to die. Stop listening to the lying voices in your heads. Each time we encountered an obstacle, we overcame it, and this is no different. It's just another problem, and no problem is too big for the Creator to solve."

Simea tensed as if he were about to argue with Kyonna, but Aibhera put a hand on his arm and said, "Ky's right. We've listened to lies and should be ashamed of ourselves. Let's continue and pray that the solution arrives before it's too late."

CHAPTER FORTY-EIGHT

SHARED DREAM

Simea and the girls awoke. They screamed, shot upright in their bedrolls, eyes wide, and trembling in terror. The campfire had turned to ash and embers. The girls clung to each other for comfort.

"The people from our dreams were in desperate distress," Simea stared across the moonlit plain as if still dreaming.

"I saw them too. It's horrible. They're skinning the older man alive. His friends are trying to rescue him, but they can't because there are so many enemies, and the big warrior lost one of his weapons," Kyonna's eyes rolled in fear, and she shivered as though chilled. "It's horrific. We must help them, or they will die, but we are too far away. What can we do?"

"They need help right now," Aibhera stood to her feet. "We don't have time to wander around any longer. We must Shift immediately to where the Abrhaani and Eniila are fighting the Nethera's followers. If we don't, the Nethera will win, and Aarda will fall under Nethera dominion."

"How is that even possible? We have never Shifted to any location we don't already know," Simea rose to his feet and threw wood on the fire. "We could end up entombed in the stone around them, or we could get lost in the Aether.

If we Shift near the Nethera… remember what happened to Eideron at the dark barrier? There are too many unknowns. It's too risky. This nightmare may only be a warning, a prophetic dream like the others we have had. It may not be happening right now."

Kyonna stood and poked Simea in the chest with a forefinger. "Do you really believe that, or is that your fear talking? I don't know about you two, but the intensity of this dream tells me it's happening now, or if not now very soon—too soon—we dare not wait any longer."

Simea opened his mouth, ready to argue, but Aibhera grabbed his arm before he got the words out. "I agree with Kyonna, this nightmare was different, stronger, more immediate. They need our help now!"

"I can't bear the thought of losing them when they seem so close, and the danger is so imminent." Kyonna stiffened and balled her fists. "It's worth the risk. They risk their lives for Aarda and *us*. How can *we* risk any less for *them*? *You* can stay behind if you want, Simea, but I'm going. Aibby, are you with me?"

Simea slumped and kicked dirt onto the campfire. "Okay, you win. Let's do it, but how can we find them? We can't see their location from the Aether. It's underground."

"That's true, but we see *them*. What if we focus on the *people* instead of the *location*? That might get us there." Aibby grasped Kyonna's hand and motioned for Simea to do the same.

"We should aim for the young warrior, he has always been the clearest to me," Kyonna said. "If we focus on the other man, we'll end up too near the Nethera. That would be bad for everyone." She grabbed Simea's hand without waiting for further discussion. A newly created prayer-song flowed from her lips.

Aibhera joined Ky once she understood the words, and Simea held tight to the two sisters. The journey was unlike their practice sessions. There were no glowing clouds of power and no flowing music. Darkness surrounded them for a moment, followed by a thunderclap when they arrived. Bodies flew in every direction, as the force of their arrival hurled both groups of combatants apart.

"Dragan's Wall, now!" Simea shouted to be heard above the ringing in their ears, an aftereffect of the deafening thunderclap. Surrounded by the smell of blood-soaked earth, he and the girls began the Dragan's Wall prayer-song. The Creator's power surged into the darkness and formed a shining wall between them, and the horde gathered near the sacrificial altar. It protected the warrior and the old woman while they recovered. The Sokai stood firm as the Nethera's minions leaped to their feet, regrouped, and battered the Creator's shield, trying to renew their attack.

Torches guttered, smoked, and cast flickering shadows across rough stone walls on both sides of the barrier. An amorphous black shape with baleful crimson eyes loomed behind a man in black robes. The robed figure, knife in hand, stepped back from the stone altar, and the man tied there.

The putrid smell of gore nearly choked the Sokai, despite the urge to vomit, they continued their prayer-song. Behind them, the young warrior and the old woman struggled to their feet, while the horde of fanatics crowded forward and blocked access to the altar where the other man lay bleeding. Kyonna stopped singing and turned toward the warrior and the older woman. The horde threw themselves against the shield. It wavered but firmed and remained unbroken.

CHAPTER FORTY-NINE

UNEXPECTED

A blast staggered Laakea, and his remaining sword spun from his hand, leaving him weaponless. Isil lay stunned. Deafened by the explosion, they waited for the end to come, the sounds of their attackers muffled and distant. Three tiny ocher-skinned people, lips moving in unison, stood between them and their foes, and suddenly a wall of light blocked the passage between the small strangers and Odium's assassins.

Isil rose, while Laakea retrieved his weapons, and wiped the blood off their grips on his pant legs. With swords in hand, he shrugged his shoulders and rolled his neck to get rid of the kinks. As his hearing returned, he could hear the little people singing. He stepped toward the small strangers who maintained the radiant barrier. One of the females turned to face him and stopped singing.

"I don't know who you are or how you got here, but thank you for your aide," he said. "I'm ready now. Can you let them through one at a time?"

"I think so, but running away is a better choice," the youngest female replied, while the older girl and the male, still singing, maintained the wall of protection.

"We will not leave without our friend Rehaak."

"Where is he?" the youngest woman asked.

"In there," Laakea pointed with his sword toward the altar chamber. "Now let them through one at a time, so I can kill them all and rescue Rehaak."

Isil used her staff for support and hobbled over to join them. "Maybe they got a better way, lad. Did you ask 'em that?"

"*They* might not, but *I* do," the younger girl said with confidence. "By the way, my name is Kyonna." She batted her eyelashes and smiled at Laakea. "That is my older sister, Aibhera, and our friend Simea."

"Ky, stop flirting and do whatever you're planning. Sim and I are tiring," Aibhera said when she stopped singing for a moment.

"Fine. Aibby and Sim, on the count of three, drop the wall and let me try this." She turned to Laakea. "And as for you, you big, strong, handsome thing," she said, laying her hand on his blood-spattered forearm. "Get ready in case this doesn't work."

"Ky, hurry!"

Kyonna knelt on the floor of the passage and picked up two fistfuls of grit and gravel. She motioned for Isil to do likewise. "Now, on the count of three, throw this stuff up high in front of us. Sim and Aibby, once you drop the wall, hug the floor. Otherwise…never mind, just duck and cover. Everybody ready?" Kyonna watched and waited until Isil and the others nodded. "One, two, three."

The glowing shield wall vanished. Simea and Aibhera dropped to the floor. Isil and Kyonna threw the gravel into the air. The gravel and sand arced toward the floor, then abruptly and violently changed direction, shooting toward Odium's men, as though Kyonna had loosed it from a sling. The assassins at the front of the pack stumbled forward as soon as the shield dropped. When the debris hit them, some fell where they stood. The stones and grit killed a few, blinded some, and wounded others. Those near the back, who remained uninjured, stood stunned and immobilized, shocked, and confused.

Before anyone could move, large furry bodies hurtled past Laakea into what remained of the crowd. Three wolves lunged at the men, snapping, and slashing at arms and legs, driving the assassins back into the chamber. The Nethera behind the altar shrieked and spat in rage, while the fellow in the black robes, knife in hand, waited to deliver a killing blow.

Laakea stood slack-jawed and gaping for a moment, shook himself free of his astonishment, then joined the mêlée. He waded into the fray, swinging his swords with the last of his strength. Isil hobbled along behind him and made sure that the wounded would never rise again. Soon only a handful remained.

Laakea and the rest of Rehaak's rescuers advanced toward the altar, the wolves, snarling and snapping like dogs herding sheep, corralled Odium's remaining fighters, and finished them off one by one. The Sokai stood immobile, staring at the wolves, their eyes wide, and jaws agape.

During the sudden lull in combat, Laakea found his bow lying on the floor. He slid his swords into his belt loops and jerked an arrow from a body.

Dreynar stood, with his knife poised for a killing stroke, ready to plunge it into Rehaak's chest.

Laakea nocked his arrow and drew the bowstring to his chin.

"Not one step closer, or I kill your friend." Dreynar placed the knifepoint against Rehaak's skin. "He'll make a fine present to Ashd'eravaak." He jerked his head toward the Nethera, who hovered behind him. "And then he'll feast on your lives too."

"Less'n it be a whole lot better at feastin' than the last Dark One we met, it might find my large muscular friend here a might tough to chew and a bit more'n he can stomach. The last o' its foul-smellin' kind got an awful case o' heartburn last night." Isil bared her teeth and pointed at Laakea. "He stuck one o' them shiny blades into its guts, and there ain't nothin' left o' it 'cept a scorch mark in the grass."

The wolves snarled and menaced the Dark One, who spat and screeched in rage before it vanished, and the nasty stench in the gallery dissipated with its departure. Dreynar stood alone over Rehaak's helpless body, so intent on the group facing him, he did not notice Ashd'eravaak's withdrawal.

"Yer phony god just abandoned you," Isil taunted.

As Dreynar turned his head to look behind him, Laakea loosed his arrow. It took Drey in the throat and drove him backward. The knife fell from his hand as he lay choking on his own blood.

Isil rushed forward and cut the unconscious Rehaak free from the altar. "He's chewed up somethin' fierce, but he'll be all right once we get him mended proper."

The three Sokai, still immobile, at the chamber entrance, stared at the wolves in astonishment.

"What's wrong?" Laakea asked.

"It's them." Aibhera's voice quavered, and she pointed a shaky finger toward the wolves. "The three members of the Bright Host. We have seen them in our dreams, and they have watched over you for many days."

"Are you talking about the green-eyed wolves? They have helped us before," Laakea shrugged. "Not sure why."

"Those are no ordinary wolves," Simea insisted.

The wolves looked at one another and transformed before Laakea's eyes. They stood upright and became three brawny men in armor that shone like Laakea's breastplate.

"We are sorry we deceived you and Rehaak," the leader said to Laakea. "It was necessary for our mission. No one was supposed to know of our involvement. We must leave you now because the Nethera have broken our blockade between the Aether and the Nether and have breached Abalon's location. Farewell, and fear not, we will return when we can."

Without further comment, the Aethera sheathed their weapons and strode toward the cave entrance.

"Wait! We need more information," Aibhera said. "If we need your help, how can we contact you? At least tell us your names."

The Aethera stopped, turning to look at Aibhera, and the leader bowed. "Since we are no longer accustomed to interacting with your kind, we forget your customs and courtesies. I am Sa'khalin, and these are my comrades, G'haelarin, and Sh'imbalaan. We cannot stay. You must find your own way forward, and may the Creator guide you. Farewell."

"But—" Aibhera sputtered, struggling to form another question, but the three Nethera turned away, strode toward the entrance, and disappeared around a bend without another word.

"Well, that was just rude," Kyonna grimaced and shook her head.

"I don't suppose we can expect the Aethera to be like us, Ky," Aibhera said. "They promised to return. Let's hold on to that promise."

"We must tend Rehaak's wounds," Laakea untied Rehaak. "Let's get him back to the house before he bleeds to death, or more of those crazies show up."

CHAPTER FIFTY

RETURN TO FORGE

While Simea and the girls stared down the passageway after the Aethera disappeared, Laakea scooped Rehaak off the altar and slung him over his shoulder. "Let's get him outside into the sunshine where Isil can tend his wounds. It's almost daybreak."

"What shall we do with these bodies?" Simea asked.

"Leave 'em here and let 'em rot, I says. Them Odium nasties don't deserve no decent burial." In contempt, Isil glowered and jabbed one body with her staff.

Laakea carried Rehaak past the carnage and led the others back toward the daylit opening ahead. "We can roll rocks across the cave entrance." He toed a body aside with a grunt, clearing a path. "This cavern will become their tomb."

"Will your friend survive?" Kyonna asked Isil. "Rehaak looks near death."

"He took a beatin', that's for sure, but he will survive this too if'n I patches him up proper," Isil said.

"What did you mean when you said, 'this too?' Does he get attacked like this frequently?" Kyonna raised her eyebrows.

"More often than anyone would expect. Trouble follows our friend Rehaak wherever he goes, and since we go with him...well...let's just say, it's dangerous to be

Rehaak's friend." Laakea grinned, his feral smile showing his teeth wolf-like. "But…it keeps life interesting." He stepped outside, blinking in the bright sunlight.

Flies circled above the bodies of the men Laakea and Isil dispatched during the night, and the stench of death hung in the air. Once outside, Aibhera and Simea, gagged and vomited on the grass. The smells and sight of Rehaak's wounds were too much for them to bear.

Isil spread a blanket on the dew-covered grass and bandaged the worst of Rehaak's injuries. Kyonna, the only Sokai with a stomach strong enough to aid Isil's efforts, tore bits of cloth for bandages from the dead assassins' clothing. When Simea and Aibhera recovered, they fetched water at the foot of the small waterfall and built a travois with poles and blankets, a tool to drag Rehaak to safety.

Laakea remained alert for other Nethera-worshipers while he blocked the cave's entrance with large stones. When he completed his task, he stood beside Kyonna and watched them treat Rehaak's wounds.

Isil pointed out Rehaak's injuries as she worked. "Them spots, where they peeled off bits o' skin, looks a might gruesome, but we ended the butchery afore they got too far, or he might o' bled to death. Rehaak's face be a mess 'cause they broke his nose and jaw." She rose and arched her back to stretch out the tension. "I's done patchin' the holes in him for now. We best haul him back to the house afore he springs more leaks. It be near noon, but if'n we hurries, we can get him to your home afore sundown."

Laakea handed Kyonna his bow and quiver. "Can you carry these for me?" She took them from his hand and slung the bow over her shoulder. Once relieved of the weapon, he eased Rehaak onto the triangular frame of the travois and picked up the narrow end. "Let's move." Laakea strode along, pulling his wounded comrade as Kyonna trotted at his side, and the others fell in behind them.

Laakea dragged the travois since no one else had enough strength for the task. While they walked, Simea and the girls shared how their dreams led them out of Abalon.

Where be this place you calls Abalon?"

"It's in the eastern part of the continent called Baradon," Simea said.

Laakea stopped and turned his head, his eyes bright with curiosity. "Baradon? That's where my folks came from." What's it like?"

Kyonna laid a hand on Laakea's arm. "A bleak wasteland surrounds Abalon, which separates it from the rest of Baradon. Sim and my sister walked for days just to reach the edge of the desert."

Laakea's face fell.

"We really never saw Baradon. We shifted from the edge of the barrens directly to your aid." Kyonna withdrew her hand in response to a stern look from Aibhera. "Tell us how your friend got himself into the fix back there."

Laakea and Isil told the Sokai about the series of attacks that led to Rehaak's capture and their rescue mission.

"We want to help," Simea said, "but I'm not sure how helpful we can be in the face of the threats you described. We are not warriors like you. We don't have your size, strength, or stamina. I still can't believe how fast you walk with your friend loaded on the travois."

Laakea laid his burden on the ground to catch his breath and faced Simea. "You may be small, but you proved both your strength and your worth in battle. The wall of light you called up was *more* than helpful—it saved our lives." He smiled at Kyonna. "The trick you did with the pebbles was amazing. Where did you learn that?"

"Yes, where *did* you learn it?" Aibhera said.

"Haven't you ever wondered how I became the best Windrider? I push things. It was an accidental discovery. I almost crashed when I first started on the gliders. I panicked and prayed for a push to force me away from the cliff face. Power flowed through me, and it worked.

"Whenever I pray for a push against the ground, it gives me more lift. That's why I can carry heavier loads with less wind than anyone else. All the other Windriders think it's because I'm so tiny and light, and there's some truth to it, but it's more than that. I expected if I prayed the same prayer against tiny things like the pebbles, I could move them instead of moving myself."

"Lucky for us it worked," Laakea cast an admiring glance at the tiny girl who stood at his side. "There's more to you than a pretty face." He blushed, embarrassed he had spoken his thoughts aloud.

Kyonna favored him with a smile and a toss of her ringlets.

"Let's get moving again." Laakea picked up the poles of Rehaak's stretcher and set a brisk pace.

After several rests along the trail, they reached the house just before nightfall. Isil and Kyonna cleaned Rehaak's wounds and rebandaged them after they smeared the worst cuts with a salve from his store of medicines. He drifted in and out of consciousness, crying out whenever the pain of their ministrations became too great to bear.

Once Kyonna and Isil finished their work, Laakea put him into Aelfric's bed to recover, while Isil stayed by the bedside and sang prayer-songs over him. Although exhausted from pulling the travois, Laakea spoke with the three young Sokai. "Thank you again for your timely arrival. You saved all our lives, but the quest is not over. Ashd'eravaak and his kind still seek to rule Aarda and will do anything to accomplish their goals."

"You are welcome. What is your plan now?" Aibhera asked. "Our dreams led us here, but we have no notion of what we must do next. We will follow your lead, just tell us what we must do."

"Not me, but once Rehaak recovers, I expect a trip to Narragan, the Abrhaani capital city. He has been on a quest for *The Aetheriad*, an ancient book."

Simea's eyes widened. "Eideron mentioned that book before he died. He said it might prove useful to combat the Nethera."

Aibhera's brow furrowed. "It appears we are on the same quest."

Laakea nodded. "Yes. Rehaak's search has centered here on Khel Braah, but he might travel soon to Baradon. That is why I asked about it earlier."

"I'm sorry, but I am so exhausted I must rest now and recover," Simea apologized.

"I feel the same," Aibhera added. "When we become conduits of the Creator's power, it takes a toll on our physical bodies. We can speak more about this tomorrow."

Laakea nodded. "I understand how you feel. My body feels as heavy as lead, and I can hardly keep my eyes open. If they attacked now, I couldn't lift my swords—it gives new meaning to the phrase, dead tired.

CHAPTER FIFTY-ONE

RECOVERY

On the fifth day after his rescue, Rehaak awakened, and although swathed in bandages, he insisted on sitting up to speak to Laakea and the others after breakfast. The Sokai sat on the benches built by Aelfric for his family, their chins barely crested the tabletop, and their feet dangled above the floor.

Rehaak spoke slowly, in obvious agony from his injuries. "Other people might blame the Creator for my suffering, but I do not. I bear the responsibility for my pain since I strayed from the path set before me. I walked away from the Creator's love and the protection He provided for me through my friends. My god has proven faithful throughout my unfaithfulness, my misery, and even outright rebellion. My entire life, to this point, has been a search for the place I belong, and one long lesson in trust.

"It shames me that it took this long, but I finally trust the Creator and the people He placed in my life." Rehaak paused to gather strength and held up his hand to silence Isil, who was about to interrupt. "Isil and Laakea, you have proved your faithfulness despite my vacillation. I realize now that my obligation for your safety ends where your choices begin. Where I have no control, I have no responsibility." He nodded to Isil. "You were right, there are things worse than death, and living, crippled by doubt, and a false sense of responsibility fits in that category."

"You have struck a courageous and decisive blow to the work of the Dark Ones. I owe you my life." Tears filled Rehaak's eyes. He bowed his head to each person gathered around the table, then folded his hands in his lap and lowered his head in humility.

Laakea broke the silence. "The fight is not over. The Nethera still desire our deaths, but I intend to make weapons to defeat them. While you recovered, we returned to the cave and collected more ehlbringa weapons from Odium." He pointed to the forge-house where the stack of several dozen ceremonial knives lay waiting. "I can reforge them for our use, and they are deadly to the Dark Ones. I can equip us all, given time, and I believe we have bought time with our victory."

Rehaak braced his hands on the tabletop and leaned forward. "I pray you are right. There are several ways we hindered Odium's work here in Khel Braah." He raised his hand, holding up his index finger. "First, we incited them to reveal their activities." He raised a second finger. "Second, the entire village of Dun Dale now knows of their plots." He winced and shifted his position in Aelfric's chair at the head of the table. "That does not seem important yet, but I expect word will spread to New Hope and other towns. News travels with remarkable speed between the settlements out here. We are not alone in this battle anymore."

"Yes, and the Aethera sprang to our aid," added Simea. "That's no trivial thing. When we worked together, it prompted them to help us and reveal themselves. The Aethera are powerful allies, but I'm concerned the Nethera have discovered Abalon's location."

Aibhera cupped Simea's shoulder. "But that might benefit us. Now we have proof of Nethera activity. If Abalon is under attack, it might force our people to join the fight."

Kyonna scowled at her sister. "Or it might not. You don't know how they'll react. They'll probably blame it on you for leaving Abalon. There's still so much we don't know. We don't understand the importance of writings like Eideron's fragment of *The Book of S*—"

Aibhera silenced Kyonna with a nudge. "But we have used our songs to receive power from the Creator. *The Book of Songs* might encourage people here to follow the Old Way again, right, Isil?"

Isil acknowledged Aibhera's comment with a nod, then said, "And as I tol' Laakea, we thinned 'em out a bunch. They is gonna be a long while collectin' more o' their followers afore they messes with us again, 'specially if they be workin' in Baradon too. They is gonna be spread mighty thin for a spell."

Rehaak winced as he stood erect. His voice gained power. "The most important thing…we are no longer alone in this struggle, and we know the enemy's objectives. To the demon and his followers, we are a significant obstacle on Ashd'eravaak's road to conquest." Vacillation had evaporated like water in a pot left on the fire. He stood determined to face his fate.

He looked at the faces of the others from behind his bandages. "Before they can win, every follower of the Old Way must die or feed their endless appetites. The Nethera hover like a thundercloud over Aarda. We stand beneath the glowering sky to avert Ashd'eravaak, the storm god's wrath, and wait for the lightning of his anger to strike, and we are its target.

"Although we are few, we still struck a powerful first blow against the Dark Ones. The Nethera deceive those who follow them, so they believe they are doing what is best for mankind. There may be hope for them if we can convince Odium's members of their error. Our aim has become clear, and we bought time to recover and prepare. We have good friends and reliable allies with new knowledge and potent weapons. Dawn is coming." His voice grew weaker with each sentence.

Rehaak paused as exhaustion overcame him. "I have never fully trusted the Creator, and I tried to follow Him without understanding that He is loving and faithful. My half-hearted commitment will no longer be enough. I can move forward now since I know how trustworthy the Creator is. My only safety lies along the path the Creator set before me." He slumped into the chair behind him.

Aibhera waited for Rehaak to continue, but when he did not, she stood and pushed up the sleeves of her garment. "Our grasp of the abilities the Creator has given us has grown. *The Book of Songs* provided information about the war in the Aetherial Realm and our part in it." She pointed upward and raised her voice. "The Creator has ceded control of Aarda to those who follow Him. Although the Nethera can do a great deal of damage, they cannot win outright. We have time to rest, recuperate, prepare for war, and trust the Faithful One to guide us."

※◆※

The voices of his followers faded away while they discussed their next moves. *It feels strange to think of them as my followers.* Rehaak whispered to his god for help as his strength waned. *Thank You. You taught me faithfulness through my friends, and thank You for those You sent to save us. They and my friends pulled me back from the brink of death. Physical pain rises and ebbs like the tides, but the sting of my wavering faith crippled my soul for most of my life. My heart is hard, and I am unfit for Your service. I am sorry that I never trusted You. Let mistrust end here.*

The buzz of conversation faded as Rehaak lost consciousness, but before the darkness overcame him, the Faithful One spoke. *"Do not call yourself inadequate. You are the person I set aside for my service. No, my son, what you need is k'harsa. I have forgiven you and called you to lead, and so you must lead. I chose you, and I will restore*

*your heart so you may serve me with confidence. I will be
your god, and you shall lead my people."*

Rehaak's spirit wept for joy as the Creator's love for him
filled his heart, and sealed his covenant. He could continue.
Rehaak's inner conflict, the awkward part of his quest, was
behind him now. Peace must wait until later, but after a
lengthy search, Rehaak had found the place he belonged, and
with it, he discovered a purpose, a family, and a home. He
had arrived bruised and broken, but adversity had sharpened
his wits and strengthened his will, and he would be forever
grateful for his family and his home.

Read on for the special bonus, the first chapter of Nocturne

Note from the author:
I hope you enjoyed Overture. As an Indie author, reviews
can easily make or break my career. Please remember to
leave a review, and upvote other positive reviews! Thank
you!
The Saga Continues
or sign up for updates and special offers at
https://www.krschultzauthor.com/
If you liked this story, sign up to receive updates and
exclusive offers on *Nocturne*, the next book in the series.
http://krschultzauthor.com

APPENDIX

THE CHARACTERS

Aamori: see the song "Aamori's House"
Aelfric: Laakea's father
Aelrin: King of the Eniila, Aelfric's twin brother
Aert: innkeeper at the Dancing Dog in Dun Dale
Ak'eldemea: Eniila god of metalcraft
Aibhera/Aibby: Sokai girl
Amoreya: Speaker of the Sokai Synod
Ashd'eravaak: the Abrhaani's god
Baeddan: Narragan's herald
Bajan Lanier: Rehaak's fellow scholar
Bram: miller's eight-year-old son
Breisha: Aert the innkeeper's youngest daughter
Digon: Golden Crown innkeeper
Dreynar Asan: Voerkett's second in command
Eideron: Sokai elder
Eskel: a Council of Barons member
Eyhan: Isil's son
Gael: the miller
Gil/Gillam: miller's eleven-year-old son
Herron: Sokai rising star
Himish: Sokai elder
Harmish: Abrhaani sea captain
Isilakari/Isil/Lucky: mithun drover, Rehaak's friend
Jesh'zed'haak: Eniila god of war
Keria: Rehaak's sister
Kett: Abrhaani businessman
Kyonna/Ky: Aibhera's younger sister, Windrider
Laakea: thirteen-year-old Eniila youth
Latonia: Raamya's wife
Leda: barmaid at the Golden Crown Inn
Leoned: Aibhera and Kyonna's stepfather

Lord Arven: a member of the Council of Barons
Mato: Raamya's fourteen-year-old youngest son
Nailah: Sokai healer, Simea's friend
Naom'han: author of *The Aetheriad*, Aethera scribe
Pippali/Pip: Sokai youth Simea's friend
Ogun: Raamya's sixteen-year-old middle son
Radik: Raamya's nineteen-year-old eldest son
Raith: chandler in North Narragan
Raamya: the sawyer
Radomir: an Abrhaani historian
Rehaak Eskolar/Spot: scholar, healer (and heretic)
Riata: the miller's wife
Riessa: Aibhera and Kyonna's mother
Rais: Sokai youth, Kyonna's friend (fellow Windrider)
Rogan: The Gilded Swan innkeeper
S'ek'zekaar: god of death
S'enkashaar: god of storms
Sahki Lorg: confectioner in Dun Dale
Sa'khalin, G'haelarin, Sh'imbalaan: Rehaak's Aethera guardians
Selvyn: the last Eniila to work with ehlbringa
Shel'gharim: Aethera in charge of the Sokai
Shelhera: Laakea's mother
Simea/Sim: Sokai youth
Steen: miller's five-year-old child
Tano: Rehaak's older brother
Uele: miller's four-year-old daughter
Voerkett Telmakus: Isil's husband
The Odium: a secret society of assassins

PEOPLES

Abrhaani/Greens: a green-skinned, nature-worshipping species
Aethera: powerful spirit-beings of the Aetherial plane
Eniila/Whites: a large, pale-skinned, warlike species
Nethera: corrupted spirits/fallen Aethera
Sokai: a vanished species

PLACES

Aetherial Plane: a plane of existence of pure energy
Aeron Suul: port on Khel Braah's south coast
Arkad: the great hall of the Eniila afterlife
Baradon: the Eniila homeland (continent)
Berossus: city abandoned by the Sokai millennia ago
Camikola: a coastal city in Baradon
Chavanel: a volcanic crater east of Lake Korath
Cherith Pass: the only pass through The Spine
Dun Dale: logging village in south Khel Braah

NOCTURNE

CHAPTER ONE

MATO

Mato raced around the corner of Mirtle's Inn, his heart thundering in his chest as he entered the mill yard, but he dared not stop for breath. He hoped he could lose his pursuers among the maze of log piles.

His father's men sweated and strained in the summer heat while they moved the massive logs to the mill and stacked the boards and timbers. The noise of their labor didn't drown out his pursuers' thundering footfalls. Their footsteps echoed like drumbeats through the dusty mill yard. *I must make it home before they catch me, or I'm done for this time.*

Each breath stung and burned in his throat. His heart hammered against his breastbone as rapidly as hummingbird wings. Nearing the limit of endurance, he raced past the stacked logs in front of the sawmill, toward River Road, home, and safety.

He streaked homeward, past the inn's woodshed, and headed down the alley toward the trail to Dun Dale and safety. His feet raised clouds of red dust as he skidded around a last corner. Workmen paused from their labors and watched the pursuit of a small fellow by two others as they thundered past. Both the little fellow's pursuers towered over him by and outweighed him by at least two stone.

One laborer looked up from the log he and his partner had just hefted onto a wheeled cart, and spat into the swirling dust, as the trio thundered past. The pursuers, hulking brutes, with almost identical stubble-covered undershot jaws, long hairy arms, and sloping foreheads gained on their smaller prey.

"Well, Flin, What'cha reckon the little bookworm done this time to get Radik and Ogun so riled?"

"Like as not he cheated them again an they got wise to it, Ferl. They looked set to give him a new set o' bruises though. If he be smart, he be headin' home to hide 'hind his momma's skirts."

"Their Pa aint' no help… eggin' 'em on like he do. Says competition builds character, he do. Ain't hardly fair to the youngest, no wonder his Ma coddles him."

"Yup, but that only makes it worse fer Mato—He's a crafty little bugger. Maybe he'll talk his way out o' a beatin'." Flin stroked his chin in mock thoughtfulness.

"Would you care to put money on that?" Ferl elbowed his buddy and raised his eyebrows.

"Nope, I works too hard fer it, not gonna lose it on a fool's wager.

Once the victim and his pursuers disappeared around the corner, the men returned to work. Common sense meant they wouldn't interfere in a family matter.

Flin paused and prodded Ferl in the ribs when the sound of the chase stopped abruptly. "Mark my words. Ramya's family'll come to grief…sure as day follows night."

Note from the author:

I hope you enjoyed Overture. As an Indie author, reviews can easily make or break my career. Please remember to leave a review, and upvote other positive reviews! Thank you!

To be continued: in Nocturne

Manufactured by Amazon.ca
Bolton, ON

27278257R00159